APR 0 2 2023

NO
SEAT
OF
LIBRARY

D0446263

"Time to open our gifts." As Jake started to reach for the gift bag near his plate, he sneezed so hard that his Santa hat slipped down over his forehead. He pushed it back, grabbed the gift bag, and looked inside. "It's a big cookie."

He held up a gingerbread man with white icing outlining bones and a skeleton head.

"That's called a ginger*dead* man," Franetta said. "We had gingerdead men for the Halloween bake sale. I don't know why anyone would bake them for Christmas."

"A gingerdead man. That's funny." Jake's belly shook when he laughed, as you might expect from a man in a Santa suit. "A cookie has only one porpoise—one purpose in life."

He was mangling his words more now than he had earlier. He decapitated the gingerdead man. "Mmm. Best cookie ever." He ate the limbs one by one and took a long drink from his flask.

Val had just brewed what she hoped was the final tea of the day. She picked up the pot and went around the table refilling everyone's cup. When she asked Jake if he wanted more tea, he didn't answer. His face contorted. She backed away, expecting him to emit another of his almighty sneezes.

Instead, he stood up, swayed, and landed on the floor with a thud . . .

APR 0 2 2023

NO LONGER PROPERTY OF
PUBLIC LIBRARY

Books by Maya Corrigan

BY COOK OR BY CROOK

SCAM CHOWDER

FINAL FONDUE

THE TELL-TALE TARTE

S'MORE MURDERS

CRYPT SUZETTE

GINGERDEAD MAN

Published by Kensington Publishing Corporation

Gingerdead Man

Maya Corrigan

KENSINGTON BOOKS
www.kensingtonbooks.com

KENSINGTON BOOKS are published by

Kensington Publishing Corp.
119 West 40th Street
New York, NY 10018

Copyright © 2020 by Mary Ann Corrigan

All rights reserved. No part of this book may be reproduced in any form or by any means without the prior written consent of the Publisher, excepting brief quotes used in reviews.

To the extent that the image or images on the cover of this book depict a person or persons, such person or persons are merely models, and are not intended to portray any character or characters featured in the book.

This book is a work of fiction. Names, characters, places, and incidents either are products of the author's imagination or are used fictitiously. Any resemblance to actual events or locales or persons living or dead is entirely coincidental.

If you purchased this book without a cover you should be aware that this book is stolen property. It was reported as "unsold and destroyed" to the Publisher and neither the Author nor the Publisher has received any payment for this "stripped book."

All Kensington titles, imprints, and distributed lines are available at special quantity discounts for bulk purchases for sales promotion, premiums, fund-raising, educational, or institutional use.

Special book excerpts or customized printings can also be created to fit specific needs. For details, write or phone the office of the Kensington Sales Manager: Attn.: Sales Department. Kensington Publishing Corp., 119 West 40th Street, New York, NY 10018. Phone: 1-800-221-2647.

Kensington and the K logo Reg. U.S. Pat. & TM Off.

First Printing: October 2020
ISBN-13: 978-1-4967-2244-7
ISBN-10: 1-4967-2244-2

ISBN-13: 978-1-4967-2245-4 (ebook)
ISBN-10: 1-4967-2245-0 (ebook)

10 9 8 7 6 5 4 3 2 1

Printed in the United States of America

I have endeavored in this Ghostly little book, to raise the Ghost of an Idea, which shall not put my readers out of humor with themselves, with each other, with the season, or with me. May it haunt their houses pleasantly, and no one wish to lay it.

—Charles Dickens, *A Christmas Carol*, Preface

The Phantom slowly, gravely, silently approached . . . In the very air through which this Spirit moved it seemed to scatter gloom and mystery. It was shrouded in a deep black garment, which concealed its head, its face, its form, and left nothing of it visible save one outstretched hand.

—Charles Dickens, *A Christmas Carol*, Stave Four

Chapter 1

Val Deniston paused at the top of the stairs in the house she shared with her grandfather. She usually dashed down the steps, but today she might trip over the long skirt she'd borrowed. Lifting the front of it, she descended at a pace suitable to her costume. She glanced at the red flyer on the hall table.

COME TO BAYPORT'S DICKENS OF A HOLIDAY FESTIVAL
WHEN 19TH-CENTURY LONDON COMES ALIVE
CAROLING, TEA PARTIES, STREET MARKETS, AND
PUB FARE
PRIZES FOR THE BEST-DRESSED VICTORIANS

Val lifted the cuff of her white blouse and glanced at her watch. Time to leave for London on the Chesapeake Bay. She knocked on the door to her grandfather's bedroom down the hall. "It's almost ten. I'll go on ahead if you're not ready yet."

"Coming!"

She rolled up the waistband of her skirt so it wouldn't sweep the sidewalk and donned the ghastly green cloak she'd found in the attic. She cringed at her reflection in the full-length mirror. The shapeless garment dwarfed her small frame. If anyone gave a prize for a tent look-alike, she would win it. She was tempted to ditch the cloak, but her parka would look out of place in Victorian London. On the plus side, the cloak's dense wool would keep her warm, and she'd have to wear it only for a short time. Most of the day she'd be indoors, serving tea and sweets at Title Wave, Bayport's new bookshop.

Granddad emerged from his room, struggling to knot a red scarf under his full white beard. In his black, high-collared coat and a top hat, he looked as if he could have stepped out of a hansom cab at Trafalgar Square.

He touched the brim of the hat he'd borrowed from a local theater group. "This is too small. But I wasn't going to shell out good dough for a hat I'll never wear again." He checked himself in the hall mirror. "Do I look silly?"

No more than any other man wearing a top hat. "*Distinguished* is the word I'd use." She slipped her arm under his and nudged him toward the front door. "You'll fit in with all the other Victorian gentlemen today. And you're the star attraction. Bayport couldn't hold its first Dickens festival without Ebenezer Scrooge."

"Humbug. Santa's the big star in any holiday celebration." He pushed his glasses up on the bridge of his nose.

He'd worn those same wire-framed bifocals as Santa last December. His arrival by barge at the marina had kicked off the town's holiday festivities for the previous five years. This year a newcomer to town was playing Santa, and Granddad resented him for usurping that role.

As he and Val walked the three blocks to Main Street, he continued to stew over his demotion from Santa to Scrooge.

"Granddad, remember that Scrooge turned into a happy man after visits from three ghosts."

"I don't get to be a happy man until the festival winds down. Until then, it's bah humbug all the way."

As they approached Main Street, Val was struck by how quiet the tourist town was. Traffic had been diverted for the weekend celebration. "Without the hum of car motors, I can almost imagine I'm in Dickens's London."

"It didn't look anything like this." Granddad gestured with an open palm toward the vendors' booths with their attractive displays of merchandise. "I've been reading up on Dickens. The London he knew was thick with smog and coal dust. The streets were full of horse manure and mud."

Val preferred the twenty-first-century Eastern Shore version of merry old England in Maryland, where she could walk on a brick sidewalk instead of a dirt road. The wood buildings along Main Street, formerly the homes of nineteenth-century merchants, now housed shops and restaurants decorated to the hilt for the holidays. Red poinsettias flanked the store entrances. Wreaths and swags adorned lampposts, windows, and doors.

The vendors were dressed in Victorian garb, as were some early-bird visitors. Men sauntered in black jackets or overcoats, bowlers or stovepipe hats on their heads, and women in long skirts and short capes stepped gingerly, some balancing large, elaborate hats. The majority of festival visitors wore blue jeans. Regardless of clothing, most of them carried a huge shopping bag with *What the Dickens?* printed on it.

The shopping bags reminded Val to look for the gifts she still hadn't bought, including Granddad's. Maybe she'd find some gifts at the festival. Managing the Cool Down Café at the athletic club and catering holiday parties left her little time to shop between now and Christmas.

Val scanned the crowd and saw a white-bearded, rotund man in a red suit coming toward them. This Santa carried a lot more weight than Granddad, especially now that he'd slimmed down. Val had made healthy meals for her grandfather ever since she moved in with him two winters ago. He'd grumbled at first, but eventually he gave up the junk food he'd subsisted on since Grandma died.

"Merry Christmas!" Santa waved to everyone he passed as he walked toward the intersection where Val and Granddad stood.

Granddad frowned. "'Every idiot who goes about with Merry Christmas on his lips, should be boiled with his own pudding, and buried with a stake of holly through his heart.'"

For the last week Val had heard him practice that line and others from *A Christmas Carol*, but he put more feeling into it today as the claimant to the Santa throne approached. He looked at least a decade younger than Granddad.

The big man smirked. "Well, if it isn't last year's Santa," he said as if dismissing an outmoded flip phone. He gave Val the once-over and thrust out his hand to her. "I'm Jake Smith."

Val knew his name and had heard nothing good of him. "Val Deniston." She shook his hand.

He turned to Granddad. "Bet you're glad I took over as Bayport's Santa. You gotta leave strenuous jobs to younger men."

"What's strenuous about picking up little ones and sitting 'em on your lap? On second thought, it might be strenuous for you." Granddad looked pointedly at Santa's belly. "Hard for you to bend down."

"You're behind the times. Seated Santas and posed shots are out of fashion. Strolling Santas and candid shots are in. Parents take pictures of their kids interacting with Santa. Even adults take selfies—or should I say elfies?—with Santa." Jake laughed at his own joke. "You would know about Santa trends if you belonged to the IBRBS."

Granddad eyed him with suspicion. "The what BS?"

"The IBRBS. The International Brotherhood of Real Bearded Santas." Jake patted his chin. "You have to admit I have a better beard than you."

Val wondered if Jake had made up the organization. She studied his facial hair. By tradition the Bayport Santa sported a real beard, and his wasn't fake, though its color was. Like the hair not hidden by his red cap, his beard had dark roots.

Granddad stroked his fluffy beard with one hand and pointed toward Santa's with the other. "Your beard is longer, but mine is thicker."

The one-upmanship could have been banter between old friends, but the tone and body language suggested otherwise. Val focused on the part of Santa's face not covered by a beard. He had no deep furrows between his brows or creases at the corners of his eyes. His nose and cheeks were deep pink to light red. He was younger than she'd assumed at first, probably in his late fifties. Not many men in that age group dyed their hair white. Either he really wanted to play Santa or he had another reason for making himself look older.

Santa's face puckered up, his eyes closed, and his mouth opened wide. "*Ahh-choo!*"

His sneeze sounded like a wild animal's distress cry. Santa hadn't covered his mouth, but at least he'd turned his head and spewed his germs to the side rather than at Val and Granddad. As Jake's eyes and his mouth widened again, Val buried her head in her cloak, Granddad pulled his scarf over his face, and they both backed away. Santa's second sneeze broke the volume record set by his first one. He pulled out a big red handkerchief, covered his nose, and honked into it.

Granddad glared at him. "With that cold, you shouldn't be near kids."

Santa flicked his wrist. "I'll keep them at arm's length, and I have cough syrup." He reached into his pocket and took out a flask.

"Jake!" a woman called from down the street. She sounded like a mother summoning a wayward child.

Santa hastily tucked away his flask. "Here comes Mrs. Claus." His tone suggested a man resigned to his fate.

Val looked around for a plump, motherly woman in granny glasses, white hair under a bonnet, and a red sack dress. Instead, a svelte woman with a pointed nose and prominent cheekbones approached them. Her straight, black hair grazed the white fur collar of her short red coat dress. The chunky heels of her thigh-high, black suede boots clicked on the brick sidewalk.

"You can't hide from me, Santa honey," she said with a drawl. "I could hear that sneeze miles away." She turned to Val and Granddad. "Hi, y'all. I'm Jewel Smith, Jake's wife."

Val and Granddad introduced themselves to her.

Red velvet was the only thing Santa and his wife had in common. She looked ten years younger. He was round and soft. She was angular and sharp. His hair was fake white and hers fake black. As she finger-combed it, Val stared at Jewel's crimson claws. Each had a tiny bow on it painted in green nail polish. If her fingernails had been cut blunt, they would have resembled miniature holiday boxes, but filed into points, they looked like sharp weapons, ten little lethal gifts.

"You can tell by her drawl," Santa said, "that she's originally from the South Pole." He chortled.

Val wondered how many times he'd tell that lame joke today.

His wife reached for his hand, her clawed fingers wrapping around it. "I just love living in the North Pole with you. I want to show you some tiny toys I'm putting on my Christmas list. See y'all later."

As Jewel led him toward a jewelry vendor, a family with two preschoolers crossed their path. Santa *interacted* with them, to use his word, and his wife handed them candy canes from her festival shopping bag. Their parents took a family "elfie" with Santa.

Val was glad for their sake that he'd turned into jolly Jake, though she was sure she'd met the genuine Jake.

She took Granddad's arm as they continued along Main Street. "I understand why you dislike this year's Santa, and you're not the only one. Irene Pritchard can't stand him either." Val's assistant manager at the café had a major gripe with Jake.

"What does she have against him?"

"He bought the house next door, cut down her prized azaleas along the lot line, and spoiled her view. Now she has to keep her curtains closed because he can look in her windows." Val glanced in the shop windows they passed, hoping for gift inspirations. "What do you think Santa had in that flask?"

"Not cough syrup. I'll keep an eye on him. If he starts acting tipsy—"

"Don't confront him. Call Chief Yardley." The police chief was the right person to deal with a smashed Santa.

"I'd enjoy putting the police onto Jake." Granddad pointed at a stack of holiday packages covered with foil wrapping paper and tied with perfect bows. "When you were a little girl and saw a pile of presents like that in a shop, you picked them up and shook each one."

"I remember. At home I always shook wrapped gifts and tried to guess what was in them. At the store I was angry when nothing rattled inside them. I demanded to know why the boxes were empty. The clerk told me the pretty boxes would put people in the Christmas spirit so they'd buy more."

That wasn't Val's idea of the Christmas spirit. Even now, in her early thirties, she loathed empty wrapped boxes. They reminded her of the hollow core of a season that had become commercialized. At least the festival's profits would go to a food bank, and Dickens would approve. "Dickens was right about Christmas. It's not about hoarding money and accumulating more stuff. What matters is family and food."

"Family, food, and *friends*."

"And friends," she echoed him to signal that she wouldn't mind if he asked a special friend to the family holiday dinner when her parents would visit. Granddad's friend, Dorothy Muir, had returned to Bayport two months ago to open the bookshop Title Wave. Inviting the widow meant including her son Bram. Val foresaw her parents' reactions. They'd have questions about her relationship with him, and she had no answers for them.

As she and Granddad stepped off the curb to cross Main Street, a middle-aged woman in an ivory fleece jacket and sweat pants bumped into him and knocked off his hat.

"Sorry." She picked up his hat and handed it to him.

Val recognized her. "Hi, Elaine."

The woman's salt-and-pepper hair looked windblown though there was no wind. She frowned in confusion. "Hi. Nice to see you." Then she rushed off like the white rabbit on a mission.

"I don't think she recognized you," Granddad said.

"We only met once. She hired me to cater tomorrow night, a birthday dinner for her father, Oliver Naiman, over on Belleview Avenue. You know him?"

"Not well. He didn't grow up here. His parents used the house as a summer home. So did he after he inherited it. He only moved here for good when he retired a few years ago. I didn't know he had a daughter in Bayport."

"She lives halfway between Annapolis and Washington. She visits him every weekend."

"That's good. His late wife was sick for a couple of years, and I've heard he's not too well himself." Granddad put on his hat. "Time for me to go bah humbug everyone." He straightened up, as if steeling himself for an ordeal, and plunged into the growing crowd on Main Street.

"Stop by the Title Wave if you need a tea break during the day. And you'll come to the volunteers' tea this evening, won't you?"

He nodded and went off.

Val hoped he wouldn't get depressed from playing a dispiriting role. He had a way of becoming what he pretended to be. Shortly after she moved in with him, he wangled a job as the newspaper's recipe columnist without knowing how to cook. He succeeded by using her recipes and cutting them down to five ingredients for his Codger Cook column. Since then, he'd learned to cook, largely through his mistakes. But he wasn't content with acquiring one new skill in his seventies. After taking an online course in private investigation, he'd touted his sleuthing skills. His reputation as a detective had soared after his illegal snooping helped to catch a killer.

Would he now take on the personality of Scrooge? He already shared at least one trait with Dickens's character. Granddad was a tightwad, reluctant to spend money on the house where he'd lived most of his life. Val had coaxed him into repairing the termite damage and remodeling a leaky bathroom, but she couldn't get him to buy new furniture.

Even if Granddad adopted other Scrooge traits, Val was sure it wouldn't last long. When Val's brother's family came from California for the holidays, Granddad would play Santa for his great-grandsons, ten and seven. And he was always generous to them.

Val spotted the booth where a friend, Chatty Ridenour, was showing her beauty products to a middle-aged couple. She worked as a massage therapist at the Bayport Racket and Fitness Club, where Val managed the café. Though Chatty wore exercise clothes most of the time, today's purple jacket and long black dress almost made her look like a Victorian matron. Her mauve lipstick and gel eyeliner spoiled that illusion.

Val stood to the side of the booth as Chatty described

moisturizers, cleansing lotions, hand creams, and heel balms to a redheaded woman. "I can give you a 30 percent discount on a gift pack of three items."

The redhead turned to her male companion. "I haven't bought a present for my sister yet. Do you think she'd like a gift pack of skin products?"

The man's smile was tight-lipped. "I think *you'd* like them. Elaine wouldn't use anything like that."

The woman sighed. "You're right. She's impossible to buy for, but now you know what you can get for me." She gave him a coquettish smile.

He chuckled. "I'll add it to your already long list."

Chatty spoke up, apparently fearing she'd lost a customer. "An experiential gift is perfect for someone who's hard to buy for." She pointed to a poster with photos showing her giving a variety of massages. "Your sister might enjoy an aromatherapy or a Swedish massage. I'm a licensed massage therapist. Here's my card."

The woman glanced at it. "You work near here. My sister lives on the other side of Annapolis. Too far to drive for a massage."

It hit Val that this couple might be Elaine Naiman's sister and brother-in-law. Elaine had mentioned they would be at the birthday dinner for their father tomorrow night, along with some neighbors.

She was about to introduce herself when Chatty said to them, "Would you two like a picture with Santa as a festival souvenir? He's right over there." Without waiting for a response, she waved Santa over to the booth.

He started toward it, stopped suddenly, and pointed down the street. "I see some kids over there. Don't want to keep them waiting for Santa." He hurried away.

The couple drifted toward the next vendor.

"You did your best to turn that couple into customers," Val said, "but it was hopeless."

Chatty sighed. "Speaking of hopeless, that cloak you're wearing . . ."

"It's warm. I was going to lend it to you because you'll be out here all day."

"No, thanks. And you should ditch it if you see Bram coming. By the way, have you gotten him a Christmas gift yet?"

"No." Val had been seeing him for barely six weeks, not enough time to guess what he'd like or what he'd give her. Buying gifts was the most stressful part of Christmas. "Maybe I'll take your advice and go for something experiential."

"I bet he'd like a massage, and I wouldn't mind kneading his shoulder muscles." Chatty grinned. "Or, even better, I can give the two of you a lesson in couples massage. Don't look horrified. It's not risqué. I just show you how to give each other a therapeutic back rub."

Val had a vision of Bram caressing her bare back. Her heart sped up. She willed it to decelerate. A massage would certainly send a message, but how would he receive it? "Thanks for the suggestion, but I'm looking for the happy medium between a couples massage and a poinsettia."

As Chatty turned to help two young women at her booth, Val waved goodbye to her and browsed at other vendors' booths without finding gifts for anyone on her list. She headed toward Title Wave, feeling guilty about leaving the tea party prep to Irene.

Granddad intercepted her.

"You'll never guess what I saw." He motioned for Val to turn the corner onto a side street, away from the crowd on the main drag. He glanced left and right as if checking if anyone was close enough to hear him. "I know why Elaine Naiman crashed into me. She wasn't paying attention to what was right in front of her because she was following someone."

Val shrugged. "Someone she wanted to catch up with, I guess."

"Nope. When the woman she was following browsed at a booth, Elaine pretended to shop until the woman walked on, and then continued to trail her. I saw that same routine three times, so wipe the doubt off your face, Val."

Her skepticism gave way to curiosity about her client. "Where did Elaine and the woman she was following go?"

Chapter 2

Granddad showered bah humbugs on several festival visitors before getting around to answering Val's question. He always enjoyed keeping her in suspense. "I don't know where Elaine ended up. When she stopped to fiddle with her phone, I took my eye off her and lost her and the other woman in the crowd."

"What did the woman she was following look like?"

"Shorter than you, with long, dark hair. I was too far away to see her face." He lowered his voice. "Maybe Elaine's husband is cheating on her with this woman."

"Elaine isn't married."

"Keep your eyes and ears open when you cater for her tomorrow night. You may pick up signs she's not what she pretends. What kind of work does she do?"

"She's a project manager for a tech firm."

"That could be a cover for what she's really up to."

He must have watched a suspense movie from his vintage video collection recently. "Just because she followed someone, Granddad, doesn't mean she's a secret agent or a hit woman. You and I have shadowed people now and then."

"Only when we suspected they were involved in a crime. Maybe Elaine thinks the woman is a crook. Even more reason for you to stay alert tomorrow night. If she spotted a criminal, she could be in danger, and so could anyone around her."

The plot had thickened in his mind. "I'll be on my guard, Granddad." She checked her watch. "Time for me to get to work on the first tea party of the day."

They went back to Main Street and headed in opposite directions.

She stopped to chat with her friend, Bethany O'Shay, who was dressed for caroling in a long, red skirt, a black jacket, and a green cape.

Val reached down to pet Bethany's dog, a mutt with the look of a cocker spaniel and the personality of a lapdog. The dog's reddish blond hair matched Bethany's. "Are you taking Muffin caroling?"

"No, she'd want to sing too. I won't get home until after dark, so I'm taking her for a long walk before we start caroling. Aren't you supposed to be at the bookshop serving tea?"

"Irene's there, getting everything ready. I should be helping her, but I've been dawdling."

"I just ran into your cousin. Monique's taking festival pictures for Bayport's Web site, but don't let her take a picture of you in that army blanket you're wearing."

Val patted her cloak. "Poor thing. Nobody loves you." She turned to go and said, "Happy caroling, Bethany!"

Within minutes, Val was standing in front of the Title Wave. She approved of the decorations in the display window—books tied with ribbons. No empty wrapped boxes here, no wasted paper.

Hard to believe she'd visited Title Wave for the first time less than two months ago, when she'd come to discuss catering the shop's grand opening party. Since then, she'd catered other get-togethers in the shop's Coffee and Tea Corner, abbreviated as CAT Corner.

Val removed her frumpy cloak before she went inside the bookshop. Dorothy was ringing up sales in a high-collared shirtwaist, reminiscent of what Mary Poppins might wear under her long jacket. With chin-length silver hair, Dorothy was older than the English nanny but shared some traits with her. An efficient, sensible, and good-natured widow, she was fearless enough to open a bookstore at an age when most people retired.

Waving to her, Val continued toward the CAT Corner at the back. Dozens of people browsed in the shelves along the side walls and the tall bookcases in between. The festival was good for Dorothy's business. Her son, Bram, stood in the children's book aisle. He wore a black cravat at the neck of his white shirt, and a black, high-collared jacket. He'd parted his wavy, brown hair far to the side, an unfashionable style today, but perfect with his Victorian clothes. He was the festival's Charles Dickens, but he looked more like Lord Byron than the grizzled Dickens shown in most portraits.

A cluster of children gathered around Bram as he performed a card trick and made a coin vanish from his hand.

Not bad. Val had never seen Bram do any magic tricks, though she knew he'd practiced them as a teen. He hadn't mentioned dusting off his skills for the festival.

"You're not a real magician," the biggest girl in the group said. "They wear capes and tall black hats."

He nodded. "Some dress like that, but not all magicians do. This is the Dickens festival, and I'm pretending to be Charles Dickens today. He gave his first magic show the same year he wrote *A Christmas Carol*."

Val was surprised to learn Dickens had practiced magic.

The girl who'd questioned Bram shook her head at his response. "I saw a picture of Dickens. You don't look anything like him. He had a funny gray beard."

Val suppressed a laugh. How would Bram react to this challenge from the audience?

He nodded. "He grew a beard when he was older, but not when he was a young man and doing magic tricks to entertain his children." Bram patted his pants pockets and looked around the room. "Does anyone remember where I put the jokers I showed you from the card deck?"

"In the pocket of your jacket," a boy said.

Bram reached into his jacket pocket. "You're right. Here they are." He offered a card facedown to the girl who'd questioned him. "Here's one joker for you and one for me. Turn yours over and show it to everyone."

She stared at the card in amazement. "It's Dickens, not a joker." She held up the card, showing the author with his straggly beard and walrus mustache.

"Mine must be a joker." Bram flipped over the other card, revealing a man whose clothes and hair looked like his. "It's a portrait of the young Charles Dickens."

"You do look a bit like him," the girl grudgingly said.

The other children nodded.

"Thank you all for watching a little Dickens magic. If you tell me what kind of books you like, I'll show you where you can find them in the shop."

Val marveled at how he'd thrown himself into jobs he'd never expected to have. After selling his tech company, he'd come to Bayport in October, intending to stay only long enough to help his mother set up Title Wave. He'd planned to return to Silicon Valley and invest his time and money in another start-up. Instead, he was still here, serving as the shop's accountant, public relations manager, head of sales, and whatever other role Dorothy needed him to take on.

After he pointed the children in various directions for books, she said, "I caught the tail end of your magic demonstration. Good show."

"I'm just glad the tricks worked. I didn't have long to practice. My mother came up with the idea yesterday. She thought magic tricks would keep the children occupied so their parents could shop for books."

"Was the girl with the questions a plant to set up your final card trick?"

He mimed effrontery like a silent movie actor. "Magicians don't do things like that . . . usually." He cocked his head toward the back of the shop. "Your second-in-command is already busy in the CAT Corner."

"You mean Irene? She's number two at the Cool Down

Café, but she's in charge of the teas today. She ran an English tea shop for years on Main Street. I'm just the helper, and I'm running late."

A woman with a child in tow approached them. "Do you have any books about dog training?"

Bram nodded. "I'll show you where they are."

"See you later." Val slipped through the curtain that covered the opening to the CAT Corner.

Irene was filling tiered trays with savory and sweet treats for festival visitors who'd bought tickets for the four afternoon teas. The open-faced finger sandwiches were on one tray. Curried chicken salad sprinkled with chopped scallions. Smoked salmon topped with capers and red onion. Cucumber and radish garnished with watercress. Irene had made scones dotted with dried cranberries, and Val had baked raspberry tartlets that she'd brought over last night.

She smiled at the woman in the food prep area behind the counter. "Hi, Irene."

The sixtyish woman looked at her over glasses that had slipped down her nose. "Good *morning*." Her tone reminded Val of a teacher reprimanding a student late for class.

The food looked more festive than Irene. Her wardrobe, like her hair, consisted of shades of gray. Today she was in her Sunday-best gray—a charcoal midi skirt and a taupe blouse. In her one concession to the season, she wore a green enamel holly pin with red crystals for berries.

Whenever Irene sported even a smidge of color, Val encouraged it. "I like your pin a lot. Where did you get it?"

Irene fingered the pin. "Roger gave it to me for Christmas a few years back."

"Your husband has good taste. Speaking of good taste, the treats look yummy. What do you want me to do?"

"Set the tables." Irene pointed at the black cat on the windowsill. "And let her out the next time she has a mind to roam. I've opened the door for her to leave or come back three times already this morning."

Val sympathized. She'd served as the cat's doorwoman when she catered for book clubs here. The cat had two favorite spots—the upstairs apartment she shared with Bram and the CAT Corner. From the windowsill here, she had a view of the churchyard, where she'd lived as a stray until Bram found and adopted her. The door at the far end of the CAT Corner gave her quick access to the graveyard whenever she became nostalgic for her former home.

Val set three tables for four and two tables for six with cups, saucers, and plates of old-fashioned china in two patterns. One set had belonged to Grandma and the other to Irene's mother. Still feeling guilty for not arriving earlier to help Irene, Val said, "Do you want me to get the food ready for the later tea parties? Then you can take a long break."

"Fine with me. I'd like to visit the festival booths and shop for gifts."

"I did that on the way here, which is one reason I'm behind schedule. Also, Granddad and I ran into Santa Claus, who had more to say than just ho ho ho."

"That man! If he comes to the tea we're doing for the volunteers this evening, I'm leaving early. I can't stand to be in the same room with him."

"I doubt if he'll last until the volunteers' tea. He has a bad cold."

* * *

Six hours and four tea parties later, Val set the table for the volunteers' tea. More than half of them had called to say they were too tired or busy to come to the tea, so one table for six would suffice.

The first volunteer to arrive was a middle-aged woman Val had glimpsed in the shop pretending to be a Dickens character. The woman wore a white gown and a lace veil that framed her small face. She greeted Val and Irene, and introduced herself as Holly Atherson.

As she sat down, Santa and Mrs. Claus arrived. Contrary to Val's prediction, Jake had either lasted all day at the festival or gone home for a nap in the middle. His nose and eyes were redder than earlier, but he was upright.

Irene, who was behind the counter with Val, scowled at him.

He didn't even glance at them. Maybe he thought women serving tea not worth his attention.

Jewel said, "Hi, y'all."

He took the seat at the head of the table, coughed without covering his mouth, and turned to the woman sitting on his left. "Hi. I'm Jake Smith under the Santa suit. And my wife, Jewel."

The woman in white studied Jake intently with her prominent eyes. "I'm Holly Atherson." Her lips barely moved as she spoke.

Jewel tapped on the table, her fingers dancing like a chorus line with asynchronous kicks. "You're dressed like a bride. I don't remember any bride in *A Christmas Carol*, and I saw the movie twice."

"The bride is Miss Havisham. She comes from a different book by Dickens, *Great Expectations*. Her fiancé jilted her on their wedding day. She wears her bridal finery for the rest of her life."

Jewel frowned. "Why? Was she too poor to afford new clothes?"

Holly shook her head. "Miss Havisham is rich. She wears her wedding gown as a reminder never to trust men. She trains her adopted daughter to break men's hearts, as her heart was broken."

Jewel looked aghast. "Why didn't she just get over it?"

"Because the story wouldn't have been as good," Holly said. "In the real world, though, getting over it would make for a happier life."

An African American woman in her forties had come quietly into the room while Holly was talking. She approached the table.

Jake eyed the newcomer, who wore a plain, long dress of coarse material. "And who are you supposed to be?"

Val was startled by his sneering tone. Did he have racial prejudices, on top of his other faults?

"My name is Shantell Defoe. I've just moved here. I'm Bayport's new head librarian." She sat down next to Jewel. After the others introduced themselves to her, Shantell said, "My Dickens name is Madame Defarge, from *A Tale of Two Cities*."

The title of the book apparently meant nothing to the Smiths, who looked blankly at her.

Holly spoke up. "It takes place during the French Revolution. Madame Defarge is a revolutionary."

Shantell reached into her festival shopping bag and pulled out knitting needles, yarn, and a piece of knitting that looked like the start of a scarf. "She vows to take revenge on a man whose noble family is responsible for the deaths of her relatives. She codes the names of the aristocrats she wants guillotined into her knitting."

Jake said, "Sounds like Dickens knew some mean women, bent on revenge." He glanced at his wife.

The black cat meowed, waiting at the door to go outside. Val crossed the room, opened it, and kept it open while the cat, with two paws out and two paws in, decided whether to visit the cold, dark graveyard after all.

At the other end of the room, the curtain between the CAT Corner and the shop floor parted. Someone stood there in a bizarre costume—a long, black garment like a monk's habit, hands encased in black gloves with 3D latex skeleton bones, and head covered with an upside-down holiday gift bag. The bag had two sets of eyeholes, one set positioned three inches lower than the other. The figure hobbled toward the table, carrying a festival shopping bag.

Val assumed this was a festival volunteer playing one of Dickens's ghosts. The ghost reached into the shopping bag for small red gift bags. Jake had a coughing fit as the ghost put a gift at each of the six places at the table.

Irene didn't like anyone messing with her tea party. "Who the Dickens are you?"

Without answering, the ghost limped toward the door Val was still holding open. She stepped aside, the cat crept out, and the ghost followed. Unable to tell if a woman or a man was in the costume, Val checked the shoes for a clue. She caught only a glimpse of white below the black robe before the figure disappeared into the darkness.

"Who was that?" Holly said.

Jake laughed heartily. "You can't guess? The gifts on the table, the gift bag on the head. That's the Ghost of Christmas Presents."

Val smiled. She suspected Bram of concocting the costume. He had a playful sense of humor.

Shantell pursed her lips. "The Ghost of Christmas Present who visits Scrooge in the Dickens story is a jolly giant in a green robe with a wreath on his head."

"Who cares? The Ghost of Christmas Presents"—Jake emphasized the *s* on the end—"made a joke, and a good one." His loud belly laugh ended in an even louder sneeze.

"Did you lose your hankie?" Jewel took a pack of tissues from her bag and pushed it toward him. "Cover your mouth so we don't all get sick."

Sitting across from her on Jake's other side, Holly slid her plate, her teacup, and even the ghost's gift to the left, moving them out of Jake's sneezing range.

Val wondered how to quarantine him for public health reasons.

Irene whispered to her, "This is one tea we can't serve family style. That man will spread his germs by passing the trays and breathing on the food. We have to prepare plates for each of them."

"Good idea." Easier than quarantine. "We'll put the food on the spare plates we have here and exchange them for the ones he's contaminated."

"After we take those germy plates away, we'd better scrub them and our hands." Irene picked up the teapot.

She went around the table, pouring tea, while Val plated the food. She'd just finished filling plates for the four volunteers when Granddad came in. He sat down at the other end of the rectangular table from Jake. Irene made up a plate for him. Then the festival's coordinator of volunteers, Franetta Frost, arrived and took the last seat at the table. She wore a white caftan and a pointed hat with a candle-shaped LED light atop it, like Dickens's Ghost of Christmas Past.

Irene sighed. "If more people keep showing up, we'll be here all night."

Remembering that Irene detested being around Jake, Val said, "I'll make up Franetta's plate while you take the ones we've already prepared to the table. Feel free to leave after that. I can handle the cleanup without you. I'll pack up your china and drop it off at your house later."

Irene lost no time making her getaway. Good thing she left before Jake started complaining.

"S'lot of food here." He slurred his words. "With tea you have bitty bites, not a whole plateful."

His wife rolled her eyes. "He usually grumbles because there's not enough food. Now there's too much. Can't make that man happy."

He took a bite of one sandwich, put it down, and bit into a different one. "None of it tastes good."

The food's lack of flavor didn't keep him from stuffing it in his mouth. He washed it down with whatever was in his flask.

Franetta took off her Ghost of Christmas Past hat and assumed the role of a woman who never did only one thing at a time. While eating, she led a discussion about the festival and took notes on her phone. What had gone well? What could they have done better? What activities should they add to next year's festival? Her note-taking lasted until she finished her food.

Granddad asked where the gift bags on the table had come from, and Val described the black-robed ghost who'd crashed the tea party and left the gifts.

Franetta's brow wrinkled. "That wasn't an official costume for the Dickens festival. The last ghost Scrooge sees is shrouded in black with a spectral hand, but the festival committee decided against anyone dressing like that. Too scary for the children." She brightened. "I think the person who left the gift bags didn't want to be recognized, an anonymous donor thanking us all for being festival volunteers."

"Time to open our gifts." As Jake started to reach for the gift bag near his plate, he sneezed so hard that his Santa hat slipped down over his forehead. He pushed it back, grabbed the gift bag, and looked inside. "It's a big cookie."

He held up a five-inch-tall gingerbread man with white icing outlining bones and a skeleton head.

"That's called a ginger*dead* man," Franetta said. "We had gingerdead men for the Halloween bake sale. I don't know why anyone would bake them for Christmas."

"A gingerdead man. That's funny." Jake's belly shook when he laughed, as you might expect from a man in a Santa suit. "A cookie has only one porpoise—one purpose in life."

He was mangling his words more now than he had earlier. He decapitated the gingerdead man. "Mmm. Best cookie ever." He ate the limbs one by one and took a long drink from his flask.

Val had just brewed what she hoped was the final tea of the day. She picked up the pot and went around the table refilling everyone's cup. When she asked Jake if he wanted more tea, he didn't answer. His face contorted. She backed away, expecting him to emit another of his almighty sneezes.

Instead, he stood up, swayed, and landed on the floor with a thud.

Chapter 3

Val assumed Jake had lost his balance or fallen down drunk.

His wife jumped out of her chair and peered at him. "Are you okay?" He didn't answer. Looking dazed, he started to roll sideways but gave up, falling back.

Val set down the teapot. Maybe he'd hit his head when he fell.

Holly crouched down next to Jake. "I think he's passed out!" She smacked his face. "Wake up!" That smack would have stung if he'd been conscious, but it didn't rouse him.

Val was amazed that the woman who'd tried so hard to avoid his sneeze eruptions was checking his pulse, her face inches from his.

"It could be an allergic reaction to something he ate." Franetta poked at her phone. "I'm calling 911."

"He doesn't have any allergies," Jewel said.

"People can develop allergies at any time." Holly slapped his cheeks and then shook his shoulders. "Come on, Jack. Wake up!"

Jack? With the man in obvious distress, no one corrected Holly when she called him by the wrong name, not even his wife.

Jewel kept her distance, peering at him from above. "Does he need mouth-to-mouth resuscita—"

"No." Holly took her fingers from his neck. "He has a pulse, and he's breathing."

"If it's a heart attack or a stroke," Shantell said, "getting medical help fast can make a big difference."

"The first responders are coming," Franetta announced. She pointed at the door to the outside. "I told the dispatcher to send them to the back door rather than go through the shop. I'll let Dorothy know what's going on." She left the room through the curtained doorway.

Everyone hovered around Jake except Granddad. He beckoned Val to the far end of the room and spoke quietly, "Except for sneezing and sniffling, Jake looked fine until he ate that cookie. Then he keeled over. Something in it made him sick."

She shook her head. "Just because he fell after eating the cookie doesn't mean that it—or any other food he ate—caused him to collapse."

"It wasn't just any cookie. It was a ginger*dead* man, left by someone who didn't want to be recognized."

At first, Val had assumed that Bram had left it, but she'd changed her mind after seeing the gingerdead man. He wouldn't have handed out a creepy cookie in his mother's shop. He might, however, have seen who did.

The Ghost of Christmas Presents had come through the shop on the way to the CAT Corner. "I want to ask Bram something. I'll be right back, Granddad."

She zipped across the room and pushed the curtain aside. Bram was talking to a pair of teenagers in a nearby aisle. He was still in his Victorian clothes, but his hair was no longer neatly parted on the side. Instead, it had reverted to its usual unruly state, wavy strands falling over his forehead.

He glanced at Val, said something to the teens, and then joined her.

He pointed to the CAT Corner. "What's going on in there? Franetta charged out, looking for my mother. And you look tense and pale, like—"

"Like I've seen a ghost?" The question was whether he'd seen one. She told him about Jake's sudden collapse. "Franetta called 911. She came out to let your mom know the emergency responders would arrive soon and go in the back door. Franetta doesn't want anyone in the shop or on Main Street to see Santa carried out on a stretcher."

"Especially kids. What can I do to help?"

"Stop your customers from poking their noses into the CAT Corner."

"Okay. I'll hang around the aisles toward the back and keep everyone out." He pointed to a sign at the CAT Corner entrance that said it was reserved for a private party. "That sign gives me an excuse to shoo them away."

Sirens wailed. Val breathed more easily. Jake would soon get emergency care. Now for the other matter Bram could help with. "Did you see anyone in the shop wearing a long, black robe and—"

"An upside-down gift bag for a mask. I couldn't miss

him. He walked straight back to the CAT Corner. I figured him for a festival volunteer going to the tea."

"Why did you say *he* and *him*? I couldn't tell if a man or a woman was under that robe."

Bram tilted his head from side to side, as if weighing evidence. "Men take longer strides than women, but that person didn't. He—or she—walked unevenly, almost limping. Franetta was in charge of the volunteers. She must know who wore that costume and what character it represented."

"She didn't. The person left gift bags for everyone at the table, so Santa named him the Ghost of Christmas Presents."

Bram brushed back a curl from his forehead. "First, you tell me about Santa's medical emergency, and then you quiz me about an incognito ghost. Is there a connection between the two?"

"Granddad thinks so. Santa hit the floor a little after eating the gingerbread cookie from his gift bag. If there's any news on Santa, I'll let you know."

Val walked back to the CAT Corner, pushed the curtain aside, and saw the emergency medical responders, a man and a woman, kneeling beside Jake. She couldn't see him or what they were doing to him.

Jewel, Holly, Shantell, and Granddad clustered near the bookshelves along the wall. Franetta stood sentry at the back door.

Granddad moved next to Val. "The emergency crew asked us to back away so they could work on Jake. He had a seizure, and when it stopped, they gave him oxygen."

A burly man at the back door wheeled in a gurney.

With his help, the other two responders got Jake on it and wheeled him toward the door.

"I'm his wife," Jewel said. "Can I go with him?"

The woman on the team shook her head. "I'm sorry. No one's allowed in the ambulance except the patient. We're transporting your husband to Treadwell Hospital. Drive there and check in at the emergency room. They'll tell you where your husband is."

Holly volunteered to drive Jewel to the hospital. The others offered their sympathy and support.

Once Jewel and Holly were out the door, Shantell said, "I have a ticket for the holiday concert in the community center and I need to get out of this costume before then. I'm roasting in it. Val, I want to thank you and Irene for the tea party." She reached for her gift bag.

"Don't touch that!" Granddad said. "No one should handle those gifts except the police."

Franetta whipped her head toward him. "Bite your tongue! Jake had a bad cold and was exhausted after a long day. He'll be fine."

Shantell looked at Granddad and then at Franetta. "I hope you're right." She slung her festival shopping bag over her shoulder and left the gift on the table.

Franetta pursed her lips. "Don't go around hinting that something he ate brought on what's ailing him."

"I won't. His wife might," Shantell said. "You did a terrific job organizing the festival, Franetta, but some things are beyond your control."

Val agreed. Not even Franetta, with all her super-powers, could contain rumors in a small town. News of Santa becoming ill at the tea would reflect badly on the festival as well as on Val and Irene.

Shantell exited through the curtain.

A moment later Dorothy entered. Usually unflappable, the shop owner had creases Val had never noticed in her forehead and around her eyes. The tension made her look all of her sixty-some years. "Thank goodness it's almost closing time. The customers in the shop earlier knew someone back here needed emergency help, but I didn't say who. Hearing that Santa Claus is sick would upset children. How is he?"

Franetta shrugged. "They took him to the hospital. That's all we know. But from now on, we should refer to him as Jake Smith, not Santa."

Dorothy approached the table and frowned. Frozen in time, the table looked exactly as it had when Jake fell down and everyone else stood up, leaving uneaten food. Jake's plate was the only empty one. All the others had at least one untouched sweet.

"I'll help you clean up, Val," Dorothy said.

If Granddad was right about the reason for Santa's illness, the police wouldn't want anything touched. Val said, "Thank you, Dorothy, I'll take care of it. It's my job."

Granddad nudged Dorothy back toward the shop floor. "You've been on your feet all day. Val and I will handle this."

Franetta studied the screen on her phone. "Now there's a mix-up about the concert tickets. I've got to go there and untangle the mess." She donned the pointed hat with the light on top, turning herself from a woman in a white caftan into the Ghost of Christmas Past. "In a few more hours the Bayport Dickens Festival will be history. We shouldn't let anything dampen our spirits or keep us from putting on a better festival next year." She marched to the back door.

Left alone with Granddad, Val eyed the unopened gifts on the table. A chill ran through her. "Maybe every gift is a gingerdead man like the one Jake ate. If he hadn't gobbled it down first—"

"I could be lying on the floor too." Granddad shuddered.

"Six people could be on the floor." No one would know what felled them. Everything they ate would come under suspicion, probably ending Val's sideline in catering. Who'd hire a caterer with even one food poisoning incident in her past? Her café at the athletic club might also lose business. "Once he's at the hospital, they can pump his stomach, and he could recover fast."

"Sometimes that works. I called Earl and told him what happened here. He said he'd stop by."

A family friend, Bayport police chief Earl Yardley would take Granddad's concerns seriously. Though the chief hadn't always welcomed Granddad's amateur sleuthing—or Val's—he tolerated it.

Granddad answered his cell phone. "Yup. We're still here. Come in the back door."

A minute later there was a knock at the door, and he opened it for Chief Yardley.

Decades ago, after the chief's father died suddenly, Granddad had taken the teenaged Earl under his wing, treating him like a son. Val remembered her first impression of the policeman. When she was a child visiting her grandparents, he'd reminded her of a gingerbread man, with his round head on a barrel-chested frame, his neck barely visible, and a big smile on his face.

Decades of police work had worn down that smile. Tonight he greeted them grim-faced. Once they were seated at a table, the chief jotted in a small spiral notebook as Val described the costume and actions of the Ghost of Christmas Presents.

The chief looked up from his notebook. "Anything else unusual about that individual?"

"The ghost walked with a hitch or a slight limp."

"Height and weight?"

Val conjured an image of the strange figure. "A weight estimate wouldn't be reliable. Someone thin could wear an overcoat under the robe and look heavier. The ghost wasn't short or very tall. The gift bag might have added a couple of inches. It rested on the ghost's shoulders and had eyeholes at two different heights, so I don't know where the eyes really were."

"Let's narrow it down. Could the ghost have been your height?"

"Five foot three? No. The ghost was a minimum of five inches taller than that."

The chief stood up. "As tall as me? I'm six foot."

"No, and the ghost wasn't as big in the shoulders as you."

"Approximately five foot eight to ten. Medium for a man, tall for a woman."

Granddad spoke up, "Coulda been a shorter woman in high heels."

"Those can give you a wobbly walk. And aching feet." Val was glad she could wear athletic shoes at the café and was grateful to be sitting now. She'd spent so much time on her feet that the low-heeled boots she'd put on this morning no longer felt comfortable.

Granddad described the gingerdead man cookie Jake had unwrapped and what happened within minutes of his eating it.

A call came in for the chief. He got up and walked across the room to take it. He returned to the table, looking even more somber than he had earlier. "That was a police officer at the hospital. Jake Smith is dead. It looks like poison."

Chapter 4

Chief Yardley surveyed the table where Jake had eaten his last meal. "Please tell me who was here for tea and where everyone sat."

"I thought you might say that, Earl." Granddad reached into his pants pocket for a festival flyer, unfolded it, and turned it to the reverse side. "I made you a seating chart."

Val peeked at his diagram as he passed it to the chief.

Jake Smith
(Santa)

Jewel Smith
(Mrs. Claus)

Holly Atherson
(Miss Havisham)

Shantell Defoe
(Madame Defarge)

Franetta Frost
(Ghost of Christmas Past)

Don Myer
(Scrooge)

The chief's eyebrows rose. "I've known you most of my life, Don, but you still surprise me." He looked at the chart and then at the table. "Which end was Jake at?"

"He was facing the food prep area." Val went over to it. "Irene Pritchard and I were facing the table as we assembled sandwiches and plated the food to take to the table."

The chief stood behind Jake's chair. "You could see Jake from there, but you weren't necessarily looking at him the whole time because you were working. Is that correct?" When she nodded, he said, "Did either of you notice a guest moving or removing food, dishware, or anything else on the table after Jake collapsed?"

Granddad whipped out his cell phone. "Nope, but I took a photo of the table right after he keeled over. You can compare it to how the table looks now."

Val stared at him, amazed. While she'd assumed at first that Jake's drinking explained his fall, Granddad had immediately suspected foul play. The recent murders in Bayport must have influenced his thinking.

The chief mimed tipping his hat to Granddad. "Send me the photo." He turned to Val. "I'd like you to give me a schedule, your best estimate, of when each person arrived for the tea. You can e-mail me that. Did Jake leave the room and come back at any time?" When Val shook her head, he said, "Was anyone near Jake's food aside from you and Irene?"

His question suggested he wasn't as convinced as Granddad that the gingerdead man had killed Santa. Val conjured an image of the ghost circling the table. "The ghost leaned over the table to put down the gift bags and had the chance to drop something into Jake's tea."

Granddad pointed to the teacup and sugar bowl to the right of Jake's plate. "His wife sat right next to him, close enough to put something in his tea. If she reached for the sugar, she could have slipped something into his tea without anyone noticing."

Val agreed. "Especially if she did it when everyone was distracted by the ghost."

The chief peered into the cup. "There's still a bit of tea there, probably enough for the lab to test for poison. I don't see any platters on the table. Did you clear those away, Val?"

"No, we didn't use platters. Jake had a cold. We didn't want his germs passed around. Irene and I made up a plate for each guest. We put exactly the same things on everyone's plate."

Dorothy came through the curtained entrance to the CAT Corner. "I heard voices in here. I thought you'd be finished by—" She stopped short at the sight of the chief. "Is there a problem?" Looking nervous, she fingered her hair.

"Yes," he said. "We have to restrict access to this room. We're treating it as a crime scene."

Dorothy's eyes widened. "A crime scene! My bookshop." As Bram came into the room, she turned to Granddad. "What happened here, Don?"

Granddad went over to her. "I'm sorry to tell you this. Santa didn't survive. He died at the hospital."

She frowned. "How did he die? Why is *this* a crime scene?"

Bram put his arm around his mother.

Chief Yardley said, "We're investigating his death as a

possible poisoning, but please keep that to yourself. Until we can get a team here—tomorrow at the latest—I'd like this area to remain as is. No one should come in here or remove anything from the room." He pointed to the doorway. "Is there any way to close off this space with something more than a curtain?"

Bram said he'd roll some tall bookcases in front of the curtained entrance to prevent access from the shop to the room. He'd also lock the back door to the CAT Corner. Then he gently led his mother out.

Val and Granddad trudged home along the same route they'd taken that morning. She'd anticipated an enjoyable festival. Granddad's expectations had been lower. When they both looked back on this day, though, Santa's poisoning would be the only thing they'd remember.

Back home, Granddad sank into his lounge chair, a gift from Val's mother and the only comfortable chair in the house. "This sure has been a long day. Dorothy was really upset about a crime connected to the bookshop, and she asked me to explain it. I hope she doesn't hold what happened against me."

A baseless fear in Val's opinion. Dorothy appeared to be as fond of him as he was of her. "She asked you to explain because she trusted you to give her a straight story. Why would she hold anything against you?"

"She's only been here a couple of months and already there have been two suspicious deaths involving groups in that back room. I was around both times. So were you. She might think we're bad luck and avoid us from now on."

"Dorothy isn't superstitious. She's logical and level-headed." Val crossed the sitting room toward the kitchen. "I'm getting myself a glass of water. You want one?"

"I'd like a beer."

When she returned with the drinks, Granddad was reading something on his phone. For years he'd rarely even answered his cell phone. Now, after her mother had given him the latest model with a bigger screen, he was addicted—snapping photos, downloading books, and surfing for information.

He looked up from the screen. "I think I know what killed Jake—cyanide. It doesn't take much to kill someone with it. It acts fast, causes symptoms like the ones he had, and leaves a distinctive odor. Not everyone can smell it, but someone at the hospital might have recognized it."

Val took Granddad's analysis with a grain of salt. He was no expert, but the fact that the police were calling the CAT Corner a crime scene meant they didn't think Santa had been poisoned earlier in the day. They had reason to believe it was a fast-acting poison.

She plopped down on the old tweed sofa. "Isn't a cyanide pill what spies carried in case they were captured?"

"Yup, so they could commit suicide before they were tortured. I can't see Jake committing suicide, but it's easy to imagine someone killing him. His wife was in the best position to poison him. She couldn't do it at home because she'd be the only suspect. She mighta got someone to play the ghost as a diversion so she could sneak poison into Jake's tea. I wonder how much money she's going to inherit."

Val put down her glass. This wasn't the first time
Granddad favored the victim's spouse as the culprit and
came up with a scenario based on little evidence. "Earlier
you thought the ghost was the culprit and the gingerdead
man contained the poison."

"I'm considering all the options." He took a long swal-
low of beer. "The woman who sat on the other side of
Jake, opposite his wife, had a chance to poison him too."

"Holly Atherson?" Val shook her head. "His cup and
glass were on the side where his wife could reach them,
not on Holly's side. And she moved her chair and place
setting farther from him because he was sneezing."

"I don't think she did it at the table. We're all assuming he was poisoned before he fell down. But maybe
something else caused him to lose his balance—too many
slugs from his flask all day long. Holly rushed to help
him before anyone else could. We couldn't see him when
she was bending over him. While she was supposedly
trying to help him, she could have slipped a cyanide pill
into his mouth."

"Which she just happened to have in hand? Why
would she do that? They introduced themselves to each
other. They behaved like strangers. She even called him
the wrong name."

"I'm working on opportunity now. We'll figure out the
motive later."

We? Val was about to dismiss his latest theory as a
flight of fancy when she remembered that Holly had
stared at Jake as if he looked familiar. Maybe he reminded
her of someone she'd once known. But to take cyanide to
the tea and use it on him required certainty about his
identity, and about her ability to slip him the poison with-

out anyone noticing. "One thing is clear—this wasn't a spur-of-the-moment crime. Cyanide means premeditation."

Granddad rubbed his chin as he often did when he was pondering an idea that popped into his head. "Did you put the food on Jake's plate or did Irene?"

Val shrugged. "We were both filling plates."

"Who took them to the table?"

"She did." Val shifted on the sofa to get away from a spring she could feel through the worn cushion. "I know what you're thinking. Irene could have poisoned something on the plate she put in front of him." And it had been Irene's idea to plate the food rather than pass it around.

"You said she didn't much like Jake."

An understatement. Irene couldn't abide him. Val believed her capable of slipping something in Jake's food to give him indigestion, but not to kill him. "Irene wouldn't tamper with any food she was preparing, and she's no murderer."

"I'm talking about the opportunity to poison Jake, and four people had it. The women on either side of him at the table—his wife and Holly." Granddad ticked them off on his fingers. "Then we have the ghost and Irene."

"Another person had the opportunity. Jake could have poisoned Jake, committing suicide in a dramatic way." Val jumped up from the sofa. "I almost forgot. I told Irene I'd drop off her china tonight, the stuff she supplied for the tea parties. I'd better call and tell her what happened."

"No! Don't call her. Let's go to her house. She's expecting you anyway." Granddad eased himself out of his lounge chair. "I want to see her face when you tell her Jake's dead."

Val sighed. Fifteen minutes ago he'd crashed on the chair in exhaustion. Now he was full of energy. Nothing animated him more than the prospect of solving a murder. Murder didn't exactly make him merry, but at least it took his mind off minor matters like playing Scrooge instead of Santa.

Chapter 5

As Granddad turned onto Creek Road, where Irene lived, Val looked out the window at the houses lit up for the season. One of them resembled a gingerbread house with multicolor lights framing the doors and windows, glowing candy canes lining the path to the front door, and gumdrop ornaments hanging from the trees.

Tonight Val couldn't even view holiday decorations without bleak thoughts intruding. Gingerbread houses had a dark history, linked to the Grimm brothers' tale of Hansel and Gretel, who kill a witch by the same cruel method she planned to use on them. Val shivered.

Granddad parked in front of Irene's one-story house decorated with a single string of white lights along the eaves. The house was plain and sturdy, like Irene and her husband.

Val rang the bell. When no one responded, she pushed the button longer, and Granddad knocked on the door.

As Irene opened it, the sound of a roaring crowd at a football game blared from the television. "It's hard for me to hear the bell when Roger watches TV. Have you been waiting long?"

Val knew from having tried to carry on a conversation with Irene's husband that he was both hard of hearing and taciturn. "We just got here. We have something important to tell you."

Irene frowned. "You didn't bring my china?"

Val shook her head. "No, and I came to explain why. Is this a good time for us to talk?"

Irene hesitated as if trying to ward off bad news. Maybe she was afraid her antique china had been stolen. Dealing with her resembled eating a loaf of day-old sourdough. You had to work your way through the crusty exterior to get to the softer middle.

Irene opened the door wider. "Come in. We can get away from the TV by sitting in the kitchen."

The front door opened directly into the living room. Val waved to Roger, who raised his hand in greeting and returned his attention to the football game. She followed Irene through the living room to the kitchen. Granddad stopped to exchange a few words with Roger, probably checking on the game score.

Val had never been in Irene's kitchen. Next to the new appliances, the cabinets and counters looked dated. Larger than the living room, the kitchen must have been extended to include an eating space and a small sitting area with an armchair and ottoman. From this room Irene would have a view of her side gardens and of the backyard that extended down to the creek. On a moonless night like this, Val couldn't see the creek, only the bare branches of the trees nearest the house.

Granddad joined them in the kitchen.

Irene pointed to the table. "Have a seat. Would you like some tea or water?"

He declined, but Val asked for water. Irene brought her a glass and put one for herself on the table. She sat down, her back erect, her hands folded.

The round table had exactly enough room for three people. The third chair must have been there for Irene and Roger's son, Jeremy, who worked afternoons at Val's Cool Down Café and evenings at the Bayport marina's crab restaurant. The young man probably visited and ate regularly with his parents, although he no longer lived with them.

Val got straight to the point. "I wanted to let you know that Jake became ill after you left the CAT Corner. An ambulance took him to the hospital. He died there."

Irene's eyes bugged out. "What was it? A heart attack?"

Granddad leaned across the table, scrutinizing Irene at closer range. "The police are keeping this under wraps for now, so don't tell anyone. He didn't die of natural causes. They're running tests for poison."

Irene looked askance. "Not by anything we gave him to eat. No one else was sick, were they?" She turned to Val for confirmation.

"No. The others were fine. The police are testing all the food in the CAT Corner. I wasn't allowed to remove anything, which is why I couldn't bring your china."

"I hope the police don't break any of it." Irene sipped her water. "I didn't much care for Jake, but when somebody dies, you gotta do what's right. I'll let the neighbors know he passed away. They'll stop in to make sure Jewel's okay for the next few days. If she has family coming, we'll pitch in and bring her some food."

Val was surprised. Irene wasn't just doing what was right, she was showing generosity toward inconsiderate neighbors. "That's good of you, Irene, especially after Jake and Jewel destroyed your plants."

"She wasn't involved. He did it in June, when he moved in. She didn't come until October." Irene ran her finger around the edge of her water glass. "Most married people move in at the same time."

Was Irene implying that Jake and Jewel weren't married? Val could think of good reasons why a woman might stay behind after her husband moved, like work or family obligations.

Granddad said, "Maybe Jewel stayed back to fix up their old house and get the best price for it. They could have taken out a bridge loan on the place here."

Irene folded her arms. "Uh-uh. My former neighbors told me Jake bought the house with cash. His name was the only one on the sales contract."

Still not proof they weren't married. Val picked up her glass. "They might have separated and then reconciled."

Irene raised a skeptical eyebrow. "After he chopped down the bushes between our houses, he could see right into our living room and kitchen. That works two ways." She pointed to the side window. "From there I have a view of the bedrooms in his place. His windows have curtains, but with the lights on at night, I could tell who was in the room. Those two slept in separate rooms, and I heard them arguing when they were sitting on their back patio."

Val wished she had a dollar for every married couple

who argued and slept apart. She could pay for all the needed improvements in Granddad's house and take a really nice vacation. "Where did Jake and Jewel come from?"

"Texas. They never said what part of the state. He sure didn't sound like he hailed from there."

Val agreed. She was no expert on regional speech differences, but he clearly didn't come from that far south.

Granddad sat back. "He ever say what line of work he was in?"

"No, but I found out what he was doing here." Irene paused for a drink of water, increasing the suspense. "He was trying to buy up some old houses on Brook Lane. He created a lot of bad blood between neighbors."

Val's friend, Bethany, just starting out as an elementary school teacher, rented a tiny house in that area. It was one of the few sections in town where people with modest incomes could afford a roof over their heads. "Why bad blood?"

"He made offers on several houses on the same block. When one person accepted his offer, Jake wouldn't go through with the sale unless the owner could convince his neighbors to sell too."

If Jake did that in Texas, Val would suspect an oil well under the houses, but what did Jake want with a bunch of small old houses in Bayport?

Granddad snapped his fingers. "He was going to tear down those houses and put up more expensive ones. That's why he's been cozying up to the town council members. He needed their support for his redevelopment plans."

Irene put her water glass down with a bang. "I get why he'd destroy houses to line his pockets, but what did he gain by killing my azaleas? I wasn't here when he cut them down, but Jeremy was. He told Jake to stop chopping down the azaleas because they were his mother's. Jake ridiculed Jeremy and said he had no reason to listen to a dumb kid."

Val knew how protective Irene was of Jeremy, who'd struggled with a learning disability. No wonder she detested Jake. Destroying her shrubs paled in comparison to dissing her son.

Irene continued. "Jake apologized and claimed he thought the shrubs were his. I told him I'd send before-and-after pictures of my garden to the newspaper and file a police complaint against him for vandalism."

"Did you do that?" Granddad said.

"No, because he said he'd pay for planting new bushes, but there's no way to replace mature plantings. It'll take years for any azaleas you plant now to grow as tall and full as the ones I had."

"Did he clear-cut on the other side of his house?" Granddad said.

"Yes, and behind it down to the creek. He said he had nothing against flowers, just against high bushes. I don't usually speak ill of the dead, but that man was a nasty piece of work."

Five minutes later, when Granddad and Val were in the car going home, he said, "That's one angry lady."

Val viewed Irene's obvious anger as a sign of innocence. "That doesn't mean she killed Jake. She did nothing to hide her hatred of him. Wouldn't the killer hide the motive for the murder?"

"After she told you and probably a lot of other folks what Jake did to her, she couldn't pretend to like him."

Once Granddad got an idea in his head, it was hard to

dislodge it, but Val would try. "Irene doesn't gain anything by killing Jake. It doesn't bring her azaleas back to life or erase his insult to her son." But the satisfaction of revenge was often its own reward.

"You're right. I'm not taking her off the list, but I'll move her to the bottom of it for now. Jewel stood to benefit most from his death, assuming that she's his wife or that he made out a will in her favor. I'll pay her a condolence visit tomorrow. You want to come along?"

"I'm serving brunch at the café until one. Then I have to get the food ready for the dinner I'm catering tomorrow night. I can squeeze in a visit with Jewel in between, but you'll have to bake something. She'll be more inclined to talk to us if our condolences come with cookies."

"I like that plan. It's a win-win for us. If she turns us away, we'll have lots of cookies to eat." He grinned. "We should also talk to the woman who could have poisoned Jake when she was down on the floor supposedly trying to help him."

"I'll tackle Holly Atherson on Monday." But Val would need an excuse to get together with her.

"You'll have to do it without me. I'm gonna be working all day on the recipes for my column."

Val had never convinced Granddad to finalize his recipes before the newspaper's Monday evening deadline.

On Sunday morning Val arrived at the café at ten. She relieved her teenage assistant, who'd served coffee and bagels to the athletic club's early birds. Still racking her brains for a pretext to visit Holly, Val had just emptied the old coffee from the carafe when Holly glided into the café.

She was as graceful in leggings and a quilted jacket as in the bridal gown she'd worn last night.

She approached the eating bar, her elfin face pinched. She glanced back at the club's reception desk outside the café alcove. "Is it okay for me to come here even if I'm not a club member?"

"Of course. The café is open to the public." Val was grateful she no longer needed an excuse to approach Holly, who apparently had a reason to talk to her. "Have a seat. Can I get you something to eat or drink?"

Holly climbed onto a stool at the eating bar, which separated the food counter from the café's bistro tables. Her nose twitched. "The coffee smells good, but I've already had my cup for the day."

She had a sensitive nose, smelling coffee after Val had emptied the carafe. "Would you like tea?"

"Herbal tea would be good. I don't care what kind. I couldn't reach Franetta this morning, so I came here, hoping you had news about Jake."

"I thought *you* were bringing *me* news about him." Val put a chamomile tea bag in a mug and added hot water from the dispenser. "Didn't you go to the hospital with Jewel?"

"No, I didn't. She wanted me to take her home so she could change out of the Mrs. Claus costume. She asked for directions to the hospital and said she'd drive her-self." Holly's eyes narrowed. "You know what happened to him, don't you?"

Val hesitated. The police hadn't yet made it public that Jake was poisoned, but surely the news of his death would be all over town before long. She put the tea in front of Holly. "Jake died last night."

Holly sighed. "I was afraid of that." She blinked rapidly, her eyes glistening.

Tears for a man she'd just met? Val resisted the temptation to conclude that Holly and Jake had known each other before last night. After all, the finality of death can bring anyone to tears. "Everyone else assumed that once Jake got emergency help, he would pull through. What made you afraid that he wouldn't?"

Holly shrugged and blew on her tea.

A nonanswer always motivated Val to persist. "Maybe you were afraid because you were a lot closer to Jake than anyone else."

Holly bit her lip, looking nervous. "What do you mean by that?"

"You might have noticed something that made you think he was beyond help. You were down on the floor, hovering over him, so the rest of us couldn't see him."

If Holly had slipped him some poison, she'd probably have taken those words as a veiled accusation and become defensive. Instead, she relaxed. Maybe Holly had interpreted being *closer to Jake than anyone else* as implying intimacy and was relieved to hear an alternate interpretation. Val now suspected Holly had known Jake *much* better than either of them had let on.

"I wasn't hovering over him," Holly snapped. "I was trying to help him when no one else was."

Not even his wife. "You certainly acted fast." But Holly hadn't continued her efforts for long. "Then, all of a sudden, you turned pale and gave up."

"Did I?" Holly's nose twitched, as it had earlier when she sniffed coffee even after it had gone down the drain.

Was the nose twitching now at the memory of an aroma?

Perhaps the distinctive odor of cyanide? "Did you smell something when you leaned close to Jake?"

Holly stared past Val. "I smelled death."

Val had trouble reading Holly. With her waiflike face, she resembled a little girl whose wrapped gift had been snatched before she could open it.

She put a few dollars on the eating bar, slid off the stool, and hurried out of the café, leaving her steaming tea untouched.

Val had more questions now than she'd had when Holly had sat down. What does death smell like? How long had she known Jake? And why hadn't she asked how he died?

Chapter 6

Val returned home in the early afternoon and parked in the driveway. She was about to go into the side vestibule when Granddad came out, ready to go visit Jewel. He carried a quiche in one hand and a cookie tin in the other. Val put both on the floor behind the driver's seat and climbed back into the car.

She waited until Granddad buckled his seat belt and then reversed out the driveway. "What's in the tin?"

"Leftover brownies and some coconut cookies I just made in case Jewel doesn't care for chocolate."

Val turned onto Main Street, where few signs remained of Victorian London. It was back to being a small town on the Eastern Shore with a steady stream of gasoline-powered traffic. "What have you heard from the chief?"

"Nothing directly from him. Today's police bulletin

said that an ambulance took a man from a business in Bayport to the hospital, where the man was pronounced dead. His death was under investigation. The bulletin also reported a burglary and a fender bender that happened yesterday. The final item was a police request for information about a person wearing a long black garment and walking unsteadily last evening in Bayport."

The lack of details surprised Val. Why had the police left out Jake's name? An explanation dawned on her. "Jake might have relatives besides his wife who need to be notified before the police make his identity public."

"News is spreading. After church this morning I heard people talking about Jake being dead. Someone said I didn't get along with him. Once word gets out that he was poisoned and you were serving the food—"

"The chief knows us too well to think we had anything to do with it." Yet town gossip could be brutal.

"We'd better figure out who killed Jake before tongues start wagging. Don't bring up poison when we talk to Jewel. The chief might not have told her how Jake died, especially if he suspects her of the murder. He'd be hoping she'd give herself away by blurting out something the police didn't reveal."

"You can give yourself away, not just by what you say, but by what you don't say. Holly Atherson stopped by the café this morning. She hadn't heard Jake was dead, but when I told her, she didn't ask how he died."

Val summarized their conversation for Granddad. By the time she finished, she was on Creek Road. She slowed down as she passed Irene's house and parked in front of the next house.

She and Granddad walked up the driveway to the Smiths' garage and then on the lawn to a small covered porch. The one-story house was similar in style to Irene's, but without the beautiful landscaping in the front yard. The yard here looked barren. The only bushes between the street and the house were low foundation plantings beneath the windows—Japanese barberries, invasive shrubs with sharp spines. There was no welcome mat at the front door.

Val rang the bell.

Jewel cracked the door open as if wary of anyone on her doorstep. "Yes?"

Val might not have recognized her if she hadn't known who lived in the house. Jewel's dark hair, brushed and sleek yesterday, now hung down uncombed and limp. She looked sickly pale without the pink blush she'd worn as Mrs. Claus.

"We were sorry to hear the bad news about Jake," Granddad said. "We brought you a meal, figuring you might not feel up to cooking."

Jewel glanced at the quiche he was carrying. "Thank you very much." She opened the door wider to reach out for it.

"We've got other food too. We'll take it inside for you." He stepped across the threshold past her and into the house. She couldn't stop him without using physical force. Val followed him inside.

They both gaped at the front room. The combination living-and-dining space looked as if a burglar had come through. Throw pillows littered the floor. Sofa cushions were upended and drawers left open.

Jewel couldn't miss their amazed looks. "Jake was sloppy. After what happened, I just couldn't bring myself to clean up. I thought of all the times we argued about his mess, and now he's gone."

Her dry eyes, with no hint of redness, didn't give the impression of someone sad and sentimental. And the room appeared to have been ransacked rather than left untidy.

Granddad strode across the living room to the dining table. The drawers in the sideboard next to it were open and papers strewn on the table. "Should I set the food here or take it to the kitchen?"

"Just leave it there." Jewel's hands fluttered as if shooing her visitors away.

She suddenly stopped and put her hands behind her back, but not before Val noticed two broken crimson fingernails, their pointy ends blunted, the tiny bows painted on them sliced through. What had Jewel been doing to break an index fingernail on each hand?

Val broke her nails most often when she was in a hurry and didn't pay attention to what she was doing. Judging by the state of this room, the person who'd gone through it had been rushed.

"I hate to trouble you," Granddad said, "but nature calls. Hope you don't mind if I use the facilities."

He hurried past the front door to what looked like a hall, the only place the bathroom could be in the small house.

The longer Val could keep the widow talking, the more time he'd have to poke around. "Do you have family coming to help you get through the next few days?"

"*Family?*" Jewel's voice dripped with scorn. "Haven't seen mine for years, and Jake's kin are dead."

So much for the idea that Jewel would talk about her relatives. "Where did you meet him?"

"Vegas. I was working at a casino."

"I've never been there." Val hoped Jewel would gush about Las Vegas and its attractions. Didn't happen. Val had no choice but to talk about herself. "I haven't been to that part of the country at all. Closest I came was California. We were a military family and moved every few years. Mostly we ended up near a coast, which makes sense because Dad was in the Navy." Val babbled about the various places her family had lived, aware that Jewel was paying no attention. Val continued. "When my father retired from the military, my parents moved to Florida— near the water, of course."

Jewel stood up. "I hope your grandfather's okay. He's taking a while."

"He's slow at his age." Val raised her voice to alert him. "*I'm sure he'll join us in a second.*"

As she'd predicted, he appeared in the hall. They said their goodbyes to Jewel and again offered their sympathies.

Granddad handed Jewel a business card. "If you need help, just give me a call. I'm good at locating things folks have lost and in burglar-proofing their houses. Without Jake here, you may want to beef up your security. Whatever problem you have, if I can't fix it, I probably know someone who can."

Val could tell by the spring in his step as he went back to the car that his snooping had yielded some results.

As she pulled away from the curb, she said, "What did you discover?"

"The bathroom cabinet had a supply of cream bleach for facial hair and some gunk you can comb into your hair and beard to whiten it. The receipt for that came from an outfit called Santa Supplies."

Having noticed Jake's dark roots, Val wasn't surprised. "He must have really wanted to play Santa."

"He didn't do it just for that. His hair was white when

he moved here six months ago, but it might not have been before that. If you're clean-shaven and dark-haired, dying your hair white and growing a full white beard would make you look totally different. I figure he changed his appearance because he was hiding from the law."

Val thought of a less dramatic reason for Jake to bolt. "He might have been running away from his wife. She didn't show up in Bayport until he'd been here three months. It could have taken her that long to find him."

"Why wouldn't he just divorce her?"

"That might have cost him more money than bolting." Val slowed down for a stop sign. "Jewel told me they met when she worked in a Las Vegas casino. Maybe he was a gambler with unpaid debts. He moved to an obscure little town on the Eastern Shore to avoid a collection agent or a mob enforcer. That would explain why he cut down all the bushes. He didn't want anyone to hide behind the shrubs and sneak up on him."

Granddad peered at her over his bifocals as if she'd lost her mind. "Hit men hide in plain sight and use guns with silencers. They don't need bushes, they don't dress like Dickens characters, and they don't kill with poisoned cookies."

"I'm not suggesting a hit man killed Jake with a cookie." She turned onto Main Street. "I'm saying he could have been afraid of someone. If you disagree, let's hear your explanation of why he aged himself, moved across the country, and got rid of all the hiding places near his house."

Granddad stroked his chin. "I think Jake did those things so he could spy on someone who lives here."

"Who? Irene and Roger Pritchard? I doubt they're secret agents from decades ago or major crime figures now."

"They aren't the only neighbors. Maybe he was watching the ones on the other side. He had to cut down the bushes on both sides so it wouldn't be obvious who he was spying on."

"We can't do anything but guess what Jake was up to because we know almost nothing about him." Val turned onto Grace Street and slowed as she approached Granddad's house. His investigation course had taught him how to dig out information on the Internet. "While I'm cooking tonight's dinner for the Naimans, you could do online research on Jake and Jewel."

"First I'm going to the bookshop to see how Dorothy is coping with the shock of a customer dying there. I'll research Jake after that, if I have time."

Val was glad he put Dorothy first. Sleuthing energized him, but he also needed someone to relax with. Most of his old friends had retired to Florida, moved to live near their children, or died.

She drove into the driveway. "Who do you suppose made the mess in the Smiths' house? Jake, Jewel, or a burglar?"

"Jewel tossed the place. She was searching for something. There's a pull-down staircase in the hallway where the bedrooms are. It wasn't completely closed. She must have gone up to the attic to search and then, after she came down, she couldn't get the wood panel that hides the staircase to go up the whole way."

"She broke two nails since last night, maybe from struggling with the pull-down stairs."

"Or with stuff in the attic."

Once they were in the house, Val headed straight for the kitchen. "After last night's tea party with a bunch of strangers dressed weirdly and tensions at the table, I'm looking forward to cooking and serving dinner to a normal family."

"Don't get your hopes up. The woman who hired you to cater tonight's dinner wasn't acting normal yesterday, unless tailing someone is normal."

Val took Granddad's interpretation of Elaine Naiman's actions with a grain of salt. He fed his imagination with Hitchcock movies, most of which involved at least one character spying on or stalking another.

"It doesn't matter what she did yesterday, Granddad. This is a happy occasion. I'm going to make a beautiful cake for Mr. Naiman's birthday. He'll be surrounded by family, old friends, and good vibes." Val hoped those vibes would help her forget the murder and put her into the Christmas spirit.

"You're setting the bar too high, Val."

Chapter 7

On Sunday evening Val climbed the porch steps at the two-story, neo-Colonial house where she would cater Oliver Naiman's birthday dinner. Before she reached the front door, Elaine Naiman opened it. She looked less harried than when she'd collided with Granddad and knocked off his hat yesterday.

She touched her mouth with her index finger and whispered, "My father is napping." She pointed to the wood staircase that led up from the center hall to the second floor. "Can I help you bring in the food?"

Val handed her two large, insulated tote bags and went back to the car for the cake. When she returned with it, Elaine led her through the hall to the kitchen door at the back of the house.

On her way there, Val glanced into the L-shaped, living-dining room. No one was in it. As she unpacked the food, she said, "Your sister and brother-in-law aren't here?"

"They are . . . sort of. Cyndi's upstairs perfecting her hair and makeup. Her husband, Kevin, borrowed our neighbor's boat and went fishing."

Val looked through the French doors to the backyard. She could just make out the river in the twilight. The houses on Belleview Avenue were prized not just for their wonderful views, but also for their easy access to the bay. Almost all the houses had docks. It was a short, scenic boat ride from here past the Bayport Marina and out to the broad expanse of the Chesapeake.

"Your sister's husband must really enjoy fishing to do it in December." Val hoped he wouldn't catch anything. Whenever Granddad caught fish, he always insisted on cooking it that day. She had no desire to add a last-minute fish course to dinner.

"Fishing's his excuse for being on a boat. I'm not even sure he baits the hook." Elaine pointed to the two coffee-makers on the counter. "After dinner, make a carafe of regular coffee and use a pod to make a single cup of decaffeinated for my father. Caffeine's bad for him. If anyone else wants decaf, you'll have to use another pod. We have only regular ground coffee."

The floor above creaked. Val glanced up and then heard quick footsteps on the stairway. A man pushing eighty wouldn't bound down the stairs like that. She expected to see Elaine's sister, the redhead who'd shopped for facial products at Chatty's booth yesterday.

Instead, a petite young woman with long, dark hair poked her head into the kitchen from the hallway. "You want any help with dinner?"

Val opened her mouth to decline the offer, but Elaine spoke first.

"Thank you for offering to help. Our caterer, Val, will take care of everything tonight. Val, this is Iska, my father's health aide."

Iska matched Granddad's description of the woman Elaine had tailed yesterday. "Nice to meet you, Iska. I'm Val Deniston."

Elaine said, "Take the rest of the evening off, Iska. We'll manage without you."

The young woman's face fell. "I have a birthday gift for Mr. Naiman."

"You can give it to him later tonight if he's still awake when you come back, or it can wait until tomorrow."

"Okay. I'll get ready and go."

As Elaine shepherded the health aide out to the hall, Val went through the doorway between the kitchen and the dining room. The only thing on the cherrywood table was a centerpiece of red and yellow chrysanthemums. The tablecloth, dishes, and glasses might be in the buffet, but Val didn't want to root around in it without asking Elaine.

A framed family picture hung above the buffet. A handsome man, a woman with a plain but pleasant face, and two girls close in age. Val guessed the bigger one, about eight years old, was Cyndi, a curly-haired redhead with porcelain skin and a smile that showed her dimples. The smaller girl with dark, straight hair must be Elaine. She stared solemnly ahead.

The girls in the photo reminded Val of fraternal twins she'd known in college. One had been blond, delicate, and vivacious. Her brunette sister, with heavy brows and coarser skin, had been the serious one. Val had expected the quieter one to resent her popular, outgoing twin, but instead she'd idolized her.

Elaine's comment about Cyndi perfecting her makeup suggested the Naiman sisters had a different dynamic than the twins from her college class.

As Elaine joined her in the dining room, Val said, "You have only six chairs at the table. I thought there would be eight for dinner."

"One couple couldn't make it. Their daughter had her baby earlier than expected, so they've left to see their new grandchild. It'll just be the four of us and our neighbors, the Frosts. You must have met Franetta. She knows everyone in this town."

"I've met her, but I didn't know where she lived." Franetta's husband had been on the town council for years, so Val wasn't surprised that they had a house on the premier street in Bayport. "I can set the table if you put out the china and cutlery you want to use."

"Cyndi will set the table. She always enjoys making it look like a work of art instead of just a surface for eating."

"Then I'll get started on the food." Val went back to the kitchen, thinking that Elaine was nibbling on sour grapes tonight.

Most of the dishes were at least partially made, but some needed time in the oven. She preheated it.

Cyndi swept into the room and introduced herself. Val had seen her from yards away at the Dickens festival yesterday. Now a close look at her face revealed that her ivory complexion had more flaws and wrinkles than her sister's less delicate skin. The few extra pounds Elaine carried plumped up her face and gave her a more youthful appearance than the thinner Cyndi. The plainer sister had blossomed in middle age while the pretty one had wilted.

"I'm so glad you're cooking," Cyndi said in her low-pitched breathy voice. "I'm hopeless in the kitchen, and Elaine isn't a lot better. My father has to eat whatever his aide, Iska, cooks. It all involves mounds of rice. Oops. I hope you're not serving rice with dinner."

"I'm not, but Elaine said your father isn't used to his dentures yet and would have trouble eating anything that's hard to chew."

"I didn't know about his dentures. He's the birthday boy, so I guess we'll all have to eat what he eats. What's on the menu?"

"Appetizers to go along with drinks in the living room, and then squash-and-parsnip soup, beef bourguignon that will almost melt in your mouth, a spinach soufflé, and a mashed potato casserole. Dessert is a lemon chiffon layer cake. I'll put French bread on the table in case someone craves crunchiness."

"That sounds wonderful!"

Elaine appeared in the doorway between the dining room and kitchen. "Weren't you going to set the table, Cyndi?"

The two went into the dining room. Though they couldn't see Val standing near the sink, their voices drifted toward her as she peeled potatoes. Elaine brought up the subject of their father's living arrangements.

Cyndi's voice carried into the kitchen. "Kevin and I talked about your suggestion. He doesn't think it's a good idea for Dad to move to the retirement village. Moving upsets older people, and Dad doesn't need to move. He has Iska to help him."

"It's hard for him to manage the stairs. Iska's a small

woman. She wouldn't be able to keep him upright if he lost his balance. He could easily fall."

Val was glad that Granddad's house had a main floor bedroom and bath. If stairs ever became a hazard for him, he wouldn't have to move.

"Kevin says we can get a stairlift," Cyndi said. "He'll install it for Dad."

"Dad won't use it. He's stubborn and thinks he can still do everything he did when he was younger. Living where there are no stairs is what he needs at this stage."

"Retirement places are ridiculously expensive, and Iska costs next to nothing."

"With his investments and the money from the sale of this house, Dad can afford years at the retirement village. The village provides free transportation to medical appointments. Iska doesn't have a license and can't drive him. If the nerve damage to his foot gets any worse, it won't be safe for him to get behind a wheel. His doctor says that's likely to happen soon."

"Soon is not now." Cyndi's voice was even huskier than usual. "To me, he doesn't look as if he's declined so much that he needs a place like that."

Listening to the sisters argue made Val uncomfortable. She dreaded the day when she might have a similar conversation with her mother or her brother.

"You don't come here often enough to judge Dad's health, Cyndi. His memory is certainly getting worse," Elaine said. "We shouldn't wait until he's forced to leave this house. Then he'd have the double whammy of a health problem and a move at the same time. I'd like him to visit the senior village, find out what kind of activities and services they offer, and talk to people who live there."

"Elaine, you're like a dog with a bone. You just keep

gnawing on it. What if Dad doesn't like the place after visiting it?"

A legitimate concern in Val's opinion. She volunteered at the retirement village, holding trivia sessions and giving talks about food history. The village residents she encountered varied widely in their opinions about the place. Some hated it, some loved it, most just tolerated it.

Elaine said, "We need to convince him it's the best option for him. You should be there too when he visits the place so he knows we're both on board with his move. Can you make time for it in the next week or so?"

"*Next week*? What's the rush?"

"I'm moving in two months. I won't be living close enough to check on Dad once or twice a week, make his doctors' appointments, and see that his prescriptions are filled. You'll have to take over those tasks. It will be easier on you if Dad is settled in the senior village by then."

Val heard slow, heavy footsteps on the stairs. Oliver Naiman's daughters would probably prefer their father not overhear their conversation.

"This is sudden," Cyndi said. "Where are you moving?"

"North Carolina. It isn't sudden. I've—"

Val poked her head into the dining room. "I think your father's on his way downstairs."

Elaine lowered her voice. "We'll talk about this later, Cyndi."

The sisters came into the kitchen from the dining room at the same time as Oliver Naiman came in the doorway from the hall. He was tall but slightly stooped, with a thicker crop of white hair than most men his age. Elaine introduced Val to him.

He smiled warmly. "I'm pleased to meet you, Val. And

grateful you're cooking so everyone can enjoy dinner." He peered into the dining room. "Where's Iska?"

"I gave her the evening off," Elaine said.

"*Why did you do that?*" Oliver bellowed.

Startled, Val took a step back, as if she'd just heard a clap of thunder on a sunny day. She and Granddad didn't always agree, but he never raised his voice.

Cyndi stared at her father, aghast.

But Elaine, the more frequent visitor here, didn't look surprised. "Iska works hard. I thought she could use some time for herself."

Her soothing words didn't soften her father's glower. "I gave her time off every day this week. I wanted her here for my birthday party."

Val relaxed. He now sounded more aggrieved than angry.

"You'll have your whole family and two old friends celebrating with you." Cyndi slipped her arm through his. "Let's go sit in the living room and wait for Kevin. Did you know the Frosts let him use their boat so he could go fishing? That was so sweet of them."

"The Frosts will do anything for me," he said as he left the kitchen.

Val wasn't sure how to interpret Oliver's comment. Was he grateful for good neighbors, disdainful of his son-in-law, or arrogant about his own influence?

Elaine followed her sister and father out of the room.

Val was glad to have the kitchen to herself. It didn't open directly to the living room, so she couldn't hear voices from there. She wouldn't be as distracted as she'd been by the conversation in the dining room. She heard the front door open and footsteps on the squeaky stairs. Soon after, she picked up the faint sound of a shower overhead. Cyndi's husband must have arrived.

Half an hour before Val was scheduled to serve dinner, she was putting the potato casserole in the oven when he came into the kitchen.

"Hello there. I'm Kevin Kenwig, tonight's wine steward and bartender." He gave her a wry half smile. "You must be the famous Chef Val."

She centered the casserole on the rack and closed the oven door. "I'm Val Deniston and not a chef. Happy to have someone handle the drinks." In his cardigan sweater with suede elbow patches, he looked more like a professor than a wine steward. He had a slight paunch and receding sandy hair.

He surveyed the trays where she was arranging the appetizers. "What have we here? Roasted sweet potato rounds with what on top? Looks like chèvre and a dollop of cranberry sauce."

She mentally tipped her hat to him. Most people would say, *What's that white and red stuff on top of the orange circle?* She smiled. "You guessed right. I usually put dried cranberries on top of the potato rounds, but with your father-in-law's teeth problems, the sauce would work better."

"What's inside the little pastry puffs?"

"Cream cheese, sun-dried tomato spread, and basil pesto."

"I'm looking forward to a dinner of the finest soft food." His ironic half smile appeared again. "Is catering your main occupation?"

"It's a sideline. I manage a café. Your appetizer analysis makes me think you work or have worked in food service."

"No. Strictly an amateur cook. High school science teacher by profession, but there's some crossover. I assign cooking experiments to illustrate chemical principles."

She figured he was probably a good teacher, thinking up creative assignments. "Where do you teach?"

"Outside Baltimore, not far from where we live." The doorbell rang. "That must be the neighbors. I'd better get to work here."

He uncorked a bottle of white wine and one of red, and filled drink orders efficiently.

Once everyone had their drinks, Val took the appetizers to the living room, where the family sat with their guests, Franetta and her husband, Thatcher, a trim man in his sixties. She'd dressed in a red sweater and black pants. He wore a crisp blue shirt and an air of authority. He paused briefly in the middle of his monologue to acknowledge Val's existence and then continued talking.

Val knew the Frosts from the athletic club, where they played in a tennis league. Val had seen them while on a court next to them. Franetta was the better player, but that didn't stop Thatcher from giving her pointers to improve her game. Now, as Val circulated with the appetizers, he regaled the group with all he'd accomplished on the town council.

When he stopped puffing up himself long enough to pop a puff pastry into his mouth, Oliver said, "How's your son these days?"

Thatcher's bushy eyebrows rose in surprise. "I can't believe you didn't hear the news. He's in line for a job at the White House."

"Franetta told us that last weekend, Dad," Elaine said. "You must have forgotten."

He shrugged. "I remember events from long ago better than recent ones."

Elaine looked pointedly at her sister, as if to say *I told you he was forgetful*.

In his booming voice, Thatcher once again gave himself a verbal pat on the back. "I have to admit I called in some favors and pulled some strings in Washington to make sure he was first in line for that job. He'll start as soon as his preliminary security clearance goes through."

Oliver raised his wineglass as if toasting. "That boy has made something of himself. I'm glad I helped him out of a fix."

"These look so yummy." Franetta took a puff pastry with one hand and a sweet potato appetizer with the other. "Did all of you get to the Dickens festival yesterday?"

Cyndi sipped her wine. "Dad didn't feel up to walking around in the cold, but we got him there briefly toward the end. When I was in the supermarket today, I overhead a clerk and customer say that someone died at the festival."

"An older man collapsed after the festival ended." Franetta held up the sweet potato round she'd nibbled. "Val, these taste even more delicious than they look."

"I might know the man who died," Oliver said. "What was his name?"

"Jake Smith. He was new in town, so you probably don't know him." Franetta leaned forward in her seat. "Now, what was everyone's favorite part of the festival?"

As they chatted about the booths and events, Val circulated again with the trays. Franetta's ability to change the subject with lightning speed kept Jake's death out of the conversation.

With more dinner prep to do, Val left the appetizers on the coffee table. Thatcher Frost seized the conversation ball again to talk about his favorite subject—himself.

She walked back to the kitchen, understanding why Franetta filled her evenings with volunteer work. Anything to get away from that man. She had talked up a storm at meetings and at the tea last night, maybe because she had little chance to exercise her vocal cords at home.

Later, when everyone was at the dining table, Thatcher had less to say. He focused on eating, taking second helpings of everything.

Val was too busy to pay attention to the table talk until she was serving the dessert. After everyone sang "Happy Birthday," she took the cake from the table, put it on the buffet, and removed the candles Oliver had blown out.

"I don't feel older than yesterday," he said, "but I've reached an age when I should set things right or I might die before I get the chance."

"Don't be so gloomy, Dad," Cyndi said. "You've got years ahead of you."

"On another subject and since we're all together," Elaine said, "I have an announcement. I'm getting married in February. It'll be a small wedding, but you're all invited."

Her knife poised over the cake, Val glanced sideways at the family. They looked stunned. She concentrated on cutting the cake and putting slices onto plates.

Franetta broke the silence by clapping. "Of course we'll come. Wonderful news! Congratulations."

"February!" Oliver said. "I'd think it was a shotgun wedding except that you're too old for that." He and Thatcher laughed, but no one else did. Then Oliver patted Elaine's hand. "I'm happy for you. Who's the lucky guy? That Navy fellow from Annapolis you brought here once?"

Elaine nodded. "Scott. He was here more than once."

Cyndi said, "So that's why you're moving away."

Val put a slice of cake in front of Oliver.

He didn't even glance at it. He turned to Elaine. "Moving away?"

"Scott just retired. Years ago he bought a house on the coast of North Carolina, and that's where we'll be living." She leaned toward her father. "I'll drive up to visit you, of course. And Cyndi will be coming to see you more often."

"Absolutely," Kevin said. "We'll both be here for you."

Franetta nodded. "So will we. You can rely on us if you need help with anything."

Thatcher spoke up. "When this place gets to be too much for you, let us know. Our son would definitely be interested in buying it as a weekend place."

Oliver smiled and gazed around the table at his family and friends. "Thank you. I'll manage here . . . with help from my new wife. Iska agreed to marry me."

Cyndi dropped her fork. It hit her plate with a clatter.

Val delivered the last piece of cake and sidled back to the kitchen. The Naimans probably didn't want outsiders around for the fallout from Oliver's bombshell. Franetta and Thatcher must have had the same thought. They finished dessert quickly, said a quick goodbye, and left. But Val couldn't do that. She still had to clean up after the dinner, an easier mess to tackle than the one the family faced.

At least this dinner, unlike the tea last evening, hadn't ended in murder.

Chapter 8

While Val loaded the dishwasher in the Naiman kitchen, the family in the dining room couldn't see her, but she could hear them.

Cyndi was the first to speak after the neighbors left. "I can't believe you're thinking about getting married, Dad. Mom has been gone less than two years. You're old enough to be Iska's grandfather."

"You're not helping," her husband said quietly to her.

Val agreed. Cyndi's attempt to guilt-trip her father might backfire.

"I loved your mother," Oliver said. "Still do. When she was sick, Iska was there day and night. Afterward, she helped me deal with my grief. She took care of us, and I'd like to take care of her too. I want to give her some security so she'll be okay once I'm gone. It's the least I can do."

"We're all grateful to Iska," Elaine said. "But you can take care of her without marrying her. Remember her in your will and leave her some cash."

Val wondered how that idea would go over with Cyndi. She'd probably object less to the cost of a retirement village if the alternative was her father's marriage.

Oliver shook his head. "Money can't buy the kind of security she needs. When she marries me, she'll be an American citizen."

Kevin chimed in. "It's not automatic. If the feds think that's the reason for the marriage, they won't confer citizenship."

"It's not the reason we're getting married," Oliver shouted. "We love each other."

"I have no doubt you love Iska." Elaine's voice was quiet, her tone soothing. "But I need to tell you something about her. When I was at the festival yesterday morning, I noticed her doing something that surprised me. I took a picture of her with my phone. I think you should see it. She was kissing a young man."

"Could be her brother or cousin," Oliver snapped.

"Look closely at the picture, Dad," Elaine said. "That's not a brotherly kiss."

A long silence followed. Val shifted her position so she could see the table. Cyndi looked over Oliver's shoulder while he peered at the phone. Then he slapped it down on the table.

"I've had enough of this birthday," he roared. "I'm going to bed."

The wood floors squeaked as he made his way to the hall stairs. Val scurried back to the sink, her stomach churning. She felt sorry for all of them.

Elaine groaned. "I hated doing that, especially on his

birthday. We're lucky he didn't elope with Iska. The only bright spot is that he may be more willing to move into the retirement village if she's not in the picture."

"Did you have any idea before tonight what was going on between them?" Kevin said.

"Lately I noticed Iska teasing him in a flirty way, and he seemed to like it. Last week he wanted to know where Mom's jewelry box was, and he never asked that before. I'm just glad I took that picture when I spotted her yesterday. I don't think Dad would have believed me without the photographic evidence."

Val gave Elaine points for evasiveness. She'd made it sound as if she'd been near Iska by chance, rather than by doggedly following her, as Granddad had reported.

"Should I go up to make sure he's okay?" Kevin said. "The photo shocked him. We don't want him to harm himself."

"Yes, check on him," Elaine said. "Make sure he stays in his room. If he doesn't go to sleep right away, sit and talk with him. I don't want him downstairs when Iska comes back. I have a plan to deal with her, and you'll both have to help."

"Kevin and I need to leave soon," Cyndi said. "I have an early flight to Chicago tomorrow. All I want to do is go home and go to sleep."

"You can't leave yet, Cyndi. Take the suitcase from the closet in Iska's room and pack her things in it. Keep an eye out for anything that looks like Mom's jewelry and set it aside. Bring everything down here. Iska can't stay here anymore."

Val wondered how Oliver would react to the disappearance of Iska. Would he be relieved or furious?

"You're throwing her out?" Cyndi said slowly as if confused. "On a cold night like this?"

"I'm not a Dickens villain, Cyndi. She has places to go. Her relatives live around here. She knows people from church. And, as we now know, she has a boyfriend. If she stays here, she'll explain away the boyfriend and tell Dad what he wants to hear. Next thing you know, they'll be secretly married."

Cyndi yawned audibly. "We have to find another aide fast."

"No, we don't. Iska went to the beach on several weekends last summer. Dad managed on his own."

"He might forget to take his meds. Will you be here tomorrow morning?"

"No, I have clients who've flown in for an early meeting with me. His meds are in a pill box labeled with the days of the week, and I'll call to remind him. I can ask the woman down the block to check that he's taking them. She's given him vitamin shots, so he knows her."

"She's a nurse?"

"Pharmacist. We won't have to worry about his meds once he's in the senior village. Before we can move him there, though, we have to get rid of Isk—" Elaine broke off. "Kevin, you're supposed to be upstairs with Dad."

"He's in bed. Exhausted."

"That makes two of us," Cyndi said.

"You do look tired, Cyndi," her husband said. "We'd better go soon."

"Would the two of you please pack Iska's belongings? You can leave after that. I'm going to stay down here to watch for her and keep her from going upstairs."

With the family taking up their battle stations, Val could finally go into the dining room without intruding on them. As she cleared the table, she noticed still-wrapped birthday gifts on the buffet. Too bad Elaine hadn't waited until after her father opened them before thrusting the photo of Iska in front of him. As long as those wrapped gifts sat there, they would remind him of his unhappy birthday. Val resisted the urge to tuck them away. It was none of her business.

She stored the leftovers in the fridge, enough for Oliver to heat up and eat for the next few days. Finally ready to leave, she went through the doorway from the kitchen to the hall, just as Iska came in the front door. Elaine confronted her. Val slipped back into the kitchen, a captive audience for the next act in a sad family drama.

When Val returned home from the Naiman house, she found Granddad in the kitchen, pouring water from the teakettle into a cup.

"You want some tea?" When she nodded, he made another cup. "How did the party go?"

"The food was a hit. No one died. That's the best I can say about it." She sat down at the table. "I can clear up one mystery. The small, dark-haired woman Elaine followed at the festival was Oliver's health aide, Iska. The big to-do at the birthday dinner revolved around her."

He brought both cups to the table and sat down across from her. She told him what had happened before, during, and after the birthday party, ending with Elaine firing Iska and barring her from the house.

"I felt sorry for Iska when Elaine gave her a carrot-and-stick ultimatum. If Iska left immediately and stayed away from Oliver, Elaine would give her a good reference so she could get another job as a health aide. But if

Iska refused or ever tried to contact Oliver, Elaine would report her to ICE as an illegal."

Granddad's eyebrows shot up. "She doesn't mess around. Did Iska put up a fight?"

"No. She called someone to pick her up. She wanted to leave Oliver a birthday gift, but Elaine wouldn't let her."

"The next few days are gonna be hard on him. Is one of his daughters staying with him?"

"No. They're both driving home tonight. Cyndi and her husband left while I was still there." Val sipped her tea. "Instead of raising my spirits, Oliver's birthday dinner left me depressed. I'd rather talk about Jake's death. Did you discover anything about him online?"

"Googling Jake Smith gave me more than a hundred million hits. When I added Texas to the search, I narrowed it down to thirty million. That's not counting the Jacob Smiths. Looking up Jewel Smith in Texas, I ended up with only thirteen million hits. I'll leave it to the police to figure out which Smiths landed here."

"We've at least learned a lesson. If you want to make yourself hard to find, use a common name." Val swirled the tea in her cup. "Any luck digging up information on the others at the tea?"

"I found another person with a motive. The librarian, Shantell Defoe, had a big beef with Jake. She lives on the block where he was making offers on houses. She formed a committee to stop him and tried to talk people out of selling. The neighbors who wanted to cash out were lobbying the others to sell. Folks who'd gotten along well for years became enemies."

"So that's why she was glaring at him across the table. But the odds are against her poisoning him. Murderous librarians are rare, and she wasn't anywhere near Jake at the table." Unlike Holly, who'd kneeled down next to him when he was on the floor. "Did you discover anything about Holly Atherson?"

"Yup. She had the know-how to kill Jake. She studied pharmacy and worked at a poison control center."

Val nearly choked on her tea. "Is she working as a pharmacist now?"

Granddad shook his head. "Her husband's a retired doctor. She never got a job after moving here from Pittsburgh a few years ago. Gotta wonder why. Maybe she mishandled drugs."

"Or she just wanted to retire along with him. Where do they live?"

"On Belleview Avenue."

"Like the Naimans." Val would bet Holly was the neighboring pharmacist who gave Oliver vitamin shots.

"So what have I got to show for my research? Nothing on Jake. Shantell the librarian with a motive to kill him but no opportunity. Holly the poison expert with no motive but the opportunity."

"We might dig up a motive for her, but her opportunity, if you can call it that, depended on two unlikely things. She happened to bring poison to a tea party. And her intended victim conveniently sank to the floor unconscious."

Granddad didn't argue with this. "We're left with Irene at the bottom of the list and Jewel at the top. She had the strongest motive—her husband's money—and the best opportunity."

"No. The Ghost of Christmas Presents had the best opportunity." Val swallowed the last of her tea and stood up. "By now the police must have some leads on who that person was. I'm going to bed with hopes that the chief will wrap up the case tomorrow and tie it with a holiday bow."

"Happy dreams."

At twelve thirty on Monday, Val was putting a quiche in the oven at the café when Franetta rushed in. She usually operated like an efficient engine, but today she was frazzled, a machine gone haywire. Her tight, gray curls resembled springs, poking out in all directions from her head.

"Hey, Val." She popped onto a stool at the eating counter. "Nothing to eat or drink for me. I'm on my way to yoga class, just stopping to give you the news."

Was the news about Jake? "I'm glad you came in. What's going on?"

Franetta sighed. "Oliver Naiman is dead."

"Oh, no!" Val's stomach knotted. Had he fallen down the stairs as his daughter had feared? "I'm so sorry."

"Me too. Elaine called me this morning and asked me to check on him because Iska wouldn't be there. I went over about nine. He didn't answer the doorbell, so I let myself in with my key and found him on the kitchen floor. I didn't think anything could be done for him. I called 911 and notified Elaine. She was in a meeting, but she rushed out and got here in an hour."

"Could you tell if Oliver had taken his meds? Cyndi was worried he might forget to take his pills." And Val was worried he might have taken too many. Maybe he'd been so depressed over losing Iska that he'd committed suicide.

"I didn't notice any meds. He'd made coffee and drunk most of a cup, but there weren't any breakfast plates or bowls on the table, only a box of chocolates with the lid off. Three pieces were missing. He must have gotten the candy as a birthday present and decided to eat it for breakfast."

"No one in his family would have given it to him. When I suggested making a fudge birthday cake, Elaine said chocolate was bad for her father." That didn't mean he hadn't bought the candy for himself. Granddad sometimes cheated on the low-fat diet his doctor had recommended. "Why do you think it was a birthday present?"

"There was a gift bag on the kitchen counter like people use when they don't want to bother wrapping a box." Franetta's tone suggested disapproval.

"Was there a card in the bag or one of those To-From tags attached to it?"

"There was a tag, but no writing on it. Maybe Iska gave it to him."

"She cooked for him. She would have known he shouldn't eat chocolate." Besides, Elaine hadn't let Iska leave Oliver a gift.

"I don't understand why Iska wasn't there this morning." Franetta's eyes widened. "I just thought of something. Last night when Oliver said he was going to marry her, I took it as a weird remark. Lately he's been saying things that had no basis in reality. But if it was true that he was going to marry her, his family would have fired Iska. Was there a big blowup after Thatcher and I went home?"

Val couldn't help but listen to the family's conversation last night, but she drew the line at telling the neighbors what happened. "I left as soon as I could." *Time to change the subject.* "How long did Oliver live next door to you?"

"About seven years. His parents lived there when we

moved into our house thirty years ago. Oliver would
bring his family to visit them. When his parents retired to
Florida, he kept the house as a vacation place. Then when
Oliver retired . . ."

Half a dozen customers had sat down at the café tables
while Franetta was giving the history of the house next to
hers. "If you'll excuse me, Franetta, I have to take some
lunch orders."

"And my yoga class is starting any minute." Franetta
climbed down from the stool. "I hope your business doesn't
go belly-up."

Val froze. "Why would it?"

"Once word gets out that two men died after eating
meals you catered, risk-adverse people might overreact."
Franetta left the café on that cheery note.

Val groaned. If anyone tried to blame her, she could
point out that others had consumed her food without ill
effects and that the deaths of Jake and Oliver had more in
common besides her catering. They'd died within two
days of each other, one after eating a gift cookie, the other
after eating gift chocolates. Val wondered if any of Oliver's neighbors had seen the Ghost of Christmas Presents
on Belleview Avenue.

Stop. She was letting her imagination run away with
her. There was no proof that the gingerdead man had made
a dead man of Jake Smith. And Oliver Naiman, a senior
with health issues, had surely died of natural causes,
nothing to do with gifts or ghosts.

She'd convinced herself of that by the time her assistant, Irene's son, came to relieve her. Jeremy would work
behind the counter for the next few hours, the café's
slowest time, and then turn the reins over to his mother,
who would manage the evening meal.

Before leaving the café, Val took a moment to call Granddad. He was sorry to hear about Oliver's death but didn't ask for details because he was in the middle of testing recipes for the column he had to submit today. As soon as she hung up, she got a call from Chief Yardley.

"Can you come by my office this afternoon?" he said.

"Sure." He must have an update on Jake, but Val was surprised he would share it with her. Most of the time she had to beg for information about ongoing cases. "I'm heading out of the café now. I'll stop at your office on the way home if that works for you, and I'll bring some coffee and cookies with me."

"I reached you at the perfect moment. While you're driving here, please refresh your memory of last night. I'd like an account of what happened at the Naiman house."

Val clutched her phone tightly. He wouldn't ask for that information if Oliver had died of natural causes. Her first instincts about the man's death might have been right.

Chapter 9

Val sat in a straight-backed metal chair facing Chief Yardley in his cushioned desk chair. "I may buy you a pad for your guest chair as a Christmas gift."

"I wouldn't accept it." He sipped his coffee. "That chair gives folks an incentive to take care of business and leave. If they were comfortable, they'd stay longer and I'd get less work done."

"Point taken." Val wouldn't dally, but she didn't intend to leave without asking about the Jake Smith investigation. "I can make this quick. What do you want to know about last night?"

"Everything you saw and heard from the time you arrived at the Naiman place."

Forget quick. She squirmed. "What I heard includes conversations the family didn't realize I could hear. I'd rather they not find out I listened to and repeated what they said." If word got out that she combined catering with eavesdropping, her business would be toast.

The chief reached for one of the cranberry oatmeal cookies she'd brought him. "No one will find out you gave me information."

While she told him what had happened Sunday night, he jotted in a bound notebook, his face showing no reaction to anything she said. She ended her account with Elaine's ultimatum to Iska.

"That's the whole story, Chief. Franetta told me she found Oliver dead this morning. I assume you're looking into his death." She took the chief's silence as assent, though he might have kept quiet because his mouth was full of an oatmeal cookie. "Franetta mentioned the gift bag and the chocolates she saw near Oliver's body. That was eerily similar to what happened to Jake."

The chief frowned. "How so?"

"Both men received gifts of sweets, both ate the sweets, and both died right afterward."

"Except Oliver wasn't poisoned. The doctor said it was a natural cardiac death."

Huh? "So why did you ask me what happened last night?"

"Families usually resist an autopsy on their loved ones. Oliver's daughter, Elaine, is asking for one, and for toxicology tests. Why? Maybe someone in the family had issues with the old man, making the daughter suspect that her father didn't die a natural death." The chief twirled his pen. "When I heard you were at the Naimans last night, I wanted your take on the family. Nothing you told me suggested one of them was a murderer."

Val couldn't argue with that. "I saw an ordinary family trying to do their best for an aging parent, though they disagreed about how. They closed ranks fast to get rid of Iska."

The chief poked his cell phone. "I asked you to come by for another reason. I want to show you something. This morning the police got word of an unattended death at the Naiman house. Officer Wade got to the house before the other responders and took pictures." The chief passed his phone to Val. "Does the kitchen look the way you left it last night?"

"I cleared the counter and the table last night. The gift bag, chocolates, mug, and water glass weren't there." Val looked more closely at the picture. "There's another difference. Take a look at the two coffeemakers on the counter." She handed the phone back to the chief.

The chief peered at the photo. "One is the newfangled type for making a cup at a time with the little pods. The other coffeemaker is the usual drip kind. The carafe has some coffee in it, but it's not full. Are you saying the carafe was empty and clean when you left?"

"Yes, but I'm saying more than that. Last night Elaine told me her father wasn't allowed caffeine. I had to use a pod to make a cup of decaf for him. The only ground coffee they had was caffeinated." Val leaned forward. "Either someone else was with Oliver and made regular coffee this morning, or he made it for himself."

The chief steepled his fingers. "Oliver's shirt had coffee stains on it, and the mug had a bit of coffee left in it. If the pod contraption was new, he probably made coffee the way he had for years."

"Or he made strong coffee for the same reason he ate the chocolate, which also contains caffeine. This morning he consumed what he wanted as if—I hate to say this—he thought it would be his last meal. I'm not saying he committed suicide, but he might not have cared whether he lived or died because he was so dejected about Iska."

"I'll ask the doctor if a mug of coffee and the few chocolates Oliver ate could trigger a cardiac event. But it doesn't change the cause of death." The chief jotted in the notebook. "Wade noticed a partially eaten chocolate on the kitchen floor and bagged it as evidence in case foul play was suspected, which it isn't. We examined the chocolates left in the box to see if anyone had tampered with them, but they were intact. No breaks in the chocolate and no holes from a hypodermic needle used to inject poison."

"Maybe Oliver ate the only pieces that contained poison."

"You can't predict which chocolates someone will choose. I'd like to ease the daughter's mind and send the chocolates for chemical analysis, but the police lab won't do the work unless it's related to an investigation. If something changes and I can make the case that Oliver Naiman's death was suspicious, I'll get that analysis done." He closed his notebook.

Val saw an opening to bring up the other poisoning. "Speaking of a suspicious death, any new information about Jake?"

"The medical examiner confirmed he was poisoned. Once poison is in the stomach, you can't tell what food contained it. All the gift bags at the table had a gingerdead man cookie like his, but none of them contained poison."

"That doesn't mean his wasn't poisoned." If everyone had opened their gifts at the same time and they all had an ordinary gingerbread man except Jake, he probably would have thought twice before eating the ginger*dead* man.

"Granddad figured that cyanide killed Jake because of his symptoms and how quickly he died."

"I'll be making a public announcement shortly about Jake's death, but I'm not going to say what kind of poison. I've already told your granddaddy not to speculate in public about it. Same goes for you."

"Did anyone come forward who saw the Ghost of Christmas Presents on Saturday night?"

"A few people on the cemetery tour glimpsed a hooded figure in black on the edge of the churchyard."

The location made sense to Val. "The ghost left the CAT Corner by the door to the outside. Not wanting to be seen, the ghost wouldn't turn toward Main Street, but go in the opposite direction, through the alley to the churchyard. Did anyone in the churchyard notice the figure limping or see his face?"

"It was dark, and they were too far away to pick up details."

Val was disappointed. Not much progress on the ghost's identity, but maybe the police had uncovered information about Jake. "Granddad had no luck when he went online to find out where Jake Smith came from. Too many people with the same name."

"His real name was John Jacob Smith. We found fake IDs for Jay Smith, J. J. Smith, and Jakob Smith with a k instead of a c."

Val remembered what Holly had called him when she was trying to revive him. "What about Jack Smith?"

"We didn't find an ID for that, but it's an obvious nickname for John. He was a legitimate real estate developer for decades, but his business changed in the last few years. He started a project with money from investors and from people who signed sales contracts for houses not yet built.

After construction began and the bills mounted, he walked away and stiffed everyone. Then he moved to a different part of the country and did the same thing again."

"So Santa was filling his sack wherever he went. Was he wanted for fraud?"

"The law wasn't after him yet. His creditors were. They could bring a civil suit against him, but first they'd have to find him. The suit might not have merit. People sign contracts without reading the fine print. Investors aren't guaranteed a return on their money. I'm not delving into his business dealings unless they have a bearing on his death."

Val thought it was worth delving into what Holly knew about him. "Did you find any pictures of him when he was younger and without a beard?"

"Not many." The chief typed on his keyboard and looked at his computer screen. "We found a few old newspaper photos of him. Why do you want them?"

Val preferred not to mention her suspicion that Jake and Holly had known each other. Her hunch might be wrong. "I'm curious how Jake ended up in Bayport. Maybe he visited relatives here years ago or even lived here himself. Some old-timers might recognize the younger Jake from a photo."

"I'll send you the link to the photos." He clicked his mouse, typed, and then looked at her. "Thank you for stopping by."

She ignored the hint to leave. "One more question, Chief. Irene Pritchard, the Smiths' neighbor, said she didn't think Jake and Jewel were married."

"Depends on what you mean by married. They had a common-law marriage. Maryland doesn't consider that a legal marriage, but Texas, where the Smiths last lived, does. States generally recognize marriages that are valid under another state's laws even if not under their own."

"So she'll inherit."

"Probably, though there may not be a lot left after his creditors get what's due to them." The chief stood up, making it clear he was going to escort Val out.

In the short time Val had been inside with Chief Yardley, a cold front had come roaring in. The air was frigid and the wind fierce as she crossed the police station parking lot. Once inside the car, she checked the photos the chief had sent her. She chose the one in which Jake looked the youngest and cropped the other people out of the picture. She couldn't see much resemblance between the white-bearded Jake in a Santa suit and the brown-haired, clean-shaven man he used to be.

Her next stop was Belleview Avenue, where she hoped to talk to two people—Elaine Naiman to offer condolences for her father's death and Holly Atherson to find out if she'd known Jake Smith years ago.

Elaine opened the door. Except for her eyes, red and puffy from crying, she looked ready for a business meeting in her slate-gray power suit and white knit top. "Hello. I was just thinking about you. Last night I was supposed to pay you the balance for catering, but I forgot. Come in and I'll write you a check." She led Val to the living room. "Please sit down."

"Thank you." Val sat in an armchair. "I forgot about the check too. I stopped by to tell you how sorry I was to hear about your father. My sympathies to you, your sister, and the rest of your family. And I brought you some cookies." She reached into her tote for them.

"I appreciate your sympathy, but save the cookies for someone else." Elaine sank onto the sofa. "Franetta brought over some grapes and muffins. I couldn't taste them. I might as well have eaten cardboard. I'm just not hungry."

"The same thing happened to my mother when my grandmother died. I guess it's the effect of grief on the body. Mom's taste buds worked after a couple of days."

This news didn't console Elaine. Apparently, she didn't care if she ever ate again. "I can't even bring myself to go into the kitchen. As long as you're here, you might as well take the leftovers from last night, including the rest of the cake."

Val was reluctant to take the remains of the birthday dinner. Elaine and her sister would be here at some point, and neither of them enjoyed cooking, according to Cyndi. "I can pack the leftovers in freezer containers for you. You can reheat them when you come back or take them home."

"No reflection on your cooking, but I'd rather not have any reminders of last night's dinner. It ended badly. I had no choice but to fire Iska, but I shouldn't have assumed Dad could take care of himself this morning. If I'd been here or arranged for Franetta to stop by early, Dad would probably be alive."

"You can't know that," Val said, though stating the obvious probably wouldn't lessen the daughter's guilt much.

Elaine leaned forward. "I do know he would have been better off with someone here. The doctor said he died of cardiac arrhythmia. He could have recovered if he'd gotten emergency treatment soon enough."

"Did he have a history of arrhythmia?" When Elaine nodded, Val continued. "Was that the reason he wasn't supposed to have caffeine?"

"Partly. He was also taking an MAO inhibitor to treat his depression, which has been a problem ever since my mother died. The doctor who prescribed it told him to lay off coffee, soft drinks, and chocolate. The caffeine in them could trigger changes in his heart rhythm."

Val thought about the middle-aged man she'd tried to resuscitate earlier this year when his heart had stopped beating. It turned out that an excess of medicine meant to treat a heart problem had killed him. Did the same thing happen to Oliver? Only an autopsy would tell. It might also tell Elaine something that would make her even more unhappy, suggesting her father had deliberately overdosed on meds after his hopes of happiness with Iska were dashed.

"Did your father chafe at his diet restrictions?"

"Who wouldn't? He stopped complaining about it after a while. We knew he had a weakness for chocolate and never put temptation in his way. Or at least I didn't." Elaine pushed her hair back from her forehead, as if it kept her from seeing clearly. "If I'd been with him this morning, he'd have eaten a healthy breakfast. Instead, he drank strong coffee and ate chocolates. I don't even know where he got them."

"Do you have any relatives who might have stopped by the house this morning with candy for your father? Nieces, nephews, cousins?"

Elaine shook her head. "My cousins live in New York. I don't have nieces or nephews. Cyndi has stepdaughters, Kevin's children by his previous wife. He divorced her to marry Cyndi. His daughters are away at college in Ohio. Poor guy doesn't see much of them, though he's paying their tuition."

"Can you think of anyone else who could have brought your father chocolate?"

Elaine hesitated, rubbing her hand along the sofa's upholstered cushion. Then she squared her shoulders with determination. "Iska Dalisay. I think she came here to wheedle her way back into his good graces with help from chocolates."

"But she wouldn't have harmed him." Not if she wanted him to marry her.

"She could have panicked when he started having symptoms. If the worst happened, the police would question her and she might be deported. So she ran off. The worst did happen, but the police aren't questioning her." Tears welled in Elaine's eyes.

To give her the chance to grieve in private, Val stood up and said, "I'll pack the leftovers."

She sympathized with Oliver's daughter but didn't find her theory convincing. Iska would have been foolish to venture near the house after Elaine had threatened to turn her in to immigration authorities.

As Val walked through the dining room toward the kitchen, she noticed that Oliver's wrapped birthday gifts were no longer on the buffet, where they'd been last night. Elaine must have tucked them away so they wouldn't remind her of the sad end to his birthday.

But she hadn't removed anything from the kitchen. Everything looked as it had in the photos Officer Wade had taken this morning. A small green gift bag and a carafe with an inch of coffee were on the counter. A glass with a splash of water, a mug with coffee residue, and an open box of chocolates were on the table. Not a typical store-bought assortment. All the chocolates were circular.

The box had room for nine, but only six nestled in pleated paper candy cups. The empty cups must have held the pieces Oliver had eaten.

Val leaned down to study the remaining bonbons close up. They had flaws that suggested an amateur candy maker, one who put a bit too much chocolate in the mold and didn't trim the edges after unmolding each piece.

But they were perfect vehicles for poison. You'd have to tamper with store-bought chocolates to make them toxic and risk your victim or the police noticing. Not so with homemade candy. You could just mix the poison with the other ingredients. Short of analyzing the candy, there was no way to tell if the chocolates had played a role in Oliver's death. This morning Officer Wade had bagged a half-eaten chocolate found on the kitchen floor. The police might send it for analysis if they knew the chocolates weren't commercially made and could contain poison without any sign of tampering.

Val would have contacted Chief Yardley immediately, but her phone was in her tote bag in the living room, and she had a problem to solve right here. She stared at the six remaining bonbons, wondering what to do with them. She didn't want to touch the box or the candy in case they had fingerprints or DNA on them. But leaving them where they were now ran the risk that someone might eat them . . . with fatal consequences.

She went with the lesser of two evils. Last night she'd seen a box of disposable gloves under the sink. She put gloves on both hands and packed the gift bag and the box of chocolates in a paper grocery sack. Then she loaded the leftovers from the refrigerator into another sack and went back to the living room. The skin around Elaine's eyes was splotchy.

Val sat down in the armchair again, putting the grocery sacks on the floor next to it. She felt sorry for Elaine, dealing with a parent's death without support. "Will your sister be coming here to help you?"

Elaine tucked a wadded tissue into her jacket pocket. "Not 'til later in the week. Cyndi's in Chicago until Wednesday for business meetings. She just started a new job and couldn't cut short her trip. I told her I didn't mind her not rushing back. There's nothing she can do here anyway."

She could have rushed home to comfort her sister. "What about your brother-in-law?"

"He teaches and doesn't have spare time during the week." Elaine reached into the leather purse next to her on the sofa and pulled out a checkbook. "What do I owe you?"

Val told her and then said, "Besides the leftovers, I packed the chocolates that were on the table. They're homemade. Unless you know who made them, you wouldn't want to take the chance of eating one."

Elaine stared round-eyed at her. "My father ate those chocolates and then he died." Her jaw clenched. "The police should test them instead of taking the doctor's word for it that a heart ailment caused his death."

"I agree. I can take the chocolates to the police chief, who's a family friend. I can't guarantee they'll be tested, but I'll do my best to convince him they should be."

"Thank you."

The chief would be more likely to order a test if Val could find a connection between Oliver's death and Jake's. If Jake had visited or lived in Bayport years ago, the two men might have met. Maybe Elaine had seen him with her father. "Franetta told me this house has been in your family for decades. Did you spend much time in Bay-port?"

Elaine shook her head. "Cyndi and I came to see our grandparents here, but we were grown up by the time our parents inherited this house and moved in. We only ever made short visits."

Val took her phone from her tote bag and brought up the photo of the younger Jake that she intended to show Holly Atherson. "My grandfather recently found a scrap of old newspaper with a photo, a man who looked famil-iar, but Granddad didn't remember his name. It's driving him crazy. He's been showing the photo to people who've been in Bayport for a while. Do you recognize this man?"

Elaine glanced at the photo. "He doesn't look familiar to me, but I'm not really good with faces."

Disappointed, Val put away her phone. Was there any-thing else that might connect Jake's death to Oliver's be-sides a sweet gift delivered by someone unknown? Yes! It hit Val like an espresso jolt. One person with expertise in making sweets had been in the vicinity when both victims died—Franetta. But why would she poison either man?

A snippet of talk Val had heard last night echoed in her mind, a conversation Franetta had nipped in the bud by changing the topic. Maybe Elaine knew why. "Your fa-ther seemed like a good man, someone who helped his neighbors. While I was serving the appetizers, he said something about helping the Frosts' son when he had a problem. Do you know how your father helped?"

Elaine frowned in concentration and then shook her head. "I don't remember Dad or anyone else ever men-tioning it. The Frosts' son is easily fifteen years younger than me. By the time he was old enough to get in trouble, I was on my own, didn't live with my parents, and came to Bayport only occasionally." Elaine tore off a check, stood up, and handed it to Val. "Thank you for catering. My father enjoyed his birthday dinner, his last meal."

Except for a breakfast of coffee, chocolates, and maybe poison.

Chapter 10

As Val left the Naiman house, she noticed a large, brown dog tugging a small woman. They were half a block away, coming in her direction. By the time Val had stowed the leftovers in her car, the chocolate Labrador retriever was trotting toward her at the end of a long leash.

She recognized the Lab, but the leash-holder wasn't the same woman Val had last seen with that dog. The woman's face was hidden inside the fur-trimmed hood of her white parka.

Val bent down to pet the Lab. "Hi, Gretel." The dog's tail wagged furiously.

"You two are old friends?" the woman said.

Val looked up to see Holly Atherson peering at her from under the parka's hood. "Yes. I got to know Gretel through the house sitter who was taking care of her and the house. Are you Gretel's owner?"

"No, Gretel's my owner." Holly gave the dog a pat. As Gretel sniffed the bushes along the sidewalk, Holly glanced at the Naiman house. "I heard that Oliver passed away and that you'd catered a dinner at his house last night."

Val gnashed her teeth. Putting the two facts in the same sentence suggested they were related. If Franetta had linked the dinner and the death when telling her neighbors the news, Val had better set the record straight. "He died after breakfast today."

"I walk Gretel around seven in the morning. We'd often see Oliver go out on his porch to check the weather and pick up the newspaper."

Val was familiar with that routine. "My grandfather does the same thing every morning."

"I didn't see Oliver today."

"It was frigid this morning. Was anyone beside you outside that early?" Val was proud of how she'd slipped this key question into the conversation.

"Not a creature was stirring, aside from us. I stopped by an hour ago to tell Elaine how sorry I was about her father. She didn't want to talk about how he died." Holly fixed Val with an intent stare. "Please tell me it was a natural death."

Val wished she could. "I heard that was the doctor's opinion."

"But maybe not Elaine's or yours. Franetta told me you've looked into some deaths that weren't what they first seemed. She also said you're tight with the local police." The dog strained against her leash, ready to move on. "Gretel wants to go home, and I'm freezing out here. We'd be a lot warmer talking inside my house. I have some questions for you."

"And I have some for you."

Holly gave in to the dog's tugging. "Which of my house sitters introduced you to Gretel?"

Val walked fast to keep up with her and the dog. "The young man who was there in April."

"He didn't keep the place as clean as other sitters I've had, but Gretel liked him right away. She usually takes more time to warm up to house sitters."

"You employ a lot of sitters?"

"We moved here four years ago after my husband retired from a medical practice in West Virginia. He didn't stay retired for long. He took a job as a cruise ship doctor."

"Wow. An ideal job for someone who likes travel."

"We both do. He's on a ship for four months and comes home for two months. I can travel with him for free. I don't stay away longer than a month at a stretch before coming home to Gretel. My husband's four-month stint will be over next week, when the ship docks in Australia. He plans it so he's always home for the winter holidays and the grandkids' summer vacation."

Gretel led the way up the path to the house where she lived. When Holly opened the door, the dog shot inside.

Holly hung her parka on a hook in the front hall, blew on her hands, and rubbed them together. "I'm ready for a cup of hot chocolate. Would you like one?"

"Yes, please."

"I made some from scratch this morning. I'll heat it up. Hang up your jacket and sit down in the living room or, if you prefer, join me in the kitchen." Holly pointed toward the back of the house.

As Val walked through the living room toward the kitchen, she lingered for a moment by the built-in shelves with photos and books. A large studio portrait showed Holly in the center, flanked by what must be her family—husband, children, and grandchildren.

Val surveyed the titles shelved with the photos. If Holly had any paperbacks, they weren't on display in the living room. Oversize books with photographs of exotic places and thick biographies of historical figures took up most of the space. One shelf held science, medical, and pharmacy textbooks and two reference books on poisons. Considering that Holly had worked at a poison control center, it made sense that she'd own such books, but Val was surprised they were so near at hand.

She went into the spacious kitchen. Shiny pots and pans hung over the granite cooking island. All the appliances gleamed. "Did you add on to the house to make this room?"

"The previous owner did." Holly stirred a saucepan containing a rich brown liquid. "The fancy equipment in this kitchen is overkill for my cooking needs. The microwave is my appliance of choice, especially when I'm just cooking for one, and except when I make hot chocolate. Have a seat." She cocked her head toward the table.

Gretel had already settled down in the corner.

Val sat down and looked out the bay window at the river behind the house. "Nice view." Not as nice as it would be if the sun were shining. The river usually meandered calmly along, but today the wind made the water choppy and the clouds turned it a dull gray. The view matched Val's mood after the last few days.

Holly poured the hot chocolate into two mugs, brought them to the table, and sat down across from Val. "What have you found out about Jake's death?"

Val had expected small talk before the interrogation,

but Holly hadn't wasted any time. The chief would soon announce Jake's death by poison, but telling her now might make her more willing to answer Val's questions. "Jake was poisoned. I assume you can make an educated guess what the poison was, based on his symptoms and your professional knowledge." Val fingered the handle of her mug. She wouldn't drink the chocolate until Holly did.

"You've looked into my background. I won't pretend to be ignorant. Jake's symptoms were consistent with cyanide poisoning. Only an autopsy will tell you that for sure."

"What did you mean yesterday when you said you smelled death?"

"I meant I knew he would die, and soon." Holly wrapped her hands around her mug. "Hospitals have cyanide antidote kits. They generally sit there unused until their expiration date because so few cyanide victims make it to the hospital in time. After Jake's breathing slowed and became more shallow, I doubted he would make it, though I hoped he would."

Was that hope for a man she'd just met or one she'd known longer than that? "I'd like to show you a picture." Val took her phone from her bag and pulled up the photo of a younger Jake Smith. "Do you recognize this man as someone you used to know?"

Holly studied the picture, her face betraying nothing. "Where did you get this?"

"From a newspaper clipping." Like Holly, Val saw no reason to pretend ignorance. "The caption identified the man as J. J. Smith. John Jacob Smith. I think you knew him as Jack Smith."

"How did you figure that out?" Holly's tone indicated curiosity, not concern.

"You called him Jack when you were trying to shake him awake. And you rushed to help him before anyone else did." No comment from Holly, so Val continued. "You must have known him well at one time. How long ago was that?"

"Thirty years." Holly hadn't paused to calculate the number of years, suggesting it was in the forefront of her mind. "I expected him to cross my path again someday, but not at a tea party where everyone was in costume."

Hard to believe they hadn't previously encountered each other in a small town like Bayport. Val tried not to show her skepticism. "He moved here six months ago. I'm surprised you didn't run into him sooner." Even with a heavy cruising schedule.

"If I'd bumped into him on the street, I wouldn't have known him. Even when I sat next to him Saturday night, I didn't recognize him at first because of the beard. His name made me look more closely at him. His face was fuller, but he had the same ice-blue eyes and high cheek-bones I remembered. And the Santa suit brought back memories."

Val tried to make sense of Holly's last comment. "He played Santa when he was younger?"

"Exactly. The first time I laid eyes on him. I was in college, volunteering at a homeless shelter. He was visit-ing the shelter dressed as Santa, wearing a fake beard, a wig, and a lot of padding. He'd bought small gifts for the children at a discount store, wrapped them, and handed them out. He made their day, and I think they made his."

That didn't fit with the image Val had formed of the

man. He must have had a soft spot for children. "Did he grow up in a large family?"

Holly shook her head. "He was an only child. His father belittled everyone around him, including his wife and son. The father was like Scrooge—ruthless in business, never happy unless he was getting the better of people. He expected his son to act the same way. Jake had a better role model in his uncle, who played Santa when the extended family got together for the holidays. The uncle died in an accident the year before I met Jake. He told me he'd vowed to play Santa one day each year in memory of his uncle."

Fast forward to this year, when Jake had elbowed out Granddad as Santa, channeling both his father and his uncle. "From what I heard about Jake's business dealings, he became more like his father."

"I'm sorry to hear that. When I knew him, he was driven to make money, but not at the expense of others. He had a quirky sense of humor, coming up with puns that made everyone groan."

"Do you think Jake recognized you at the tea?"

"Unlikely. My hair used to be long and dark." Holly fingered her frosted, pixie-cut hair. "My name was different too. He knew me as Holiday Brooks."

Her first name was even more unusual than Val's. "My parents called me Valentine because I was born on February 14. Like you, I went with a nickname. Which holiday were you born on?"

"My birthday had nothing to do with it. Holiday was my grandmother's maiden name. I thought it was cool. It set me apart from all the Jennifers and Amys I went to school with. But it was too breezy a name for a professional woman."

"Most people enjoy catching up with someone they knew decades ago. Why didn't you tell Jake who you were?"

"I intended to, but not with an audience. Jake's sneezing gave me an excuse to move my chair away from him and turn my face in the other direction. Dressed the way I was, if I'd identified myself to him, he'd have drawn the wrong conclusion."

The wrong conclusion because she'd worn a bridal outfit? Maybe she'd wanted to get married three decades ago and Jake hadn't. "You two were seeing each other years ago?"

"We were engaged." Holly took a few sips of hot chocolate slowly and then thumped down her mug on the table as if finalizing a decision. "You have a reputation for unearthing facts, so I'll save you the trouble of digging for them. Jake didn't show up for our wedding."

Val gasped. "Like Miss Havisham's fiancé." Had Holly responded the same way as her literary counterpart, dwelling for years on her aborted wedding and her fiancé's villainy?

"Jake wasn't as ruthless as Miss Havisham's fiancé. He just got cold feet. It was all for the best, though I didn't think so at the time. It took me a while to trust any man after that."

"Understandable." Val's ex-fiancé had merely cheated on her, not left her at the altar, and after two years she still had scars that made her leery of commitments. Holly had made a commitment, marrying another man. Yet she'd dressed as Miss Havisham. Did she still think of herself as a scorned woman? "Why did you choose to be Miss Havisham for the Dickens festival?"

"I was late to the festival volunteer meeting, and Miss

Havisham was one of the few remaining roles. I had a white gown from a charity ball we'd attended a few years back. It was easy to add a few touches and make it look like a wedding gown."

"So it was a practical decision, saving you the time and expense of a costume." Val wasn't surprised that Holly had a white gown in her closet. She also had a white parka hanging in the hall. She was in a white dress in the family portrait. No, she wasn't exactly like the Dickens character, who'd worn bridal attire for the rest of her life, but Holly certainly gravitated toward white.

She leaned across the table toward Val. "Miss Havisham was warped by being jilted. I'm not. Jake did me a favor, and I waited years for the chance to tell him that. I was going to thank him for standing me up. I was going to show him pictures of my wonderful husband, my three beautiful children, and my darling grandchildren." Holly looked annoyed. "Whoever killed him robbed me of that pleasure."

Val realized now why Holly had talked so freely about her relationship with Jake. With his life under scrutiny after his suspicious death, her past with him was bound to come out. So she'd put her own slant on it, stressing that she bore him no ill will and even wanted him alive. While Val had been digging for information here, Holly had been planting it.

As they finished their hot chocolates, Val asked about Holly's children and grandchildren, a subject on which Holly had a lot to say.

When she collected the empty mugs, Val took the hint and stood up. "Thank you for inviting me in for the chocolate and the chat."

Holly walked her to the door. "You wondered if I'd seen anyone near Oliver's house this morning."

Val perked up. Was she about to get new information, a takeaway gift from Holly? "You did see someone there?"

"Not someone, but something in front of Oliver's door— a gift bag."

Val went directly from Holly's house to Chief Yardley's office and told him about her conversation with Holly and the gift bag she'd seen on Oliver's doorstep. "The bag she described matches the one in the kitchen at the Naiman house. It was there early this morning, in front of the sidelight by the door. It would have been visible to Oliver when he came downstairs."

"So Oliver probably took it inside."

"Someone put the bag there under cover of darkness, an anonymous gift-giver, like the Ghost of Christmas Presents with the gingerbread cookies. The box of chocolates must have been inside the gift bag. As for the chocolates—"

The chief held up his hand like a crossing guard stopping traffic. "The doctor says chocolate and coffee might have affected Oliver and led to his death, but no one could predict that result. You can't hold the person who gave him the chocolates responsible for his death."

"Unless something else went into them that could kill him. I saw those bonbons in the kitchen. I could tell they were homemade. A chocolate maker could easily add another ingredient to the recipe for the shell or the filling, and you wouldn't be able to tell by looking at it."

"The piece of chocolate Wade found in the kitchen did have a filling." The chief frowned. "How hard is it to make filled chocolates?"

"It's easy. You can use a mold, like a flexible miniature muffin pan. For each candy, you brush melted chocolate around the edges of each little cup in a thin layer, put it in the fridge so it hardens, and then brush on the next layer. Once you have a thick base layer of chocolate on the bottom and sides of the mold, you add the filling and the chocolate on top of it."

"How long would it take to make chocolates like that?"

"At least an hour, maybe two. Most chocolate molds have cups for fifteen or eighteen pieces." Val pointed to the grocery sack she'd put on the floor next to the chair. "I took the chocolates from the Naiman kitchen to make sure no one ate them. I wore plastic gloves when I put the box and the gift bag in this sack."

"Did you share your suspicions about the chocolates with Elaine Naiman?"

"I had to explain why I was taking the candy with me."

"She'll want it tested. I'll try to make a case for the lab to test the partly eaten chocolate that Officer Wade bagged at the scene. I can't say if and when they'll do it. It would help if I could tell them what to test for. If the chocolate tests positive for any added substance that would affect the heart, we'll get the autopsy. I expect the test will come out negative, and the daughter will have no reason to agitate for an autopsy."

"I'm not sure she'll give up on it. She'd like the autopsy to relieve the guilt she feels for not being there to help him. An autopsy that shows he died instantly of cardiac arrest would suit her. It would be worse if someone deliberately poisoned him, but she couldn't blame herself for that either."

"We don't do guilt-relieving autopsies. She'll have to pay a private lab for that." He pointed to his watch. "I have a conference call any minute now. If you have anything else to say, make it quick."

"About Jake. He jilted Holly Atherson on their wedding day thirty years ago. She's a pharmacist and poison specialist, and she got close enough to him on Saturday night to slip him poison." Val had learned that when the chief found anything she said worth pursuing, he jotted it down. This time he didn't even pick up his pen.

"A lot of people had more recent grudges against him," he said. "We're looking into the folks he cheated and anyone who gained by his death."

The spouse, who usually had the most to gain, made an obvious suspect. If the police were investigating other possibilities, it was because they didn't have enough evidence against Jewel. Val stood up. "Thanks for taking the time to see me, Chief."

Val climbed into her car in the police station parking area and checked the time. Five thirty already. By now, Granddad would have left to meet his friend, Ned, for pizza. And she was supposed to meet Bram for dinner in half an hour.

She called him and asked how his mother was doing.

"She's busy. That keeps her mind off what happened here Saturday night. The police announced Jake Smith was poisoned. Mom's glad they didn't say where it happened. They've gotten what they needed from the CAT Corner, so it's no longer blocked off."

"Great. Are we still on for dinner tonight?"

"Yes. It's your turn to pick the restaurant. Where do you want to go?"

Val glanced at the bag of leftovers from Oliver's birthday on the passenger seat. "How about coming over for dinner? Granddad won't be there. It'll just be the two of us."

"Wouldn't you like a night off from cooking?"

A night off from murder would be even better. "This is the food I cooked yesterday for the party I catered. All I have to do tonight is make a salad."

"We're having a romantic dinner of leftovers?"

She laughed. "Really yummy leftovers."

"Anything I can bring?"

"'A jug of wine, a loaf of bread, and thou.' By which I mean a hearty red wine, a crusty French bread, and Bram Muir."

"All three will be at your place by six thirty."

Chapter 11

Val and Bram sat at the small table in the kitchen where she always ate with Granddad. Eating at the big mahogany table in the dining room wouldn't have been cozy for two. She'd made the table more festive by putting on a white tablecloth and setting it with Grandma's good china and crystal instead of the everyday dishes she and Granddad used.

"Did you get to do anything today, Bram, besides restocking the books and ringing up holiday sales?"

"I renewed my passport. I can't believe ten years have gone by since my first one." He broke off a piece of the baguette. "Do you have a passport?"

"Yes, and it has a few years left on it." The last overseas trip she'd intended to take had been a honeymoon in Greece, but breaking her engagement had put an end to that. A canceled vacation was the only negative part of ditching Tony. "Are you planning to travel abroad?"

"I'd like to go to Europe, but I don't have anything specific set up yet. Have you been there?"

"When my father was stationed in England, we traveled around the British Isles. My parents went to the romantic places like Paris and Rome when my brother and I were spending our summers here in Bayport with our grandparents." Val sipped her wine. "You think your mom's ready to run the bookshop without your help?"

"Once we find an assistant manager who can handle shelving and selling." He put down his fork. "I've made a big decision. I'm moving."

Moving? Val felt a sinking sensation in her stomach, surprised at his news and at her own reaction to it. She would miss him. Though they'd known each other only six weeks, she'd begun to think he might be Mr. Right. And she'd looked forward to introducing him to her parents when they came for Christmas.

She slid a piece of French bread around her plate, letting it soak up gravy and trying to look unconcerned about his departure. "When are you moving?"

"As soon as possible. But in December not many places are available. I'll have to wait until after New Year's at the earliest."

Happy New Year, Val's cynical inner voice said. Early last month he'd told her he would be staying in Bayport, but he didn't say for how long. She should have known that a man who'd spent the last decade in Silicon Valley would think of California as home, not the Eastern Shore town where his mother had grown up.

Afraid that her face would betray her sadness, Val popped out of her seat. "I meant to put water on the table.

I'll get us both some." What had made him change his mind about staying here? Maybe she'd been mistaken in thinking he'd fallen for her as she had for him. As she filled two glasses, she pondered what to say next. She could ask where and why he was moving, but she'd rather not dwell on it.

Time to change the subject. Focusing on other people's woes would help her forget her own problems. She brought the water to the table. "The birthday dinner I catered last night ended badly."

"The food didn't fall short. This beef dish is fantastic." He scooped a second helping from the serving dish. "What happened at the dinner?"

She began with Oliver's bombshell about marrying his aide, the reaction of his daughters, and the banishment of the aide. "This morning a neighbor found Oliver dead."

"That must have been a shock to this family. To you too." Bram reached across the small table to pat her hand. "Was he in bad health?"

"He had a heart condition, but it seemed to be under control."

"At least the poor guy had a really good final meal on earth."

"The dinner I made wasn't his last meal. He had a rather less healthy one this morning—chocolates that someone left on his doorstep." Val put down her fork. "His death was a little like Jake's."

Bram's jaw dropped. "Are you saying two people died of poison in Bayport within two days?"

"Not two days in a row. Sunday went by without anyone dying of poison," she said wryly. She shouldn't have shared her suspicions with Bram. After two murders, he'd probably want to leave town even faster, and take his mother with him. "Oliver's doctor says he died of natural causes, but only an autopsy would tell for sure, and the police haven't ordered one . . . yet."

"If they thought there was any chance Oliver was poisoned like Jake, they'd get an autopsy. Not every death in this town is a murder." Bram sipped some wine. "The last time you got involved in a murder investigation, it was personal. Not this time. Why do you even care who killed Jake?"

A fair question. She took a moment to think about why Jake's death bothered her. "Jake was killed in a horrible way. Food is supposed to nourish and give joy. His murderer turned something good into evil, using it as a weapon. Oliver also died after eating something sweet. Someone else might die if the killer isn't stopped."

Bram buttered a piece of bread. "You don't know for sure that Oliver's death is connected to Jake's. We're in the biggest gifting season of the year. Sweets are common gifts, and Oliver had a birthday."

"People who give gifts don't usually hide their identities behind elaborate costumes or drop off their gifts in the dark."

Bram finished chewing his bread before he spoke. "Did Jake and Oliver know each other?"

She shrugged. "They didn't move in the same circles. Oliver's family has owned a house for decades on Bayport's classiest street. Jake moved into a modest neighborhood a few months ago. They had nothing obvious in common. One was a slightly cranky widower who probably never hurt anyone, the other was a crook who made enemies wherever he went."

"What did Jake do to make enemies?" Bram forked another piece of beef into his mouth.

His plate was all but licked clean by the time she finished telling him about Jake's crooked real estate dealings and his practice of decamping when his creditors got wise to him. "Then he'd relocate and run another real estate scheme. He's been trying to buy up older houses in Bayport, probably with intent to defraud."

"He sounds more like Scrooge than Santa."

Yet he'd played Santa. Ironic that he was killed on the one day a year when he tried to do good. Val took the dinner plates to the sink. Unlike Bram's, hers still had food on it. Hearing that Bram was leaving and talking about Jake had made her lose her appetite, but she regained it as she sliced the lemon chiffon cake. "Do you want coffee or tea with dessert?"

"Don't bother. I'll just finish my wine. You think someone Jake cheated caught up with him?"

"Possibly." Val placed the dessert plates on the table, sat down, and picked up her fork. "Jake was rotten in other ways besides fleecing people. For example, he cut down Irene's prized shrubs. That's small potatoes compared to what he did thirty years ago. He jilted his fiancée right before the wedding. Exactly what you'd expect from a jerk like that."

She dug into her cake. Sweet, tangy, and melt-in-your-mouth delicious, even after sitting around for a day. This was the food she needed now. She took another bite and another, savoring each one. She looked across the table, and saw that Bram had eaten almost none of his dessert. He stared at his plate. Maybe he didn't like lemon cake. "We have some apple pie if you'd prefer that."

"No, no. I love the cake." As if to prove the point, he took two quick bites, the second one even before he'd finished the first. Then he laid down his fork and put a hand on his stomach. "I've eaten too much and too fast. I'd better walk it off." He stood up and turned away from the table.

She was about to say she'd go along on the walk, but he was already out of the kitchen. She followed him through the dining room and living room.

He hastily put on his fleece-lined black jacket. "I'll be fine after a brisk walk. That was a terrific dinner. Thank you." He closed the door behind him.

She'd never seen him leave any uneaten dessert on his plate. He must feel really sick. Strange how it had come on so suddenly . . . or maybe not. Her laser focus on the two suspicious deaths might have kept her from noticing what was going on across the table.

As she turned to go back to the kitchen, Granddad opened the front door. "I just saw someone who looked like Bram hurrying toward Main Street. Was he here?"

"Yes. We ate leftovers from last night's birthday party. We'd just started dessert when he said he'd eaten too much and insisted on leaving."

"He might have a stomach bug. There's one going around." Granddad hung up his parka. "Ned wanted to catch the Monday night football game, so we skipped dessert at the pizza place. You got any left?"

"I saved you a slice of Oliver's birthday cake. How about some tea with it?"

After they settled down at the table, Val told him what she'd learned about Jake from the chief and Holly.

When she finishing talking, Granddad was scraping the last of his dessert from the plate. "Mighty fine cake. I can't say I'm surprised by Jake's history. Someone he cheated could have tracked him down, disguised himself to leave the poisoned cookie, and then skedaddled out of Bayport."

Val sipped her tea. "I agree that someone Jake defrauded might have killed him, but not an out-of-towner on a brief visit. Only a local would know that Jake was playing Santa and that he'd go to the volunteers' tea in the bookshop. That tea wasn't listed in the festival's public schedule. And where does a visitor to town bake a poisoned gingerbread cookie?"

"So we're looking for someone Jake swindled who was either a festival volunteer or tight with one. Could be anybody." He shrugged. "Let's focus on the people we know would benefit from Jake's death, starting with his wife."

"Jewel may not benefit much, between her not-quite-legal marriage and Jake's many creditors. But if she thought she would benefit, she had a motive. She also had the opportunity to drop poison in his tea. But did she have the means to do it? Where would she—or anybody else—get cyanide?"

"I did some online research on that. Chemical supply houses sell cyanide. It's used for metal polishing, jewelry making, and photography."

"The police could check if a suspect bought cyanide. Chemical suppliers must keep records of their buyers." Val put down her mug. "Of course, the buyer could have used an alias."

"Chemical suppliers aren't the only sources. Cyanide was used in rat poisons and pesticides until it was outlawed. People may still have it in their garden sheds." Granddad sipped some tea. "You can even make it yourself from apple seeds or the pits of other fruits. You need a lot of pits and patience, but you can do it."

"Would Jewel know how to do that and leave no trace? The police must have had a forensic team crawling all over Jake's place."

"Jewel mighta had an accomplice, a lover, who got the cyanide for her. Once they were rid of Jake, they could live off his money."

No surprise that Granddad had come up with that film-noir plot. He never tired of re-watching 1940s and '50s crime classics from his video collection. But Granddad could be right. Jewel hadn't shown up in Bayport until Jake had been here for months. She could have been with another man during that interlude. "I think the police are watching Jewel closely. If there's any sign of a lover, they'll be on it."

"Let's not forget Holly, the pharmacist and poison specialist. She'd know where to get cyanide and how to extract it. She had the chance to poison Jake after he keeled over, but her motive isn't as strong as Jewel's."

Val thought Holly had a perfectly fine motive. "There are other ways to benefit from a man's death beside inheriting money. Though Holly insisted she wanted Jake alive, what she said convinced me that she's been thinking about him for thirty years. And revenge is a dish best served cold."

"If she served Jake that dish, she must have known he was Santa before she came to the tea. Why else would she have brought cyanide with her?"

"Exactly. She told me she didn't know Jake was in Bayport until he sat next to her on Saturday night. Of course, she could be lying, but there's no way to prove it." Val loaded her fork with another bite of cake. "Not counting Irene, who I'm sure isn't a murderer, we've gone through everyone who had the opportunity to poison Jake—Jewel, Holly, and the ghost."

"Don't count out Irene. And there's someone else who had the opportunity. Franetta could have been the ghost. She wasn't at the tea yet when the ghost came. She knows how to make really good cookies. At bake sales I always ask which ones she made. Jake raved about the ginger-dead man, and he didn't say anything nice about the food you and Irene made."

"On the plus side, our food didn't kill him. I agree that Franetta would be a good suspect, but what's her motive for murdering Jake?"

Granddad carried his plate and mug to the sink. "Maybe he swindled her or someone in her family. Or he had a hold over her. That would explain why she gave him the Santa job."

Val rolled her eyes. Would Granddad ever get over being replaced as Santa? She joined him by the sink and opened the dishwasher. "Sit down, Granddad. I'll take care of cleaning up tonight." When he went back to the table, she said, "Let's put Jake aside and talk about Oliver."

She'd phoned Granddad from the café with the news of Oliver's death. Now she told him about her talk with Elaine, her observations about the chocolate, and the chief's response.

"So Earl might or might not get the chocolates tested," Granddad said. "One thing I'd like to do as soon as possible is locate Iska."

"Why?"

"Even if the chocolates weren't poisoned, Elaine would say the candy contributed to Oliver's death and blame

Iska for giving it to him. Iska might have an alibi proving she couldn't have left the chocolates, but she's afraid to come out of the shadows since Elaine threatened to report her to ICE. She can't get another job if she's hiding out."

Val loaded the utensils into the dishwasher. "What will you do if you find her?"

"Try to get her to talk to the police, but only if Earl promises that he won't turn her over to ICE."

"What if the chocolates were poisoned?"

"They weren't poisoned by her." Granddad removed the tablecloth. "She had nothing to gain. She wanted to stay in this country, but not in prison."

Val nodded. "As long as Oliver was alive, she had a chance, however slim, of marrying him. How are you going to reach her?"

"I have a few ideas. Did she see you at the Naiman house or did you just catch a glimpse of her and overhear her talking with Elaine?"

"She saw me. Why does that matter?"

Granddad's phone rang before he could answer. He pulled it from his shirt pocket and glanced at the display. "Gotta take this one."

After he left the kitchen to talk on his phone, she took out hers, called Bram, and asked him whether he was feeling better.

"Yes, thanks. I probably just ate too fast. Are you up for a do-over later this week? I'll pick out the restaurant."

"Sounds good." By then she ought to be able to discuss his move away from Bayport with more composure than she could manage today. "I promise not to talk about men eating sweets and crumpling to the floor."

He laughed. "At least hold off until after dessert. I'm really sorry for running out tonight."

"You can't help it if you're sick. Talk to you soon."
She hung up.

She was wiping the counter when Granddad returned.

He tucked his phone back in his pocket. "That call
proves that it pays to give out business cards."

An image popped into Val's mind—Granddad distrib-
uting business cards to people on a haunted house tour, in
case they had any ghosts they wanted to get rid of. Amaz-
ingly, he'd gotten some ghost-busting gigs. But that *skill*
wasn't listed on his business card, where he described
himself as a senior sleuth and problem solver. "Who was
on the phone?"

"Jake's widow. She wants to hire me."

Val looked up from wiping the counter. Last spring a
widow had asked Granddad to look into her husband's
suspicious death. Could that be happening again? "Is
Jewel hiring you to investigate Jake's murder?"

"Nope." He rubbed his chin. "And you gotta wonder
why not. Either she already knows who murdered him or
she doesn't care."

"Or she thinks the police can do it without your help."
Meanwhile, the police were doing their best to find evidence against her. Was she clueless about that or secure in
her own innocence? "What does Jewel want from you?"

"I think she's hoping I'll find her a fortune."

Chapter 12

Val couldn't imagine where Granddad would find the widow a fortune. "Does Jewel want you to dig up treasure that Jake buried in the yard?"

"Come into the sitting room and I'll tell you what she said."

Val followed him into the room and sat down gingerly on the sagging sofa, hoping to land in a spot with some cushioning.

Granddad made himself comfortable in his reclining chair. "Jewel asked me if I knew anything about computers. I was afraid she had a broken computer she wanted me to fix. That wasn't it. She wants me to bring over a computer and check something for her."

"Doesn't she have one?"

"The police took Jake's computer. That was the only one in the house. Even if it was there, I'm not sure she'd know what to do with it. She'd like me to locate what she called a thingie you plug into a computer. She knew the police hadn't taken it because they gave her a list of everything they removed after they searched through Jake's things."

"And there's no thingie on the list?" Val chuckled. "Why does she think you can locate it?"

"She's looked all over for it and now she hopes a man might have better luck finding it than a woman. When she told me how big it was and said Jake used an abbreviation for it, I figured she must mean a thumb drive, except Jake called it a USB flash drive. She said that's where he kept his financial records."

Val sat up straighter. "She asked you to bring over your computer so she can see what's on the thumb drive. That could be a trove of information. When are you going over there?"

"Tomorrow at three. Can you come along and keep her occupied? I don't want her standing over me if I'm poking around her stuff searching for something."

"I'll go with you. I was planning to visit the library to chat with Shantell, but I can put that off."

"Jewel thanked me for the quiche and hinted she wouldn't mind some other dish that's easy to heat up. She said the food the neighbors brought her didn't taste as good as mine."

Val laughed. "She's buttering you up. Are you going to keep feeding her?"

"One more time. I ran across a recipe today that your grandmother liked, a chicken casserole for a crowd. I'll give some to Jewel, and we'll have enough for a couple of dinners." He took an index card from his shirt pocket and handed it to Val. "What do you think of the recipe?"

Val skimmed it and saw it included one ingredient she hardly ever used—canned soup. It also contained more fat and salt than Granddad should have. She remembered liking the casserole when Grandma made it, so it was worth tweaking, cutting down on the fat and salt in keeping with Granddad's healthier diet. "How about upgrading the ingredients? Add some sliced mushrooms to the sauce. Skip the bacon so the dish doesn't look greasy."

He scrutinized the recipe card. "If I take out the bacon, the recipe has five ingredients. I'll use it in next week's Codger Cook column. Jewel can be the taster, but she'll have to make her own rice to go with it."

Val smiled. "Good idea not to let Jewel depend on your cooking. Try to convince her of what you claimed when you started your recipe column. *Anyone can cook. All you need is five ingredients.*" With that rash statement, he'd boxed himself in for the life of the column.

He tucked the index card back in his pocket and got out of the chair. "I need to make some calls."

Val expected him to use the landline phone in the hall, as he generally did at home, instead of his cell phone. But as she went toward the stairs to her room, she could hear him talking to someone in his bedroom behind a closed door. His words were too muffled for her to make them out.

He rarely cared about privacy when he talked on the phone. But a few times in the past, he'd kept her from overhearing his conversation when planning a caper he suspected she would discourage. This time of year, though, he could have another reason for secrecy. Maybe he was talking about what to get her for Christmas and asking her mother for suggestions. And Val had yet to come up with a gift idea for him.

* * *

On Tuesday morning Val overheard a lot of chatter about Jake Smith's poisoning from the customers at the Cool Down Café. The police had given out his name, announcing only that he'd died on Saturday evening after being at the festival. A few customers had heard that she'd been on the scene when he collapsed. In answer to their nosy questions, she said only that he'd fallen ill and been taken to the hospital.

She also received a call from a client who'd tentatively scheduled her to cater a dinner in January. The woman now wanted to back out of it and gave no reason. Val suspected that rumors she'd catered a poison victim's last meal had influenced that client. How much more business would she lose because of Jake's death?

As she left work at two, her friend Chatty was waiting for her outside the café alcove. Val hadn't seen her since stopping at her festival booth.

"I'm glad I caught you before you left the building." Chatty was so hoarse that she was barely audible.

"You sound terrible." Her friend might be sick, but she looked as color coordinated as usual, with violet lipstick and eye shadow the same shade as her scarf.

"You should have heard me yesterday. Actually, you couldn't have heard me. I had no voice at all. I was fighting off a cold last week, but after spending all day outside at the festival, I had no resistance and lost my voice."

Laryngitis had to be the worst cold symptom Chatty could imagine. She'd acquired her nickname because she loved gossip. The inability to spread any for the last two days must have made her miserable, and disappointed the people who depended on it. "You'd better not tax your voice today or you may lose it again."

"I know something about the guy who was poisoned. Come to my treatment room. I don't want to have to talk over that." She pointed to a speaker blaring music with a pounding beat intended to encourage rigorous exercise. Val felt the vibrations inside her from the bass notes as they skirted the cavernous area devoted to exercise equipment and weights.

The windowless room where Chatty gave her clients facials and therapeutic massages was quieter. Smaller than most walk-in closets, the space aroused Val's mild claustrophobia. She hoped the news about Jake was worth the uneasiness she felt there. She sat down in the room's only chair.

Chatty perched on the long, narrow massage table. "Jewel Smith comes here for a massage three times a week."

Val leaned forward in her chair, her curiosity overcoming her claustrophobia. When Chatty kneaded their muscles, her clients became totally relaxed and uninhibited. They said things they wouldn't tell anyone else. Too bad Jake hadn't come in for a massage, but his wife was the next best thing. "I've never seen Jewel at the club. How did I miss her?"

"Her standing appointment is at four, and you've left by then. I was sorry when her husband didn't visit my booth on Saturday. I really wanted to see what he was like. After what she told me about him, I wouldn't have expected a man like him to play Santa Claus." Chatty took a long swig of water from a reusable water bottle the same violet color as her lipstick. "What's the latest on the investigation into his poisoning?"

Val suppressed a groan. Chatty didn't give out information without demanding some in return. "The police don't yet know how and exactly when he was poisoned."

"Weren't you there when it happened?"

How did Chatty discover that? Though she'd been home sick and unable to talk for the last two days, she must have been in receiving mode. The gossip had come to her. "I was there when he fell over, but some poisons take a while to work." A true though misleading statement.

"The police always suspect the wife, but Jewel had reasons to want him alive. She finally had him where she wanted him." Chatty paused to savor Val's rapt attention. "Last spring, when the Smiths lived in Texas, Jewel went away to visit an old friend. When she returned a week later, Jake had gone. He'd cleared out their joint account and hocked what he could, including jewelry he'd given her and antiques she'd bought."

"They'd had a fight?"

"She didn't say that. People who'd lent him money for a building project were suing and threatening him after it went belly-up. One of them said he'd have Jake arrested. She figured that's why he ran off." Chatty gulped down some more water. "Jewel got a temporary job to pay the rent until the lease was up. Then she went to find him."

"How did she know where to look?"

"He'd been researching boats online. She was sure he'd stashed enough money in offshore accounts to buy a yacht and drop anchor in some island tax haven like the Bahamas. So she headed for the East Coast."

"Why not Florida? It's closer to the islands."

Chatty shrugged. "Annapolis was where the next big boat show was. She spotted him there and confronted him. When he denied being Jake Smith, she said, *You can grow a beard and dye your hair, but you can't change how you walk.*" Chatty did a good imitation of Jewel's Southern drawl. "Bottom line, she moved in with him."

"You said she had him where she wanted him?"

"She knew where the bodies were buried." Chatty grinned. "Don't look shocked, Val. I don't think she meant real bodies. He skipped out on her and she made him pay. If he didn't support her in style, she'd tell his creditors and the police where to find him."

"He's been treating her well. Your massages don't come cheap."

"Cheap compared with the new car she's driving and the jewelry she wears," Chatty croaked, her voice giving out.

Jewel's demands might have been the issue in the arguments between her and Jake that Irene could hear from her house. Blackmail was often hazardous for the one doing it, not the one buckling under. How ironic that he was dead and she wasn't.

Val's phone rang as she pulled into the driveway at home. It was Elaine Naiman. Val hoped she wouldn't ask what the police were doing about the chocolates. Val had no answer and that wouldn't make Elaine happy.

"Hi, Val. Cyndi managed to get an early plane out of Chicago. I'm going to meet her and Kevin at Dad's house. We have to decide what type of arrangements to make for my father, what to do about the house, what to keep, what to sell."

"It's good you can all be together to tackle those

issues." Val wondered why Elaine was sharing her evening plans with her.

"It is, and I don't want to talk about those things at a restaurant. I wish now that I'd kept the leftovers from Sunday night's dinner. Do you still have them?"

Uh-oh. Val didn't feel guilty about eating the food Elaine had insisted she take, but she hated adding to Elaine's burdens today. "I'm sorry, Elaine. The leftovers are gone. You can get pizza delivered or pick up something at the Chinese carryout place."

"Cyndi and Kevin won't be happy with that. Do you have time tonight to make a family dinner for the three of us? You don't need to bother with appetizers like we had for the party with the neighbors. Just simple food and a dessert, between seven and seven thirty. Will that work for you?"

"That's fine." Val would need to fit in a trip to the supermarket before making dinner. But first she had to go to Jewel's house with Granddad. "By the way, I took the chocolates to the police chief and did my best to convince him to test them."

"Thank you. I'll call him too and urge him to do it."

"Good idea." The squeaky wheel gets attention. "See you later, Elaine."

Val climbed out of the car, went inside the house, and found Granddad in the kitchen. "It smells good in here."

He pointed to the large casserole pan on the counter containing the chicken blanketed in a light cream sauce. "I'll scoop out some to bring to Jewel. I invited Dorothy to have dinner with us tomorrow night. Bram's going to take care of the bookshop and give her an evening off."

Val eyed the chicken casserole. Enough for ten people.

"Elaine Naiman called and asked me to cater a dinner for her, her sister, and her brother-in-law tonight at her father's house. I might have to cut short my visit with Jewel to shop for the food. But if you can spare three helpings of this chicken, I can stay longer with Jewel and still have time to make side dishes and a dessert for this evening."

He grinned. "This is a first. You've never let me cook anything for your catering gigs. There's plenty of chicken for Jewel, the Naiman clan tonight, and the three of us tomorrow night. How long will you be gone tonight?"

"An hour and a half, from around six thirty to eight-ish." Val assumed he was wondering what he'd do for dinner. "There's still a helping of beef bourguignon in the fridge. With salad and French bread, you'll have a good meal. I'll make do with an omelet." She glanced at her watch. "I have enough time before we leave for Jewel's house to make the filling for Key lime tartlets. I'll take three to the Naimans tonight, and you can have one for dessert."

He scooped a portion of the chicken casserole into a plastic container, put it and the casserole dish in the fridge, and left the kitchen. She was going to tell him what she'd learned from Chatty, but he didn't return to the kitchen.

By ten minutes to three, she'd mixed the filling for the tarts and put it in the fridge to set. She would make the tart shells later and fill them. She picked up the plastic container with Jewel's chicken dinner and went into the sitting room.

Granddad wasn't where she expected him to be, napping in his lounge chair as he often did in the afternoon. He wasn't in the study either, though he'd already taken the laptop computer from there, put it in a case to take to

Jewel's house, and set it by the front door. Val glanced down the hall toward his bedroom. His door opened and he came out, tucking his phone into his shirt pocket. He'd made another call that he hadn't wanted her to overhear.

He put on his parka. "We gotta go to Jewel's house in your car to explain why you came with me. I'll tell her my car wouldn't start. And when we get there, we're gonna leave the computer in the car."

"Why?"

"If I find Jake's thumb drive, I'm going to make a copy of what's on it before I show it to Jewel. It might contain evidence I can turn over to the police. I don't want her to destroy it accidentally or on purpose."

Val wasn't sure the police could use evidence Grand-dad had acquired illegally, but that was preferable to having it disappear. "While we're driving, I'll fill you in on what Chatty heard from Jewel. In essence, the glue that kept Jake and Jewel stuck together was blackmail."

Chapter 13

When Val and Granddad arrived at Jewel's house, she asked them into her small living room, thanked him for the chicken dinner, and left to put it in the refrigerator. By the time she returned to the living room, Granddad and Val were sitting in the two chairs that faced the window. They'd deliberately left Jewel only one place to sit—on the sofa with her back to the window. From that position, she'd be less likely to notice if Granddad went to the car to copy files to the laptop.

Jewel had pulled herself together in the two days since they'd last visited her. She'd trimmed the jagged edges of the nails she'd broken, but the polish on them was still chipped. They were conspicuous next to her other nails, still pointy and shiny with little gifts painted on them. In her all-black outfit, slacks and a snug pullover sweater, she might have passed for a woman in mourning, but the heavy gold jewelry on her wrists, around her neck, and dangling from her ears suggested a widow ready to be merry.

"When did you last see the thingie you want me to find?" Granddad said.

"Thursday or Friday. Jake plugged it in when he was working on the computer and took it out when he finished. He always stuck it in his pocket, but he never left it there. I know because I checked his pockets now and then. He must have had a hiding place for it."

Granddad said, "Do you know exactly what kind of information he put on it?"

Jewel nodded. "Where his money was, account numbers, passwords. He was afraid someone might break in and steal his computer, so he didn't want to put that stuff on it."

Or he was afraid Jewel might get her hands on it. Val exchanged a look with Granddad, knowing he was thinking the same thing. She would sit quietly and let him ask questions. She'd get her turn while he searched for the thumb drive.

Jewel fidgeted. "I need money to tide me over until I can sell this house. It's not fair that I can't get to it. One of the neighbors told me I'd have to fill out forms and list the value of Jake's estate in order to inherit. I have no idea what the value is."

Granddad stroked his chin. "Did he leave a will?"

"I looked all over for it. It didn't turn up. I guess he didn't figure on dying."

The hint of sarcasm in Jewel's comment didn't surprise Val. From what she'd heard about the Smiths' relationship, she would have been suspicious if Jewel had pretended sorrow over Jake's death. Instead, she seemed mainly concerned about her own financial situation. Hard to believe she'd kill him when she was so dependent on him for money. On second thought, maybe she was pretending she had nothing to gain by his death. If so, she was shrewder than Val had given her credit for.

"Do you have any idea who might have killed him?" Granddad said.

"The person in the costume who left him a poisoned cookie. It must have been someone who followed him from where we used to live. A couple of people were after him for money. He was always on the lookout, moving the curtain aside and peeking through the window to see if anyone was out there."

Granddad pointed to the window behind the sofa where Jewel sat. "Did you ever see anyone out there?"

"Not until Jake was dead. On Sunday morning I saw a guy in a sweat suit hanging out across the street. When the police came by to talk to me and I opened the door for them, he jogged away."

Val assumed the man had been warming up for jogging, not watching Jewel's house. An avid runner who lived near Granddad's house always walked up one side of the street, crossed, and then walked along the other side before breaking into a trot. Val had also seen him doing a cool-down walk when he returned from his run.

"Was that the only time you saw the man in the sweat suit?" When she nodded, Granddad continued. "Can you describe him?"

"No. His jacket had a hood and I couldn't see his face."

"How tall was he? Was he slim or heavy?"

"He wasn't tall or especially thin or fat, just normal-size. He didn't limp like the guy who poisoned Jake, so I wasn't superworried. He looked a little familiar. That's why I thought he might be someone Jake knew in Texas." Jewel tapped her fingertips on the sofa arm. "Where do you want to start your search?"

Granddad stood up. "I'll look in the study first." He crossed the hall to the small room with a big desk visible through the open door.

"I went through everything in there. I hope you'll see something I missed." Jewel turned to Val. "You don't have to stay. I'll be glad to drive your grandfather home."

"I don't mind waiting for him. How did you and Jake end up in this area?"

"He liked the Chesapeake Bay. When he was young, his uncle took him here a few times. They went out on boats to fish and drove to the beach at Ocean City. Lately, Jake's been shopping for a boat."

"He had good memories here. Any special reason he chose Bayport?"

"I asked him that once. As a kid he read books about two brothers who had adventures in a place called Bayport."

Val nodded. "The Hardy Boys. I read a few of those books." When a Nancy Drew wasn't nearby. "My brother was a real fan of the Hardy Boys . . . like Jake, I guess."

He might have been trying to recapture his childhood innocence, returning to a place he'd enjoyed when young, settling in a town that reminded him of the one in his favorite books. Val stopped herself from sentimentalizing Jake. His actions as an adult suggested he'd lost that innocence for good.

Granddad came in. "I didn't find the thumb drive, I mean the thingie, in the study. Do you have an outdoor shed, Jewel?"

"It's a lean-to against the house. I took a quick look in there, but I didn't want to poke around because of the spiders. I'll get you the key." She fetched it from the kitchen and gave it to Granddad. As he left the house, she said to Val, "You must have other things to do. I'd be glad to give your grandfather a lift home."

Val wondered if Jewel had made up the missing thingie as a way to lure Granddad here. Maybe she wanted a replacement Santa. "Granddad will be finished soon. You might face complications in getting access to Jake's funds. The people who said he owed them money might sue for part of his estate. You should probably consult a lawyer. I have a friend who's a lawyer here in Bayport, Althea Johnson."

"I can't afford a lawyer. I might not even be able to keep a roof over my head." Jewel glanced up at the ceiling.

If she hocked her jewelry, she'd stave off poverty for at least a few months. "Althea won't charge much, if anything, to meet with you once," Val said. "She'll give you basic information on what you need to do and then explain how she can help you. Sometimes lawyers are willing to wait to be paid until a client comes into the money. I don't know if that would apply in your case, but it never hurts to ask."

Val noticed Granddad through the window behind the sofa. He opened the door to her car and climbed inside. Apparently, he'd found the thumb drive in the shed, and now he was going to copy the files from it to the laptop.

Jewel chewed on her lip. "What did you say your lawyer friend's name is?"

"I'll write it down for you." Val took out one of her

business cards and scrawled Althea's name on the reverse side.

Jewel took the business card from Val. "Thank you. I hope your friend gives me a break on this."

"I hope she does too. Once you settle the issues related to Jake's estate, will you stay in Bayport?"

"No. It's too cold here. Besides, the people who hounded him might come after me too. I'll leave this town as soon as I can." Jewel stood up. "It's almost happy hour. Would you like some wine or beer?"

"No, thank you. If you're getting yourself a drink, I wouldn't mind a glass of water, please." Val checked her watch. A little early for happy hour, but high time she went home to finish preparing tonight's dinner for Elaine, Cyndi, and Kevin.

"I'll get some snacks too."

While Jewel was in the kitchen, Granddad came back into the house with the laptop in one hand and the thumb drive in the other.

"You found it," Val said quietly. "That didn't take long."

He whispered back, "I saw a new pair of garden gloves hanging on a hook and a pair of grungy ones on a shelf. The new ones still had tags on them. I took them off the hook and felt something hard in the thumb. What better place to hide a thumb drive?"

Val smiled. Jake had a childlike sense of humor. She remembered that Jewel's drawl had prompted his comment that Mrs. Claus came from the South Pole. "He enjoyed his own jokes even if no one else did."

When Jewel returned from the kitchen and heard about Granddad's find, she asked him to plug the thingie into his computer and show her what was on it. He sat at Jake's desk in the study with Jewel next to him. Val hovered behind them, despite Jewel's glares. Granddad opened the most recently updated spreadsheet on Jake's thumb drive and found exactly what Jewel had wanted. Abbreviations for big banks or brokerage houses, their physical and Web addresses, and what appeared to be account numbers, user names, and passwords. Judging by the amount of money Jake listed for each institution, he was worth easily a million dollars.

At Jewel's request, Granddad attached the printer cable to the laptop and printed a hard copy of the spreadsheet for her. Then she wanted to try to access the bank records. He talked her through the process of getting to the Web site for a bank and how to log in to the accounts. But the password in the spreadsheet didn't work.

After trying without success to get into accounts at three different institutions, Granddad said, "Jake probably entered coded versions of his passwords. I can take a look at them to see if anything strikes me, but you may need expert help decoding them."

Jewel pouted. "There must be a way to get to the money without a password. People die all the time, and their families don't have passwords."

"You'll have to go through the process of being recognized by the court as the executor and heir. Then you'll need to send your credentials and Jake's death certificate to the banks and brokers, and they'll arrange for the transfer of funds, if everything checks out."

"That means I won't get the money any time soon."

Val said, "At least now you can estimate the value of Jake's estate." Assuming he didn't have another thumb drive somewhere with information about more accounts.

Jewel wanted Granddad to try getting into another bank account before he left. Val left him on his own and walked home to finish the dessert for Oliver Naiman's family.

On the way she thought about the irony of her visits with Holly and Jewel. They each had an apparent motive and the opportunity to kill Jake at the tea, but also a reason for wanting Jake alive. Though Val couldn't rule out either of them as Jake's poisoner, they weren't at the top of her list. That honor still belonged to the Ghost of Christmas Presents. How had a black-robed person with a gift bag on his head become as invisible as a ghost after leaving the bookshop? What, if anything, connected Jake's death to Oliver's?

No answers came to her as she finalized the dinner for Oliver Naiman's family. Unlike the last time she'd made dinner for them, this time she didn't anticipate a happy evening. The family would have a harder time dealing with Oliver's death than Jewel had reconciling herself to Jake's murder.

Granddad still hadn't returned with her car by the time Val had to leave for the Naiman house. But as she was carrying the food to his Buick, he drove up. She quickly loaded the food into her car instead and drove to Belleview Avenue.

She arrived at Oliver's house as Cyndi and Kevin were climbing out of a silver compact car in the driveway.

Cyndi looked surprised to see her. "Elaine didn't tell me *you'd* be here again."

Val wasn't sure how to respond. She couldn't tell from Cyndi's tone if she resented the intrusion of any nonfamily member tonight or of Val in particular. "Hello, Cyndi. Hi, Kevin."

He smiled at her. "Nice to see you again, Val."

Later, when the family was in the living room and Val was cooking the rice, he came in to make drinks. "I'm glad you're making dinner tonight. The pretzels, chips, and store-bought dip Elaine put out tells you how little the Naiman women care about food. I love them both, but not in the kitchen. What's for dinner?"

She told him as he opened a bottle of wine and poured it into glasses. He offered her one, but she declined.

Val couldn't hear any of the conversation from the living room until five minutes after he left the kitchen and Cyndi raised her voice.

"What! You want an autopsy? You want Dad cut up? Are you nuts, Elaine?"

Val couldn't hear Elaine's reply, but Cyndi apparently didn't like it.

"No," she screamed. "I won't allow it. I'm older than you. It's my decision."

They conversed for a minute loudly enough for Val to catch their hostile tones but not their words.

Then Cyndi yelled, "Where is the candy now?" A moment later she appeared at the doorway to the kitchen, her face a mask of fury. She marched up to Val. "You have some nerve coming in here, feeding my sister's fantasies. You stole something from our house and gave it to the police. How dare you? You pretend to be a caterer. You're nothing but a meddler and a troublemaker. And I'm going to make sure the people in this town know it."

Her sister and her husband had come up behind her during her tirade.

Kevin put an arm around her. "Calm down, Cyndi."

She pointed at Val and screamed all the louder. "I'll make sure nobody ever hires you again, you snooping nutjob!"

Kevin hustled her out of kitchen.

Elaine spoke through compressed lips. "I'm sorry, Val. You'd better go. Cyndi's grieving and out of control."

Val calmed herself long enough to pack the casserole and take the rice off the burner. She hurried to the car, realized she'd left the dessert, and drove off instead of going back for it. Two blocks away she pulled to the curb, shaking too much to drive.

She took deep breaths. Was it fair to say she'd stolen the chocolates? She *had* put the box in a bag even before telling his daughter it should go to the police. But Elaine had welcomed the idea, possibly because Val had fed her fantasies, as Cyndi had said. Or had Elaine anticipated Cyndi's response and brought in Val to bear the brunt of it?

Val rubbed her throbbing head. Despite her good intentions, she'd added to the burdens of a family already in sorrow. Now she'd have to live with the consequences. If Cyndi made good on her threat, Val would lose income she and Granddad needed to maintain the old Victorian house. There was only one thing that could justify her interference—proof that Oliver had been poisoned with those chocolates.

When she stopped trembling, she drove the short distance home, pulled into the driveway, and went to the side door. She was startled to see her friend Bethany there.

"You can't come in!" Bethany said. "You weren't supposed to be here until eight."

An explanation occurred to Val. "Are you helping Granddad wrap my Christmas gift?"

"I wish. He lured Iska here. I'm part of his cover story. You'll spoil it if you come in. She just arrived a few minutes ago."

Val now had an explanation for Granddad's secretive phone calls. "My grandfather called you and roped you into this, didn't he?"

Bethany could handle a classroom full of six-year-olds without losing her cool, but tonight she looked jittery. "I don't mind helping him."

But for some reason Granddad thought Val would mind. She didn't dare interfere with his scheme now. "I'm not standing out in the cold. I'll stay in the side vestibule. Leave the inside door to it open so I can hear what's going on in the sitting room."

What did he have up his sleeve and how much more trouble would he get her into with the Naimans?

Chapter 14

Val hid herself behind the partly open door between the vestibule and the living area.

Bethany hurried back to the sitting room. "Sorry for running out. My phone vibrated and I had to take that call. Now, where were we? Oh, yes, I was telling you about my uncle's health issues. He needs a caregiver."

Val had never heard of this uncle. Granddad had probably invented Bethany's relative as a pretext for talking to Iska. No wonder Bethany was so jumpy. She wasn't used to lying.

Granddad said, "I'm helping Bethany interview caregivers. We'll choose a few to meet her uncle, and he'll decide which one to hire."

"Do you have any health care training, Iska?" Bethany's question sounded rehearsed.

"I took classes in the Philippines. I want to continue

my studies here, but I have to save some money first. Does your uncle need a live-in aide or someone to come in each day?"

"Well, um . . ."

Val imagined Bethany shooting Granddad a panicky look, unsure of the right response to Iska's question.

He spoke up. "Her uncle hasn't decided yet. What kind of experience do you have taking care of older people?"

"I was a live-in aide for a woman who had cancer. She was older than seventy when she died. Her husband was even older and also had health problems. He did not want to live alone after she died and asked me to keep on working. I shopped, cooked, and cleaned for him. I also made sure he took his medicines and went to doctors' appointments."

Like most people at a job interview, Iska was ready for a question about her experience and handled it fluently. Val was sure, though, that Granddad would throw a curveball before long.

"What was your work schedule as a live-in?" he said.

"I was there every night and most days. I had one full day free on the weekend. That's usually when his family would visit. On the other days I was always there for meals. I had a few hours off afternoons or evenings during the week."

"Was that your most recent job?" Granddad said. Iska must have nodded because he continued. "Why did you leave it?"

"Something went wrong with the man's heart, and he died. That is what I heard. I was not working that day."

"You must have felt *terrible*," Bethany said. "Did this happen recently?"

After a long silence, Iska said, "Yesterday."

"Yesterday! Oliver Naiman died yesterday. Were you taking care of him?" Granddad didn't wait for an answer. "Yesterday was Monday. Why weren't you working?"

The silence in the room told Val that Iska hadn't expected that question.

"I will explain," Iska said. "On Sunday evening the man's daughter told me I was not needed to take care of him anymore. She wanted him to move to the retirement village where he would have doctors and nurses nearby."

"Did you hear about Oliver's death from his daughter?" Granddad said.

"No, my friend who works at the retirement village told me. Some of the people who live there knew Oliver and were talking about what happened to him. I was very sorry to hear he died. I hope his daughter was with him."

"She wasn't," Granddad said. "I heard that his aide was at the house yesterday morning and gave him a gift."

"That is not true." Iska emphasized each syllable. "I still have the gift I bought for Oliver's birthday. A scarf. He will never wear it now." Her voice broke. After a moment she said, "Bethany, when can I meet your uncle?"

"I'm not sure. I . . . I don't feel good. Excuse me."

Val peeked into the sitting room as Bethany rushed to the front hall and turned toward the first-floor bathroom. Was she really unwell? Or had she decided to stop playing along with Granddad's deceit? Val was losing patience with it too. Granddad had dangled a possible job to get Iska here. But if she figured out she'd been tricked, she might leave before Granddad wheedled any information from her.

Val opened the door from the vestibule to the outside and slammed it closed. "I'm back." She walked into the sitting room. "Hello, Iska. Remember me?"

"Yes." The aide frowned. "What are you doing here?"

"Mr. Myer is my grandfather. Did I just hear Bethany's voice in here?" When Granddad nodded, Val turned to Iska. "Bethany is my best friend. I didn't expect to see you here, Iska, but I'm glad you are. Some questions came up about Oliver's death that you might be able to answer. Someone left, uh, food for him yesterday morning. Elaine is convinced it was bad for him, and she believes you left it."

Iska's eyes grew round. "It wasn't me. I didn't go near the house after Sunday night."

"That's good. Were you with anyone that night and the next morning?" When Iska nodded, Val continued. "My grandfather has a good friend who would like to talk to you about what happened."

Iska frowned in confusion. "Why?"

Granddad said, "He's trying to find out how Oliver died."

"A doctor?"

"No, my friend is in charge of the police in Bayport." Granddad must have noticed Iska turn rigid. "Don't be afraid. You can trust him. He has nothing to do with immigration. He needs to talk to all the people who knew Oliver, including you. If you don't mind answering a few questions, I'll call him, and he'll come here to meet you. That way you won't have to go to the police station."

Iska stared at Granddad, possibly wondering if she could trust him. "And then we can speak more to Bethany about her uncle?"

Granddad nodded and gave Val a stern look, a silent warning not to contradict his nod. Then he stood up. "I'll call my friend. Sit and talk to Iska, Val." He pointed with his thumb toward a side chair halfway between the hall and the sofa, where Iska sat rigid.

Val sat on the edge of the chair. Granddad apparently expected her to tackle the aide if she tried to bolt. It would be better to convince Iska that she had nothing to fear. "When the police chief was a boy, his father died. My grandfather acted like a second father to him. The chief owes my grandfather a lot and promised not to give your name to ICE, and he won't." Though Chief Yardley wouldn't hesitate to arrest Iska if he had proof she'd murdered someone.

"Thank you. I am happy to hear that." Yet she looked more tense than happy, lacing and unlacing her fingers.

"Oliver's death must be hard on you, Iska, after all the years you were with him."

"I will miss him." Her eyes filled with tears. She wiped them away and looked nervously at Val. "You were there when Elaine fired me. I want you to know I didn't do anything wrong. Please don't say to Bethany that her uncle shouldn't hire me. Elaine was always happy with my work until a few days ago. I believe she changed because Oliver said something that wasn't true."

"About what?"

"Last month he started asking me to marry him. I would never marry such an old man, but I couldn't say that to him. I pretended he was joking. I think Elaine fired me because he said he would marry me." Iska sniffed. "She shouldn't have blamed me for that."

Val could believe that Oliver proposed to Iska and, after not hearing a definite no, might have assumed it was a done deal. Possibly, though, she really had agreed to marry him and was now lying so she'd have a chance at working for another older man. "Did Oliver often lie to his daughter?"

"No, but sometimes he got mixed up and said crazy things, especially in the last year. My grandmother was like that too when she was very old."

And yet weird comments could have a basis in facts. "What do you mean by crazy things?"

"Like what he said about the woman down the street who gave him shots. Holly. Nobody likes to get shots, but he was okay with her until last month. Last month he got sick after she gave him a shot. He told Elaine that Holly tried to poison him and he didn't want her near him. Once Oliver got a silly idea in his head, he said it over and over until he believed it himself."

Oliver must have known that Holly had worked at a poison center. Connecting his sickness with her, he'd come up with a bizarre theory to explain it, but the accusation made no sense. Holly was smart enough not to put poison in a hypodermic needle she herself wielded. "I've met Holly. I'm sure she would have been upset by what Oliver said. Did she know about it?"

"I didn't tell her because it would hurt her feelings. Elaine wouldn't either. She didn't want people to think Oliver was getting funny in the head." Iska rubbed her hands along her thighs, still nervous.

Val came up with a story that might create some rapport with her and yield more information about Oliver's family and friends. "My grandfather doesn't say crazy things, but I had a friend whose grandfather did. When he was really old, he decided his daughter's husband was a bad man and told her to divorce him. Did Oliver do anything like that?"

"No, he said Kevin was better than Cyndi's last husband."

So Kevin didn't have a hard act to follow. Val hoped the give-and-take between her and Iska would continue. "Oliver was lucky to have you helping him and to have good neighbors like Franetta and Thatcher looking after him."

"Franetta is a good neighbor. She brought Oliver cookies and cupcakes. He liked her, but not her husband. Oliver said Thatcher was like all politicians. He looked out for his own good and covered up things he didn't want people to know."

"Did Oliver ever say what kind of things Thatcher covered up?"

"A couple of times, but I didn't understand the words he used. He said something about the drowning business. I don't know what a drowning business is."

Val wasn't sure how to interpret those words either. Oliver could have meant a business on the verge of bankruptcy or a literal drowning. At the birthday party, when he talked about helping his neighbors' son, Franetta had shut him down. Iska might know something about the son.

"The police might want you to give them a list of people who came to see Oliver," Val said. Maybe that was even true. "Did Thatcher and Franetta's son ever visit him?"

"Not while I was with him."

Val had one more name on her list of Oliver's possible contacts. "Did Oliver ever have a visitor called Jake or Jack? Or even talk about anyone with a name like that?"

Iska frowned in concentration. "No. Is that the name of Franetta's son?"

Telling her that Jake was a recent murder victim's name might add to her jitters. "I'm not sure."

Granddad came into the sitting room. "My friend is on his way here to talk to you, Iska. Would you like something to drink?"

"No." Iska glanced toward the hall as if she wanted to make a run for it.

"Don't be worried, Iska. He's a good man." Val stood up. "I'm going to check on how Bethany's feeling." Val went to the hall bathroom and knocked. "Are you okay, Bethany? Can I get you anything?"

Bethany opened the door. "I was nauseous. I stayed here rather than be sick somewhere else. I'm feeling a little better now." She lowered her voice. "Did your grandfather get Iska to tell him what he wanted to know?"

Val whispered, "He coaxed her into talking with Chief Yardley, but I don't understand how Granddad made contact with her."

"I helped him. I got to know some Filipinos through a church fundraiser. One of them works in home health care. I called her and asked if she knew anyone who could cook and run errands for an older man. She got back to me right away, and we set up this meeting. Your grandfather told me Iska might suspect a trap if you were here because she'd met you. That's why he needed me to play along with him."

"I'm sorry he dragged you into this. I can see that it upset you."

Bethany looked down at her trembling hands. "I don't know why I'm so shaky. I wasn't that nervous about playing the part."

Val was getting concerned about her friend. Bethany's

pale complexion verged on white. "You might have the flu. I'll drive you home."

"Good idea. I walked here, but I'm feeling a bit light-headed."

The chief arrived at that moment. He and Iska went into the study and closed the door so they could talk in private. When she came out, Granddad would have to break the news to her that Bethany was sick and the job interview over.

After Val backed out of the driveway, she saw that Bethany was taking her own pulse. "Why are you doing that?"

"I felt like my heart was pounding and then slowing down. With my fingers here I can feel it skipping a beat, and then pounding again."

A pang of fear shot through Val. "Instead of driving you home, Bethany, I'd like to take you to the hospital to get checked."

"Why? I catch all kinds of bugs from my first-graders. This is probably just a twenty-four-hour virus."

"You can't be sure. And your symptoms—nausea, light-headedness, irregular heartbeat—could be a sign of something serious. I'm not trying to scare you, but even young women can develop heart problems."

Bethany wrapped her arms around herself as if warding off frigid air. "Okay. I'll go, just to be on the safe side."

Val made the turn toward Treadwell and the hospital. As she left town for the two-lane highway, a less frightening explanation for Bethany's symptoms occurred to her. Maybe she'd gone on a new fad diet, and it was wreaking havoc with her system. "Did you have a chance to eat before you came to our house?"

"I had a bowl of chili and a salad. I skipped dessert because I'm trying to lose some weight before Christmas. But I did indulge in a piece of chocolate."

Val gripped the steering wheel tightly. After yesterday, the word *chocolate* was enough to cause her anxiety. "A chocolate bar?" she said hopefully.

"No, a bonbon. Someone left a small box of them on my doorstep, probably a neighbor."

Val froze for a moment and then pressed hard on the accelerator. The car lurched forward. "Sorry." She let up on the pedal, but not much.

She decided against explaining why she'd sped up. With Bethany's heart beating erratically, hearing about possibly poisoned chocolates would give her a jolt she didn't need.

Despite Bethany's fidgeting in the passenger seat, Val tried to stay calm. Even if the worst was true—that Oliver had died because of poisoned chocolates and Bethany had eaten similar ones—Bethany had consumed less than half as much chocolate. She was young and robust. His age and health had doubtless contributed to his death. She'd survive. If she didn't—no, Val couldn't bear to think about losing her best friend.

She stared at the dark road ahead through misty eyes. Bethany would make it. She had to.

Chapter 15

Val stopped in front of the hospital's emergency room entrance, took Bethany inside to the registration desk, and then cruised the hospital's lot for an empty space. Parking was tight with two rows blocked for construction. A car backing out of a space hit her front fender. The damage was minimal to her ancient Saturn and the other car, but the driver insisted on following protocol, exchanging contact and insurance information with her.

Twenty minutes later, Val returned to the emergency waiting room and looked around. She saw a few people she'd noticed when she'd gone in there earlier, including a man with a listless-looking child and a woman with a teenage boy clutching his wrist. Bethany wasn't there. Fear gripped Val. Had her friend taken a turn for the worse and been rushed inside?

Val stood in line at the registration desk while people needing emergency care were checked in. When she finally got to the front of the line, the man behind the desk would give her no information because privacy rules prohibited it. He asked for her name and the name of her friend. He'd relay the information and, if the patient and the patient's doctor permitted it, she could go to the treatment area. He told her to have a seat in the waiting room until someone called her name.

Val was too nervous to sit and paced the room. Granddad called to find out why she hadn't returned home yet. She explained where she was and shared her fear about the chocolate Bethany had eaten.

He questioned her about Bethany's symptoms and expressed his concern. "Do you want me at the hospital to wait with you?"

"No, I'll call you when I find out what Bethany's problem is. It might have nothing to do with the chocolate she ate." Val guessed what he'd do next. "Don't alert the chief yet. He can't do anything here. By the way, how did the meeting between him and Iska go?"

"I didn't get a report from either of them. Earl didn't stick around, and she left after finding out Bethany had gone. I'm glad you were here when Bethany needed your help, but why did you come back so early from the dinner you were catering?"

Val briefly described what had happened at the Naiman house.

"I understand the daughter balking at an autopsy for her father," Granddad said. "But you gotta wonder why she doesn't want the chocolates tested."

"Because she resented my interference. I don't think

Cyndi would kill her father, if that's what you're suggesting."

"Maybe she suspects her husband did."

"If I thought my husband poisoned my father, I'd get the chocolates tested. Anyway, Kevin didn't have the opportunity to leave them at the doorstep. Neither of them did. He and Cyndi left Oliver's house to drive home even before I did. Elaine didn't leave until later, but she would have noticed if there was a gift bag by the door."

"Where do Cyndi and Kevin live?"

"Outside Baltimore." Val heard her name called. "Gotta go, Granddad. Someone's calling me. I hope they're taking me back to see Bethany."

"If the doctors don't know what's wrong with her, tell them she might have been poisoned."

"I will."

Bethany was propped up in bed. Her tiny room was filled with equipment tracking her vital signs. One finger had a plastic clip on it and one arm was encircled by a blood pressure cuff.

Val hugged her first and then took a good look at her. "I think you have more color in your face. Are you feeling any better?"

"Yes. As you can see on the monitor, my heart rate is steady. I've had all kinds of tests, but they haven't told me the results." Bethany adjusted her bedclothes. "I've been lying here feeling bad about tricking Iska. What happened with her?"

"Granddad succeeded in his goal. She talked to Chief Yardley."

"But she went away with no job."

A fortyish woman bustled into the room. She introduced herself as the ER doctor and said she had good news for Bethany. Her blood tests and EKG were normal, and her heart rate had stabilized during the time she'd been in the ER.

Tears of joy filled Val's eyes. She squeezed Bethany's hand.

The doctor continued. "I recommend you schedule a stress test to make sure you have no underlying problems that didn't show up in the EKG."

"I'll do that," Bethany said. "Was this just a random thing?"

"Maybe. Occasional episodes of arrhythmia can occur when the heart's electrical system gets out of whack. If it happens again, make an appointment with a cardiologist, who'll run additional tests." The doctor flipped through pages on her clipboard. "Your symptoms could have been caused by a stimulant. Did you have a lot of coffee, colas, or energy drinks today?"

Val stiffened. Those drinks all contained caffeine.

Bethany said, "I drank two coffees in the morning and one around noon, same as always."

The doctor made a note on the chart. "Did you take any diet or stay-awake pills, like college kids do when they pull an all-nighter?"

Bethany looked offended. "No, not today or ever. I don't like swallowing pills."

"I wasn't talking only about pills. Dietary supplements to enhance weight loss, athletic performance, and alertness are also sold in powder form for dissolving in liquids. Some of those are highly concentrated caffeine, particularly dangerous because it's easy to overdose."

If Val were in a comic strip, she'd have a light bulb over her head. Did Bethany end up in the hospital and

Oliver dead on the floor because of chocolate laced with caffeine powder?

Val restrained herself from rushing out of the room and calling Chief Yardley. He'd say she was jumping to a conclusion. Before calling him, she'd look at the chocolates Bethany had received. If they were homemade like Oliver's, or commercially made and tampered with, Val would contact the chief right away. Otherwise, she'd wait until tomorrow.

"I don't take any supplements," Bethany said.

The doctor nodded approval. "Good. Drink a lot of water to flush your system. Skip the coffee tomorrow, or at least cut down on it."

"Is it okay for me to go to work tomorrow?"

"If you feel back to normal in the morning and you don't have a stressful job."

"I teach first grade."

The doctor smiled. "You might want to take a day off." She headed for the door and said over her shoulder, "The nurse will bring you paperwork to sign and then you're free to leave."

"I'm so happy you're okay." Val hugged her friend again. "While you wait for the paperwork, I'll get you a large bottle of water in the cafeteria so you can follow doctor's orders. And I'll call Granddad, because he's worried about you too."

After updating Granddad on Bethany's status, Val told him what the doctor had said about powdered caffeine. "Bethany ate only one chocolate. I'll check the rest. If they look fishy to me, I'll call the chief."

"Call me too. I'll go online and research powdered caffeine."

                            *   *   *

Forty minutes later Val parked at the curb in front of
Bethany's tiny house. Not wanting to upset her friend,
she'd said nothing yet about the possibility that the chocolates left on her doorstep could have been poisoned.

Val accepted Bethany's invitation to come in for an
herbal tea nightcap. Her dog welcomed them when they
went inside, swished her tail furiously, and leaped for joy.

Bethany bent down to hug the dog. "Hello, Muffin.
I've missed you."

Val scanned the surfaces in the living area to the left
and the dining area to the right. A small white box sat on
the dining table next to a silver gift bag. The box looked
the same to Val as the one she'd seen in the Naiman
kitchen, though Oliver's gift had come in a green bag.

Bethany broke away from the dog, hung up her coat
and Val's, and said, "I'll boil some water." She took the
lid off the box. "Have a bonbon while you're waiting.
They're delicious."

Muffin followed her into the kitchen.

One glance at the candy confirmed Val's suspicions.
The eight chocolates remaining in the box were the same
size and shape as the ones she'd seen in Oliver's kitchen,
and had similar irregularities on the bottom edge. His
chocolates and Bethany's had probably come from the
same mold and batch. Molds for eighteen pieces were
common, and they'd each received nine. "I'll join you in
the kitchen for tea, Bethany, but first I have to make a
phone call."

Val walked across the living area to the end farthest
from the kitchen and called Chief Yardley's cell phone.

She spoke to him with her hand cupped over her mouth so Bethany wouldn't overhear. The chief said he'd come right over. She then made a quick call to update Granddad about the chocolates. He had some news for her too. What he'd discovered about caffeine powder chilled her to the bone. A teaspoon of it had more caffeine than twenty cups of coffee, and a tablespoon could be lethal. What's more, the powder was odorless and tasteless.

After hanging up, Val went into the kitchen, sat across the tiny kitchen table from Bethany, and explained why Chief Yardley was coming.

Bethany blanched. "You mean if I'd eaten another bonbon, I'd have been sicker?"

Or maybe even dead. "Until the police test the chocolates, we won't know for sure what's in them, but with your symptoms and Oliver's sensitivity to caffeine, it's hard to believe those bonbons weren't laced with caffeine."

The doorbell rang. Bethany held Muffin while Val opened the door to Chief Yardley.

Bethany had a tiny living room, filled to capacity with oversize furniture. The chief looked like the last big thing that could fit in it. Officer Wade came in right behind the chief. Fortunately, he was slim and stayed in the dining area, collecting the candy and the gift bag.

Val perched on the pouf ottoman, the chief sat in an overstuffed chair, and Bethany sank into the plump couch with Muffin's head in her lap.

The chief peppered her with questions. When and where had she found the gift bag? This evening, when she returned from school late after a faculty meeting, she'd spotted it to the side of the front door. Could she have missed seeing it on her way out this morning? Yes, she was always in a rush in the morning. The bag hadn't been on the side of the door where it opened, but on the hinged side, and she could have missed it. Had she ever before found a gift bag near the front door? She hadn't.

The chief sat forward on the chair. "We don't know for sure that the chocolate was laced with anything, but I can't take a chance. I'm putting out a bulletin tonight, warning against eating anything from an anonymous source. People don't always hear police bulletins, so you two should also spread the word. Contact your friends and coworkers, and get the news out there as soon as possible."

"I'll alert the neighbors," Bethany said.

"Not necessary," the chief said. "We'll have officers canvassing this street tonight to find out if anyone noticed that gift bag or any strangers in the neighborhood. The officer will give your neighbors the warning."

"I'll call my school principal. She can activate the telephone tree to warn all the parents."

Val said, "I'll tell my café customers tomorrow."

The chief grunted. "I hope tomorrow is soon enough. After three nights in a row, I don't want it to happen again tonight."

Val was surprised. "Three nights? You're including Jake's gift even though it wasn't chocolate?" And had cyanide, not caffeine, in it.

"The last thing Jake and Oliver ate came from a gift bag. That could have been a coincidence. Now, with a third case of an unidentified person leaving a sweet that sickened or killed someone, we have a possible copycat crime or a serial killer. That means I can put the chocolate analysis and Oliver's autopsy on the fast track. And I may get more law enforcement assigned to the case."

Val studied Bethany's face. How was she handling the news that a serial killer might have gone after her? "Are you okay?"

Bethany took a deep breath and released it. "Lightning never strikes the same place twice. The bolt struck, and I'm still here, right?" She made a feeble attempt at a smile.

She was understandably worried, as was Val. The adage about lightning would apply to the poisonings only if chance dictated who the victims were, but did it? "Chief, do you think all three poison victims were random?"

He shrugged. "I only know one thing for sure—the two of you need to be very careful." The chief stood up and pointed to the front door. "I see you have a peephole in your door, Bethany. If you hear a knock or a doorbell, check who's outside before you open the door. Val, make sure you and your granddaddy look through the sidelight before unlocking the door."

Val hugged herself, feeling chilled. "You think the serial killer, if we have one, might change tactics?"

"Our announcement will tell folks to beware of anonymous gifts. The killer will hear that warning, know we're on to him, and possibly use a different weapon."

"You used the word *him*, Chief," Val said. "Is there a reason you think a man is behind this?"

"Serial killers—and murderers of any kind—are overwhelmingly male."

"Isn't poison considered a woman's weapon?" Bethany said.

"Men are responsible for about half of all poisonings." The chief walked to the door and then turned back. "I hope we find out that the chocolate was just chocolate. Until we do, don't let your guard down." He closed the door behind him.

Chapter 16

Val sighed and caught her friend's eye across the coffee table. "Why don't you come home with me, Bethany, so you don't have to be alone tonight?"

Bethany petted Muffin. "I don't expect a restful night, but I'll do better in my own bed."

"Then I'd like to stay here with you."

"I appreciate that. The guest room's ready, and I'll leave a nightgown for you on the bed."

"Tomorrow you can come with me to the café."

Bethany shook her head. "I'm going to school in the morning."

"Even though the doctor said to take it easy?"

"Sticking to the routine will take my mind off all this. And it's better for the children not to have a substitute teacher. I'll call my principal right now. She'll make sure all the parents are warned. We don't want a child to leave for school, see a gift of candy on a doorstep, and eat poisoned chocolates." Bethany stood up and hugged Val. "Thank you for taking care of me." She headed toward the bedrooms at the back of the house.

Val called Granddad to tell him she would spend the night at Bethany's house and stop by the house in the morning to change clothes. She also passed on the chief's advice to check who was at the door before opening it.

Next she called her cousin Monique. Val could imagine Monique's two preschoolers gobbling up candy they'd found in a gift bag without telling their mommy, who frowned on unhealthy sweets. Val told her what had happened to Bethany and asked her cousin to warn other parents to check their doorsteps for anonymous gifts. She also asked Monique for any photos of Santa she'd taken at the festival. Val didn't need to explain why. Monique had heard that Santa had been the poison victim and could guess that Val was trying to figure out who'd killed him. A photo of Santa with one of the suspects could suggest what type of relationship they'd had.

After talking with Monique, Val put her phone away. Last night she'd fretted that Bram's departure from Bayport would ruin the holidays for her. Tonight the chances of a merry Christmas had gone from bad to worse. She paced from the living room to the kitchen and back, trying to contain the anger welling within her. Until now she'd viewed Jake's murder as a puzzle to solve and Oliver's death as a possible piece of that puzzle. But with Bethany threatened, Val had a personal reason to expose the culprit.

* * *

By the next afternoon Val would have been surprised to find anyone in the vicinity of Bayport unaware of the police bulletin. She'd heard it first on the radio while driving to work and several times on the café's TV. The local station had interrupted regular programming all morning to repeat the police announcement.

The Bayport Police Department issued a warning against eating food from unknown sources. Town residents have become seriously ill after consuming candy left for them in a gift bag. Anyone who sees an unattended bag or box should notify the police. Investigations are underway to determine if these incidents are related to the poisoning death of a man last Saturday during the Bayport Dickens festival.

An effective warning, short and punchy, but it left out key information—that one of the candy eaters hadn't just gotten sick, but had died. She assumed the chief was waiting for the chocolate to be tested before blaming Oliver's death on it.

The café was busier than usual for a Wednesday, possibly because the frightening news had driven people together and made them crave company and comfort food. Val worked steadily from the time she opened the café until two in the afternoon, when she turned it over to Jeremy.

Her phone rang as she was climbing into her car. A woman who lived on Belleview Avenue canceled a holiday party Val was supposed to cater. She chalked up the cancellation to mischief by Elaine's sister. Cyndi had apparently talked to a neighbor and made good on her threat to ruin Val's reputation. If this was the first stone in an avalanche of cancellations, it would be a leaner Christmas than Val had planned. She'd have to reduce her gift budget, but that was the least of her problems.

On the way home she stopped at the library to talk with the new head librarian, Shantell, the only person from the volunteers' tea Val hadn't seen since the night Jake died. She spotted the middle-aged, dark-skinned woman through the glass partition behind the book check-out counter. Sitting at a computer, Shantell looked attractive and efficient in a navy and light blue sweater over gray slacks, a far cry from the frump in the shapeless dress she'd worn as Madame Defarge.

As a library volunteer wheeled a book cart into the room, Shantell turned away from the computer. She glanced through the glass wall, made eye contact with Val, and hurried out to greet her. "I'm glad to see you again. Do you have a few minutes to talk?"

Exactly the question Val would have asked Shantell. "Yes." She glanced at the library's main room filled with bookshelves and library patrons. "Can we talk here or should we go outside?"

Shantell smiled. "Librarians don't hush people the way they used to. Yes, we can talk here, but our meeting room isn't reserved. Let's go there." She spoke to the woman checking out books and then led Val to a room with folding chairs around an oblong table.

Shantell sat straight in her chair as if on the witness stand. "I live around the corner from Bethany O'Shay. My dogs and Muffin are good buddies. When I was walking my dogs last night, I saw you go into the house with her. Later, the police knocked on every door in the neighborhood. From their questions and this morning's police bulletin, I assume Bethany was one of the people who became ill from candy someone left for her. How's she doing?"

"She felt bad last night so I took her to the emergency room. After a few hours, she recovered. She even taught school today."

"I'm glad she's okay, but the police announcement worries me. It suggested a connection between Jake, who died after eating a cookie, and the poison victims who got sick after eating candy. I can't imagine two people with less in common than Jake and Bethany."

"I agree." Val didn't understand Shantell's point. "Are you saying that you don't think there's any connection?"

"Not exactly. Like the current Librarian of Congress, I enjoy reading mysteries. When I heard the police bulletin, an Agatha Christie book came to mind. It involves a killer who murders seemingly random people. The series of crimes distracts the police so they don't focus on the one murder for which the killer has a motive."

"The police aren't distracted from Jake's murder. He made a lot of enemies in the short time he lived here as you know. You and the neighbors who banded together to stop his real estate scheme won't mourn him."

"The neighbors who expected him to buy their houses might mourn him." A note of bitterness had crept into Shantell's voice. "Some of them have even implied I might have poisoned him. I was just trying to protect them from a bad deal. Jake was going to pay the sellers only half of the money upfront. They'd have to wait for the rest of it until he put up new houses and made a profit on them, a time that might never come. I managed to talk two people out of selling to him."

"You were right to mistrust him." Val summarized

what the chief had told her about Jake's previous real estate ventures. "With his track record, the chance of his paying what he owed your neighbors was slim. If they knew that, they'd be less likely to mourn him."

"The wounds he opened up will take a while to heal. When they do, I'll still be here. I'll never sell the property I inherited from my grandmother to anyone for any price."

"You must have fond memories of visiting the house."

"I have fond memories of the garden. My life revolves around books, but my roots are in the ground. When my grandmother was young, during the Depression, the yard behind the house kept my family alive." Shantell gazed out the window as if it offered a view into the past. "They grew their own food and raised chickens. The land is part of my family history. Bulldozing it to make room for a big house would be like digging up my grandmother's bones."

"I understand what you mean." Val had similar feelings about the kitchen in Granddad's house. It was where Grandma's spirit remained alive.

"Librarians are good researchers, so I know all about your involvement in other murder investigations." Shantell's prominent brown eyes bore into Val. "I suspect you came here to pursue your research into Jake's murder. I hope you got what you wanted from me."

"Your view of Jake was what I wanted and got," Val said. Shantell had pursued her own agenda, making it clear that she had nothing to gain by killing Jake. In fact, he had a motive to kill her, the holdout who could prevent his real estate scheme from going forward.

The librarian glanced at her watch and stood up. "My break is about over, but I have one more thing to say.

Whoever killed Jake and tried to poison two other people is ruthless and won't hesitate to kill again. You'd be wise to leave this case to the police."

"Thank you. I appreciate the warning, and I'll be careful."

Those weren't empty words. A couple of times in the past, Val had gone toe-to-toe with a murderer. She'd rather avoid that trauma, especially with a serial killer. Yet she couldn't stop thinking about who was behind the poisonings and why anyone would target Bethany.

Each time she'd talked to a woman with an apparent motive to kill Jake—his wife Jewel, his jilted fiancée Holly, and his business nemesis Shantell—Val came away doubting that the woman had killed him. They were all sitting at the table when the ghost delivered the gifts. But Franetta hadn't yet arrived for the tea. She'd had the opportunity to disguise herself as the ghost, but no apparent motive for killing Jake. Maybe the files on Jake's thumb drive would point to someone else as his murderer.

Val stopped at the grocery store on the way home. Granddad had the main dish ready for tonight's dinner with Dorothy, but he might not have thought about what else to serve, except maybe dessert. Val picked up basmati rice, spinach, crackers, hummus, cheese, and nuts. In case Granddad hadn't made dessert, she put cream and semisweet chocolate into her basket. It was barely four o'clock, so she would have enough time before dinner to make a warm chocolate tart.

Back home, Val found Granddad in his lounge chair with his eyes closed. He opened them as she tiptoed by him. She told him about her meeting with Shantell and then asked, "Did you have a chance to look at the files you copied from Jake's thumb drive?"

"Yup. Mostly they're old spreadsheets with dates, numbers, and nonsense words you'd need a decoder ring to crack. The police might be able to decipher it if they cared. Jake also kept a calendar on the thumb drive."

The calendar piqued her interest. "An old one or a current one?"

"Up-to-date. I'll show you." He slowly got out of his recliner, went into the study, and sat at the desk. He jiggled the mouse, clicked around, and brought up a December calendar on the screen. "Jake used codes or abbreviations in his calendar entries like in his spreadsheet, but I could decipher some of those. I looked at the ones for the last six weeks. He had a few evening appointments labeled CC in the second half of November and the first week in December. I think it stands for Community Center, where the festival volunteer meetings were held. If I didn't already know when and where the meetings were, I couldn't have figured that out."

Val peered at the screen. "For last Saturday he blocked off the whole day as DF. That must mean Dickens festival."

Granddad pointed to the day following that. "Here's one appointment he didn't keep because he was already dead. He had something planned for Sunday morning at ten thirty—*marina O*. The O could mean the Osprey Point Marina. That's more than an hour from here. It might refer to the name of a boat at the marina in Bayport."

"Or he planned to meet someone at the marina whose name starts with an O." Val could think of only one person with that initial. "I doubt Oliver was going to meet Jake at the marina. It's a long way from the parking lot to the marina, and Oliver was having trouble walking."

Val's phone rang. She checked the caller ID. Bethany.

"Hey, Bethany. How was your day at school?"

"Fine, but it's gone downhill in the last few minutes. Chief Yardley called me." She sounded breathless. "He said my chocolates came from the same batch as the ones Oliver Naiman ate. They contained a massive amount of caffeine."

Val shuddered, though the news didn't surprise her. "That's horrible."

"I'm lucky I ate only one."

Val wouldn't want to be alone after finding out she'd escaped death by resisting another chocolate. Poor Bethany. "Come over and have dinner with us. Bring Muffin with you. You're both welcome to stay the night too, as many nights as you want."

"Okay, but I don't want to impose."

"You're not. Granddad invited Dorothy Muir to dinner. We have lots to eat." And lots to talk about. With four of them brainstorming, they might come closer to identifying Bayport's Christmas killer . . . or killers.

Chapter 17

Val took out the chicken casserole that was warming in the oven and put in the chocolate tart while Granddad grated carrots for the salad. Bethany paced the room, agitated by the chief's news that the chocolates left for her contained enough caffeine to kill her several times over. Though Bethany had offered to help with dinner, Val didn't want anyone as nervous and preoccupied as her friend near a knife or the stove. Muffin watched Bethany pace for a while and then went for a snooze on the cushion her mistress had brought for her.

Granddad had refused Dorothy's offer of help. She now sat at the small kitchen table, sipping wine. Usually cheerful and energetic, the bookshop owner had bags under her eyes. Perhaps she hadn't been sleeping well since Jake's murder in the shop's back room.

Her face sagged even more when she heard about

Oliver's fatal poisoning and Bethany's brush with death. "It was bad enough when one man was poisoned in Bayport. Now there's a serial killer."

Val couldn't imagine that anything would lighten tonight's mood, but analyzing the poisonings as a puzzle to be solved would be better than dwelling on the horror of multiple murders. "Let's get the serial killer elephant out of the room before we sit down to dinner. I've come up with different scenarios that might explain what happened, and random poisonings by a serial killer is the least likely of them."

Granddad looked up. "The statistics say that most murderers kill people they know, not strangers. I'll bet there are more serial killers in books and movies than in the real world."

Bethany went over to the table and took a handful of nuts. "I always liked scary books and movies with creative serial killers, but not anymore. From now on I'm reading only cozy mysteries."

"You'll find more poisonings in *them* than in other books," Dorothy said.

Bethany sighed. "That's true. Cozy readers don't like blood and gore, so there aren't as many guns, knives, and bombs as in thrillers. That leaves poison."

Val moved the pot of rice off the burner. "The Bayport murderer not only didn't like blood and gore, but also couldn't stand to be around when the victim died. That might be why the poisoned sweets were left in a gift bag that wouldn't be opened until the killer was gone."

Bethany put down her mug. "There's more to it than that. The Bayport murderer hates the holidays, or at least the gift-giving part. Look who the first victim was—Santa Claus, the gift-bringer."

Val figured Jake's character, or rather the lack of it, had more to do with his death than the Santa suit, but Bethany wasn't aware of Jake's background. "The first poisoning had a specific target. The murderer delivered the poisoned cookie directly to him. Of course, Jake could have chosen not to eat the cookie, but he gobbled up all his sweets. Maybe his killer knew his eating habits. Leaving candy on Oliver's doorstep was less of a sure thing."

Granddad added the carrots to the lettuce in the salad bowl. "And the poison used on Jake, cyanide, was guaranteed to be lethal and kill fast. Caffeine isn't, unless your victim is someone whose doctor warned against the dangers of caffeine."

"Caffeine is lethal enough," Bethany said. "A few more chocolates and I'd have been dead too. I'm not convinced Jake, Oliver, and I are random victims of the same murderer. Don't most serial killers stick to the same method? The Tylenol killer didn't tamper with other kinds of capsules. And the police never figured out who was responsible for those poisonings."

Dorothy leaned across the table toward Bethany. "They'll figure it out this time. They have a lot more information than the police had about the Tylenol killer. The two different poisons in this case must mean something. We have either two murderers or one who had a reason to switch from cyanide to caffeine. What could that reason be?"

Val was glad that Dorothy was now puzzling over the murders, not just brooding about them.

Granddad tossed the salad. "Cyanide is harder to acquire and handle. Caffeine powder is easy to order online, no questions asked. That's a big difference."

Val spooned the spinach into a serving bowl. "Dinner's ready. Grab a drink and we'll adjourn to the dining room."

They clustered at one end of the long table. Granddad sat at the head of the table with Dorothy on his right, Bethany on his left, and Val next to her.

After everyone had filled their plates, Granddad said, "I don't think we can rule out a serial killer of random victims just because he or she doesn't follow a pattern. Random is random. So one poison might be used twice and another one only once. Two victims might get a gift on the doorstep and one not, two get candy and one gets a cookie."

"And two victims might be random and one not." Val heaped rice on her plate. "That's the second scenario. Bayport's new librarian, Shantell, suggested it to me. She based it on an Agatha Christie plot. The murderer has a reason to kill one of the victims and kills the others to distract the police and make them think all the victims are random. If that's what's going on here, who is the primary victim?"

"Not me." Bethany speared some lettuce. "No one gains anything if I die. I have no money and no enemies."

"Jake had both," Granddad said. "The killer put the poisoned cookie under his nose. And there are more suspects and motives for his murder than you can shake a stick at. He's gotta be the primary victim."

Val took a bite of the chicken casserole, wondering if anyone else noticed the flaw in Granddad's theory.

Dorothy cleared her throat. "If the reason to kill more than one person is to distract the police from investigating the primary victim's death, the primary victim can't be the first one killed. The police would assume that's the one and only murder and really focus on it."

Val nodded. "That's exactly what happened here. Jake was poisoned on Saturday night. Oliver died on Monday morning, supposedly from natural causes. The police didn't even think to investigate his death until Tuesday night, after Bethany came back from the hospital. For three days they focused on Jake's murder."

Granddad threw up his hands. "Okay, so it wasn't Jake. But Oliver doesn't fit the bill as a primary victim either. His murderer was sitting pretty when Oliver's doctor said he died from cardiac arrest. It doesn't make sense to try and kill Bethany the same way. Doing that focused attention on Oliver's death as a deliberate poisoning."

"But only because one person"—Val pointed to herself—"saw the same chocolates in two places, recognized them as homemade, and knew caffeine was the suspected trigger both times. That was the killer's bad luck."

Dorothy frowned. "That doesn't explain why the killer left the chocolates at Bethany's place."

"True. I'll get to that in another scenario." Val wanted to cover the options in an orderly way. "So far we've talked about a traditional serial killer with random victims and the Christie version of the serial killer with one main victim and a bunch of random ones. There are flaws in both of those explanations. What else could be going on?"

Granddad heaped some chicken on his fork. "Two different murderers. That would explain why there are different poisons. The only similarity is the gift bag. Jake died after he ate what was in a gift bag, and Oliver's murder could have been a copycat crime."

Bethany frowned. "The police didn't say anything

about a gift bag when they announced Jake's death. So how would Oliver's killer know about it?"

Granddad took a sip of wine. "Everybody at the volunteer tea knew that the ghost left a gift bag, and that Jake keeled over after he ate the cookie in the gift bag. News travels fast in Bayport."

Val glanced sideways at Bethany. She was pushing the food around her plate as if assembling a jigsaw puzzle with something missing—the piece that would explain how she fit into the picture.

She made a small pile of the remaining spinach on her plate. "One murderer killed Jake. Another one killed Oliver and also gave me poisoned chocolates from the same batch. But when the chocolates were left at my house, the doctor and the police thought Oliver had died of natural causes. His murderer had no reason to create the illusion that a serial killer was operating in Bayport. So why try to poison me?"

A variation on the question Dorothy had asked. Val looked at the blank faces around her.

Granddad spoke up. "I'll take a stab at answering that. Maybe the killer, who'd just gotten away with murder, enjoyed having power over life and death."

Dorothy fidgeted as if she were itchy all over. "That's grim. Is there another explanation?"

Val nodded. Coming up with these scenarios had been like looking for the perfect recipe. Each one seemed to have something not quite right about it. Her final one was the best fit for the facts, but Val very much wanted someone to shoot holes into it. "One killer with a motive for each poisoning."

Dorothy countered with a question. "Is there any connection between Jake and Oliver?"

Granddad shrugged. "None I could find. I'm not even sure they knew each other, though maybe the murderer knew both of them. We could make a list of suspects in each murder and see who's on both lists."

The problem in this plan was obvious to Val. "That would work only if we have a list of all possible people with reasons to kill either of them. I have a feeling we're missing a few suspects for Jake, if not Oliver."

Bethany was again pushing her food around the plate with her fork. "I don't see where I fit in this scenario. Am I the only random victim?"

"You could be, but there's another possibility, and it might be the key to figuring out who the killer is." Val waited until she made eye contact with her friend. "The murderer had a good reason to get rid of Jake, Oliver, *and* you."

Bethany squawked. Muffin, napping near the heating vent in the corner, woke up, trotted over to Bethany, and gazed up at her, as if asking if she were okay. "Why would anyone want to get rid of me?" She bent down to pet Muffin.

Val could only guess why a murderer would have targeted Bethany. "Maybe you're a threat to the killer. You might have seen or heard something in the last few days that connects the murderer to the earlier poisonings."

Bethany chewed on her lower lip. "I can't think of what."

Granddad glanced down at Muffin now sitting on the floor between his chair and Bethany's. "Do you ever walk Muffin along Belleview Avenue, where Oliver lived? Or along Creek Road, where Jake lived?"

"I've walked Muffin along Belleview Avenue when

the weather's nice, but we haven't gone there lately. It's a longer walk than we take in cold weather. Creek Road is even farther. I can't remember ever taking Muffin there."

Val sipped her wine. "You and Jake were at the festival most of the day. You must have seen him while you were caroling and he was parading around in his red suit."

"I caught a glimpse of him now and then. He was doing the Santa thing, posing for photos and giving out gifts to the kids." Bethany rubbed her forehead. "I'm trying to replay in my mind who he was with and what was happening. I didn't notice him arguing with anybody or doing anything that would explain someone killing him. Maybe if I thought harder about this, I could be more helpful."

Dorothy said, "Don't dwell on it, Bethany. Let your mind drift. If there's anything to remember, it may come to you, perhaps in the middle of the night or tomorrow morning, not when you're tense. Let's talk about something else."

Granddad glanced at Val's plate. "The rest of us are nearly finished with dinner, Val, and you've hardly started. You're holding up dessert."

"Sorry." She ate mechanically, barely tasting her food, more worried about her friend now than before discussing the scenarios. A murderer with a motive who'd failed to kill Bethany the first time might try again and, as the chief had warned, with a different weapon.

"I'd just as soon postpone dessert until after our movie," Dorothy said.

Val sipped her wine. Whenever Dorothy came over for dinner, she and Granddad watched a video from his collection of classic films, often a Hitchcock because both of them were fans. "After our dinner table conversation, Granddad, you might want to pick out something less nail-biting than Hitchcock."

Granddad waved away her advice. "Hitch has a few light movies. We could watch the one about the train."

Dorothy looked askance. "I wouldn't call that one light."

"I mean the 1930s train movie, *The Lady Vanishes*. Lots of comedy mixed with suspense and some romance."

"I'd like to see it too," Bethany said. "I could use a few laughs, not to mention romance."

Bethany had just broken up with her boyfriend from the choir. Val gave her a sympathetic look and reserved some sympathy for herself too. Her romance was about to fizzle out of existence. "I'll clear the table while the rest of you get settled in front of the TV. Does anyone want coffee or tea?"

No one did. Granddad and Dorothy went into the sitting room, while Bethany refilled Muffin's water dish and Val stacked the dishes on the kitchen counter. When she returned to the dining room for the wineglasses, Dorothy was shifting a side chair to face the television.

"Are you sure you want to sit there?" Granddad said. "You and I can sit on the sofa."

"When was the last time you sat on that sofa, Don?"

"I don't remember."

"I've tried it a few times. This straight-back chair is a lot more comfortable."

Val did an internal jig for joy. Dorothy would be an ally in the struggle to convince Granddad to replace the sofa and, if he really wanted to sit closer to her, he'd have to buy a new one.

Granddad lowered himself into his recliner. Val sat at

one end of the sofa and ceded the rest of it to Bethany and Muffin.

Everyone was soon riveted by the suspense of a woman who'd vanished on a train. The other passengers denied she'd ever existed, except for the adamant heroine. About an hour into the movie, Muffin jerked up, barked, and ran to the front door. A second later the doorbell rang.

Val and Bethany both jumped up.

"Stay where you are." Granddad pressed the Pause button on the remote. "I'll get the door."

Bethany frowned. "Look through the sidelight before you open it, Mr. Myer."

Muffin continued to bark as Granddad made his way toward the hall. He didn't turn on the hall light. That way he could see whoever was standing on the porch without being visible himself through the sidelight. He called back to them, "Don't worry. It's a friend, not a foe."

The front door creaked open.

As Val flipped on the lamp next to the sofa, Bram came into the sitting room. His smile, as he locked eyes with her, made her catch her breath. She could control her breathing, but managing her heart would be more difficult. She'd better start hardening it now so that when he left Bayport it wouldn't hurt as much.

Muffin sniffed around him. He crouched to pet her.

"You're a little early, Bram." Dorothy turned from her son to the others in the room. "My car battery died, so I walked here from the bookshop this evening. Bram insisted on picking me up and driving me home."

"One of us would have driven you home," Val said, though she was glad not to have to do that. With the poisonings it was better for them to sit tight with Bethany.

Granddad said, "There's another half hour to go in the movie. Do you want to save the rest of it for another day, Dorothy?"

She shook her head. "If you don't mind waiting, Bram, you might get a piece of chocolate tart when the movie's over."

He got up from his crouch as Muffin abandoned him for Bethany. "Chocolate tart is worth waiting for."

Bethany eyed the dog gazing up at her. "Muffin is giving me her take-me-for-a-walk look. It's the last thing she does before going to sleep for the night. I have to take her."

"I'll take Muffin," Bram said. "If she'll have me."

Once Bethany handed Bram the leash, Muffin accepted him as the anointed dog walker. Granddad locked the door behind them, returned to his lounger, and clicked the remote to resume the video.

Half an hour later, when the movie ended, Bram and Muffin still hadn't returned from the walk. When Val turned on the lamp in the sitting room, she saw her own anxiety mirrored in Dorothy's face and in Bethany's. The poisonings had not only killed two people, they'd destroyed the peace and security of everyone in town. A week ago no one would have thought twice about a man and a dog going for a long walk at night in Bayport.

Dorothy stood up. "I'll call him. My phone's in the kitchen." She returned in less than a minute, looking relaxed. "Bram said Muffin took him for a long walk. They'll be back in fifteen minutes."

Granddad levered himself out of the lounger. "I'll slice the chocolate tart."

Val followed him into the kitchen, made a pot of tea, and brought it to the dining room table. They sat around it and talked about the movie. Despite a few humorous characters, Bethany found the film rather dark and scary.

"What struck me most," Val said, "was why so many train passengers denied seeing the lady who vanished. Some of them lied because they were evil, but most did it because they were afraid the train would be delayed or they'd be involved in a controversy. They wanted to mind their own business. I wonder how many festival visitors ignored the police request for information about the Ghost of Christmas Presents for similar reasons."

Granddad loaded his fork with a chunk of tart. "Talking to the police would take up their precious time. They might even have to go to court as witnesses."

Bethany poured tea in her cup. "The ghost I saw didn't limp or I would have contacted the police."

Dorothy looked across the table at her. "Where and when did you see that ghost?"

"When I left the festival Saturday evening, I walked home along Pine Street. I passed the church and got as far as the next cross street, Dixon Lane. The ghost was down that street."

Suddenly alert, Val put down her fork. "What time was that on Saturday evening?"

Bethany took a moment to answer. "Six thirty or a quarter to seven."

Val hadn't checked her watch when the ghost crashed the volunteers' tea party, but it had been around that time or shortly before. And witnesses had reported seeing a black-robed figure skirting the churchyard and walking toward Pine Street. "What did the ghost look like, Bethany?"

"Like a black blob at first. When I saw it, I was afraid someone had fallen and needed help. I turned onto Dixon

Lane and as I got closer to the blob, I could tell it was a person bending down near a big bush along the sidewalk. I said, 'Are you okay?' After straightening up, the person looked at me with a ghost mask on. I jumped back. It was a smiling ghost mask, not scary, but creepy, like clowns are with their smiling faces."

"What was the ghost wearing?" Dorothy said.

"A long black robe with the hood up, like the Grim Reaper. I figured the ghost had worn the costume for the cemetery tour and missed the entrance, so I pointed it out. The ghost headed toward the church, and I continued home."

Val conjured a vision of the ghost who delivered the gingerbread cookies. "Was the ghost you saw carrying anything?"

Bethany nodded. "One of the big Dickens festival shopping bags."

"Like the ghost who crashed the tea party. After delivering the gingerbread cookie gifts and leaving the bookshop, that ghost might have taken the gift bag off his head and—"

"You mean off *her* head," Bethany corrected. "The ghost I saw was a woman. She said 'Happy Holidays' in a cheerful voice when I asked if she was okay. The words were a bit muffled, but it was definitely a woman's voice."

Val hadn't been able to tell if the ghost who crashed the tea party had been male or female. "I guess I used *he* and *him* to refer to the ghost because all the ghosts in *A Christmas Carol* are males."

Granddad rested his fork on a plate that had only crumbs left on it. "Dickens's ghosts have been women in some of the movie versions."

Bethany said, "We already know that the ghost I saw was a woman. The only question is whether it's the same ghost that gave out gingerbread cookies."

Val shook her head. "I don't think it's a question, Bethany. It's an answer."

"To what?"

"Why the murderer tried to poison you."

Chapter 18

For the first time since Bethany had been poisoned, Val had an inkling of the reason. "Assuming the person you ran into Saturday night had just delivered a poisoned gingerbread cookie, you might be able to identify him—I mean, her."

Bethany threw up her hands. "How am I supposed to identify someone whose face I couldn't see?"

"You heard a voice," Granddad said.

"I heard two words. The voice didn't sound familiar."

That made sense to Val. "People can disguise their voices. Listen to this." She took a deep breath, pitched her voice higher than usual, and injected a note of forced joviality. "*Happy Holidays!*"

Granddad covered his ears. "I'm glad you don't talk like that all the time."

"Your voice isn't even close to how the ghost sounded, Val. But you're right, anyone could speak in a different voice." The color drained from Bethany's face. "If the ghost bothered to change her voice, it's because she thought I might recognize it. That means I must know her."

Val cast around for another explanation and found one. "Not necessarily, Bethany. The ghost went to a lot of trouble to be unrecognizable with a totally covered body and face. So she wouldn't want to use her own voice. It's another way she could be identified if she's ever a suspect in the murder."

Granddad nodded. "It's called a voice lineup. Witnesses listen to several people speak and pick out any voice they've heard before." Granddad turned to Dorothy. "You've been awfully quiet. Any thoughts about the ghost?"

"Val, did the ghost say anything in the CAT Corner?" When Val shook her head, Dorothy continued. "I don't understand the reason for saying 'Happy Holidays' when the ghost could have just stayed silent."

Val replayed in her mind the scene when the ghost arrived at the tea. "The ghost who delivered the cookies wasn't frightening. A head covered with a gift bag is whimsical, part of the costume's visual pun. With the gift bag off and the black hood up, the ghost looks threatening, even with a smiling mask. The last thing someone who's just committed a murder wants is to encounter someone who'll scream, attract attention, and bring people rushing to her aid."

Bethany nodded. "I almost did that."

And it would have been effective. Val had heard

Bethany's piercing shriek when they visited the haunted corn maze last year. "I'll bet you were less scared after a chirpy woman wished you 'Happy Holidays.'"

"Yes, and I was surprised. Until then I thought the ghost was a man."

"Why?"

Bethany shrugged.

The doorbell rang. Val went to the hall and looked though the sidelight before opening the door to Muffin and Bram. The dog shot by her, heading straight for Bethany. As Bram took off his jacket and hung it over the banister, Val summarized the conversation they'd had at the table about the ghost Bethany had seen.

"I missed a lot," he said.

"You missed even more earlier in the evening—multiple murder scenarios. Your mother can tell you about them. Your chocolate tart is on the table waiting for you."

Bram took the empty seat next to his mother and dug into the tart.

Muffin's pleading gaze at Bethany suggested she wouldn't mind a piece of tart herself.

Bethany looked down at the dog. "Don't give me that look. You're not allowed to eat in the dining room or to have chocolate with a buttery crust. Now, go to your bed." She pointed to the small room between the kitchen and dining room, the butler's pantry, where a cushion on the floor awaited the dog.

Muffin trotted around the table and eyed Bram's fork as it moved from plate to mouth.

Bram said, "You heard what Bethany said, Muffin. Bed."

Muffin must have heard a firmness in his tone that was

missing from Bethany's. The dog gave up and padded to the other room.

Val took a bite of the tart, trying to remember what she was about to say when the doorbell rang. Something about the ghost. "You said you didn't notice the ghost limping, Bethany, but when did you see her walking?"

"After I pointed out the churchyard, I went the other way, took a few steps, and then turned around. The ghost was walking without a limp toward the churchyard."

Granddad said, "How many times did you check behind you to see if the ghost was following you?"

"Only once. I know what you're thinking. That the ghost could have reversed direction, followed me, and found out where I lived. Why was I such a threat that the ghost poisoned me?"

Val rubbed her forehead. "I'm guessing here. When you came along, the ghost was bending down with the robe covering her. You couldn't see what was going on, but she was afraid you could. It must have been something that suggested her identity."

Dorothy sipped her tea. "Maybe Bethany came up when the ghost was putting on the mask or adjusting it. The ghost would have hunched down to make her face less visible."

Bethany twirled a ringlet of her ginger hair around her finger. "The ghost wasn't hunching but bending down, like you do to tie your shoes."

"Shoes!" Granddad snapped his fingers. "I know how the ghost made the limp disappear, and she'd have to bend down to do it. You can change your voice or the style and color of your hair, but not the way you walk. People who don't want to be identified—like spies, for example—put a pebble in their shoe. Because it hurts to step on a pebble, they put less weight on that foot and end up limping."

Dorothy's eyes narrowed. "How do you know about putting a pebble in a shoe? Did you work for the CIA, Don?" She paused. "I guess you wouldn't tell me if you did."

Granddad chuckled. "I saw a movie about a spy who did that to fool the assassins who were after him."

His honesty delighted Val. Around Halloween he'd touted his ghost-hunting experience. She wouldn't have been surprised if he claimed espionage experience now, but telling Dorothy the truth was a sign that he valued her friendship too much to lie to her. "A woman wouldn't have to use a pebble to limp," Val said. "She could wear shoes with different heel heights. To stop limping, she just had to take off one shoe and put on the mate to the other."

Bethany frowned. "I understand why someone would want to stop limping, but not the reason for doing it in the first place."

"It drew everyone's attention and kept them from noticing much else about the ghost," Val said.

Bram piped up, "That's true, but I think there's more to it. Someone at the tea might have identified the ghost by her walk, and that's why the ghost decided to limp."

"Wouldn't the long robe have hidden how the ghost walked?" Bethany said.

Bram shook his head. "Gait recognition technology analyzes the whole body in motion—hips, arms, shoulders, head—not just the legs. When people recognize someone by their walk, they're processing all of those things too. But a limp causes most people to screen out those data points, though it can't fool the technology."

Val stared at him across the table. "I've never heard you talk tech before, Bram."

He grinned. "If you like it, I have lots more where that came from."

"I've had enough for the moment." She stood up. "I'm going to call Chief Yardley. He'll want to interview Bethany."

She went into the study to call the chief. As soon as she told him about Bethany's encounter with a robed figure, the chief said he'd come right over.

When Val left the study, the others were in the hall. Dorothy and Bram were getting ready to leave.

Dorothy buttoned her peacoat. "Dinner and dessert were wonderful. Thank you for inviting me and for the stimulating conversation at the table. I just hope I can sleep tonight. Bethany, please be watchful."

"Don't walk Muffin after dark," Bram said. "I'll come over and do that until the police arrest the murderer."

Granddad nodded. "We don't want Bethany walking the dog at all. I'll take Muffin for daytime walks."

Bethany's eyes glistened with tears. "Thank you both. But I can't be under house arrest. I have a bunch of first graders and their parents who expect me to show up every day."

Val slipped past Granddad and reached into the closet for the cloak she'd worn to the festival. "Whenever you go out, you can wear this and put on a knitted cap. Wrapped in the cloak, with your hair hidden under the hat, and wearing sunglasses, no one will recognize you unless they know you well and see you up close." Val rehung the cloak. "Are you okay with this, Bethany?"

"My grandfather had an army blanket the same color and texture as that thing, but okay. I'll do anything to disguise myself except put a stone in my shoe."

"I don't think you should drive your car," Granddad said. "The person who left the chocolates might have seen it parked in front of your house. We'll park it around the corner when you're here."

Bram and Dorothy left, and the chief arrived a minute later. As he had with Iska, he interviewed Bethany in the study.

When they came out, the chief said, "Bethany's safety is my main concern. I'll announce that the poison victim who has recovered reported speaking to a black-robed and masked individual on Saturday evening, but didn't see any identifying features or recognize the individual's voice. I'll give the time and location and ask anyone who saw such a figure in that vicinity to come forward."

Granddad's worry lines smoothed out. "You're telling the poisoner that Bethany has already spilled the beans to the police and there's no reason to go after her again."

"Yes, but there's no guarantee that the culprit will hear that announcement or believe it." The chief turned from Granddad to Bethany. "What time do you leave for work?"

"Around seven thirty."

"I'll send an officer to drive you there tomorrow morning. You can arrange with him what time you want to be picked up in the afternoon."

Bethany looked askance. "I can't arrive in a squad car. The whole school will be talking about the teacher dropped off by the police. Parents will be calling the principal and the superintendent."

"The officer will drive an unmarked vehicle and won't be in uniform. You can say he's your boyfriend or your cousin or whatever. I'll send Officer Wade. Val and her grandfather know him. Keep a low profile and be vigilant until we have this murderer in custody."

"I'll be careful," Bethany said. "Right now, I'm exhausted and going to bed." She roused Muffin and carried the dog's cushion upstairs with her, leaving Granddad and Val with the chief.

Val hoped he would answer a few questions. She had just the incentive to induce him to stay. "We have some chocolate tart left over from dinner, Chief. Sit down and I'll cut you a piece of it."

He didn't resist.

She brought him a slice and sat down on the sofa near the armchair where he sat. Then she waited until he'd taken two bites before asking her first question. "Did anyone else report seeing the figure in black with a ghost mask Saturday evening?"

"No, but we were asking for someone in a long garment who was limping. We'll put out a new description tomorrow. Get rid of the limp and add the mask."

Val had trouble making sense of the killer's timing. "Bethany posed a threat from the moment she ran into the ghost on Saturday night. The poisoned chocolate she ate came from the same batch as Oliver's. Those were at his doorstep by Monday morning. Why did it take until Tuesday for the poisoned chocolates to show up at her house?"

Her question hung in the air while the chief munched another piece of tart.

Granddad said, "Maybe the killer delivered the gift bags to both Oliver and Bethany by Monday morning and Bethany missed seeing hers until Tuesday?"

"I doubt it." Only one bite of tart remained on the chief's plate. He loaded it on his fork. "None of Bethany's neighbors observed the bag at her house on Monday, but two of them spotted it there during the day on Tuesday. Bethany didn't notice it until she came home after school. And her dog barked around one in the morning on Tuesday. She says the dog rarely barks at night."

Val straightened up and moved to the edge of the sofa. "That must be when the killer left the chocolates. At home Muffin sleeps on the sofa in the living room, near the front door, and probably heard someone on the doorstep."

"Bethany didn't tell us about the dog barking," Granddad said.

"You didn't ask her the question I did—whether the dog did anything unusual in the last few days. Dogs could solve a lot of crimes with their acute hearing and sense of smell, if only they could talk." The chief put his plate on the end table and stood up. "Thank you for dessert. You all have a good evening."

Val walked him to the door. "The investigation might go faster now that you know you're looking for one murderer."

"I don't *know* that. The chocolate from the same batch is evidence that ties Oliver's poisoning to Bethany's. The connection to Jake's death rests on Bethany running into someone who *might* have given him a poisoned cookie. It's a theory in need of evidence. Just remember that it's my job to get that evidence, not yours."

"I'll remember." Val tried to read between the chief's lines. "You think there are two killers?"

"I have an open mind and will go where the evidence leads."

She thanked him for stopping by and closed the door

behind him, reminding herself that she needed to keep an open mind too. She went back to the sitting room. "I'm going to clean up the kitchen, Granddad."

He joined her, loading the dessert plates into the dishwasher as she scrubbed the pie pan and the casserole dish.

"I'd like to believe there's only one poisoner, Granddad, but there's no one with a motive to kill both Jake and Oliver. Three people have obvious motives for getting rid of Jake." Val ticked off the suspects with her soapy fingers. "Jewel to inherit his money, Holly to get revenge for jilting her, and Shantell to stop him from destroying her neighborhood. But they were all in the room when the ghost came."

"One of them could have hired a kid from out of town to play the ghost. Or the ghost might have been someone Jake defrauded whose identity we don't know." Granddad closed the dishwasher door. "That takes care of Jake. What about Oliver? The two daughters and the son-in-law have a financial motive. Anyone else?"

Iska had revealed a possible motive for Oliver's neighbors. Val turned off the faucet and faced him. "I forgot to tell you what Iska said when you were out of the room last night. Oliver disliked Franetta's husband because Thatcher was self-serving and swept things under the rug like a typical politician. And Oliver talked about a *drowning* in reference to Thatcher. Mean anything to you?" When Granddad shook his head, Val continued. "It might have something to do with Franetta and Thatcher's son. The night I catered the birthday party, Franetta cut off Oliver when he mentioned helping her son get out of a fix."

"The Frosts' son and a drowning? Hmm. It's coming back to me." Granddad stroked his chin. "Yeah, I get why Franetta and Thatcher might want to shut Oliver up."

Val felt a chill. Had the Frosts, those pillars of the community, shut Oliver up permanently?

Chapter 19

Val beckoned Granddad to the kitchen table. "Tell me what you remember about the Frosts' son and a drowning."

"The details are hazy." Granddad looked at the ceiling as if his memories were stored in the attic with all the other things he'd accumulated in three-quarters of a century. Judging by his small, satisfied smile, he'd hit on something. "Must've been around twenty-five years ago. Summertime. Young folks from Bayport and Treadwell got together for parties every chance they got. The morning after one of them, a college student was found in the river down toward the bay. Her body had snagged on a branch. Based on the tides, investigators figured she went into the river near Bayport."

"Did she live in Bayport?"

"No. Her family had a weekend place outside Tread-well."

"How awful for them." Val sighed. "Was it an accident or something worse?"

"It was a toss-up between an accident and suicide. No sign of foul play. The police tried to find out where and how she'd gone into the river. The Frosts' son was questioned. He'd often taken his dates boating on the river. Toasting the sunset on a pontoon. Paddling by moonlight."

"Did the son have any connection to the woman who drowned?"

"He was at the same party, but so were a lot of others. After the police questioned him, a neighbor came forward and gave him an alibi. Based on when the neighbor saw him, the boy had come straight home from the party, and no one was with him."

Val straightened in her chair, feeling a surge of energy. "Who was the neighbor?"

"I don't remember. If the neighbor had been a year-rounder, I think the name would have stuck with me. It could have been Oliver Naiman."

"Who else might remember the drowning?" Val doubted Chief Yardley could shed any light on it. He'd only recently returned to Bayport after decades doing police work in other jurisdictions.

"I'll check with Ned tomorrow. Even if he can't recall it, he could ask the other folks in the retirement village if they do."

But some residents there might know the Frosts and tell them someone was curious about the incident. "On second thought, Granddad, let's hold off on asking other people. The Frosts are prominent, and word might get back to them."

He shrugged. "Okay, but why would the Frosts care what Oliver rambled about after all these years?"

"Their son is up for a White House job. That probably means a thorough background investigation. I'm not sure how far back it would go, but it won't look good if the person who gave him an alibi twenty-five years ago confesses to lying about it." Val remembered another remark by Oliver that might have made the Frosts nervous. "As I was bringing Oliver's birthday cake to the table, he commented that he was at a point in his life to set things right, and he might not get a chance to do it if he postponed it. A few minutes later he announced he was going to marry Iska. She'd taken care of his wife and him, and he wanted to provide for her. I thought that's what he meant by setting things right."

"But it coulda meant something different to the Frosts." Granddad leaned his elbow on the table and propped his chin on his fist. "Thatcher is more likely to ask someone else to fix his problems than to do his own dirty work."

"I can't see him baking poison into a cookie or molding it into chocolates, but Franetta, the bake sale queen, has the expertise to do it." Her chocolates would have been flawless, but she might have made them deliberately ugly to suggest that someone less adept had made them. "If Oliver were the only poison victim, Franetta would be a good suspect."

"Yup. She had the know-how and a possible motive."

"And she didn't show up at the tea until ten minutes after the ghost delivered the cookies." Val imagined what might have happened. "As the Ghost of Christmas Past,

Franetta wore a long, white tunic and cape. The black robe was full enough that she could wear it over that costume."

"If she put a pebble in one shoe or swapped one shoe for another, she'd have done it in a place where no one could see her."

Val nodded. "After giving out the cookies, she'd have to go back there or to another out-of-the-way spot to reverse the process. She could have been the ghost Bethany ran into. The intersection of Pine and Dixon isn't more than a three-minute walk from the bookshop. Limping would have slowed Franetta in one direction, but even so she had enough time, after Bethany continued home, to return to that secluded spot, shed the black robe and the mask, and walk to the tea at the bookshop. The logistics work, but what was her motive for killing Jake?"

"Maybe the Frosts' son had a connection to Jake. I'll try to find out more about him tomorrow. If he's up for an important job, there should be something online about him. What's his first name?" When Val shrugged, he stood up. "I'll work on it tomorrow."

"Good night, Granddad."

He kissed her on the top of the head. "Good night." He took a few steps and then wheeled around, his eyes wide and shiny with excitement. "I remember the son's name— Owen."

"You have a good mem—" Val broke off as the reason for his elation hit her. "The O in Jake's calendar?"

"Could be. Jewel might recognize the name Owen. She left me two messages asking if I could help her decipher the spreadsheets on Jake's thumb drive. I was going to ignore her, but now I have a reason to go over there."

Val winked at him. "She's taken a shine to you."

He groaned. "I'll find an excuse to bring up what's in Jake's calendar and ask if she heard him talk about a man named Owen." He left the kitchen.

Val rushed after him. "Don't feed her his name. That's leading the witness. Just ask her who O might be."

"If she doesn't come up with any names, I'll throw out a bunch of them and slip in Oliver and Owen."

"If Jake was so secretive that he only used an initial in his calendar, why would he mention the man's name to his wife?"

Granddad continued down the hall to his bedroom. "The abbreviation doesn't necessarily mean he was secretive. He could have been too lazy to type the rest of the name."

"Good point, Granddad, but don't get your hopes up. The O might refer to a woman he didn't want Jewel to know he was meeting."

"No harm in asking. Sleep well." He closed the door to his room.

Val went upstairs to her room with little hope of sleeping well until the murderer was caught and Bethany was safe.

The next morning Officer Wade drove Bethany to school and Val left soon after for the café. Her morning there was uneventful except for a phone call from a client who called off a party that Val was supposed to cater in January. Val suspected the cancellation stemmed from Cyndi Naiman's smear campaign against her. At least customers were still visiting the café.

One of them was Franetta, who arrived as the lunch rush was ending. She took off her hooded down jacket and finger-combed her frosted curls. She was dressed for yoga, as she'd been on Monday when she'd come in to report that Oliver was dead. Sitting on a stool at the eating bar, she looked up at the TV mounted on the wall. The noon news ended with a repetition of the police bulletin that had been broadcast at the start of the show. Val watched Franetta as the newscaster read the bulletin.

"The Bayport Police Department and state crime units continue to investigate three area poisonings, two of them fatal. The surviving victim reported speaking to a masked individual in a long, black garment on Saturday evening between six thirty and seven on Dixon Lane near Pine Street. The poison survivor was unable to see the costumed person's face or other identifying characteristics. Police would like to speak to anyone who has information about or saw such a figure on Saturday."

The bulletin ended with the phone number and e-mail address anyone with information should use to contact the police.

Val had seen no reaction from Franetta to the bulletin. Maybe she'd heard it earlier.

"Can I get you something to eat or drink, Franetta?"

"Just a decaf." She blew on her hands and rubbed them together. "I left without my gloves this morning." She pointed to the TV. "Hard to believe that sweet old Oliver was poisoned."

Val put a mug of coffee in front of Franetta. "I met Oliver for the first time on Sunday night and didn't notice the sweet side of him. He was hard on his daughters and complained a lot. Maybe he was having a bad day."

"His personality changed after his wife died." Franetta added cream to her coffee. "He blamed her death on poor medical care. She had cancer, and they did what they could for her. Elaine and Cyndi had to talk him out of suing doctors and nurses. And recently he was faulting other people for all kinds of things."

"Like what?"

"Mostly his ailments. Holly Atherson was giving him shots for more than a year. Then he got sick after one of them and blamed her. He told me that he was going to sue her."

Iska had said Oliver believed Holly had poisoned him. A lawsuit meant he was acting on his belief. Even if it was a frivolous lawsuit, it would consume time and money. "Did he say that to Holly?"

"No, but I told her. I thought she might want to talk to him and smooth things over."

"Did he actually go through with a suit against her?"

Franetta shrugged. "It wasn't that long ago. He might have died before he got the chance."

Was she trying to suggest that Holly had a motive to kill Oliver? If Franetta had killed him to protect her son, she'd have a reason to add names to the suspect pot. Val noticed a customer at a table signaling for more coffee. "Excuse me. I'll be right back."

Hoping Franetta would name other people with motives to poison Oliver, Val quickly refilled the customer's cup, put back the carafe, and returned to Franetta. "Did Oliver have issues with other people in the neighborhood?"

"Not that I know of, but if he sued, it would be a matter of public record." Franetta drank the last of her coffee.

"I made a mistake choosing Jake as Santa instead of your grandfather. Jake wouldn't take any other position, and I was desperate for volunteers. He said his wife would act as Mrs. Claus if he were Santa, but not if someone else was."

"Two for the price of one."

"But it was no bargain. They both turned out totally inappropriate. Mrs. Claus is supposed to look motherly, not like an aging pinup girl. He was drinking on the job. Then somebody poisoned him. No one would have poisoned your grandfather."

With that she slid off the stool, picked up her athletic bag, and went out of the café, leaving Val amazed that Franetta could still obsess about her Santa choice days after the festival.

Granddad was leaving the house with Muffin on a leash when Val pulled into the driveway.

She joined them on the walk and told him about her conversation with Franetta.

"A lawsuit's a nuisance," he said, "not a reason to murder an old man. Franetta's ginning up a motive for Holly. You gotta wonder why."

"Did you find a connection between Franetta's son and Jake?"

"Nope, but I made progress with Jewel, though it took a while. I had to spend time scrolling through Jake's spreadsheets so Jewel would think I was there to help her find his money. I told her I couldn't make sense of them. Then I suggested we look at Jake's calendar to see if he'd made appointments at banks or with financial planners."

"That was clever, Granddad. You pointed to the O in his calendar."

"Yup. There were three O's, the first two in October and the last one on Sunday morning after Jake was already dead, where the entry said *marina O*. I asked if she knew any friends Jake had whose names began with an O. She said he didn't have any friends. He went to Chamber of Commerce and town council meetings, sat around bars, and volunteered for the festival and other fundraisers, but he never invited anyone to the house."

"No friends. Why am I not surprised?"

Granddad smiled. "I asked if Jake had ever mentioned anyone whose name started with an O. She said he had trouble remembering names, though he never forgot a face. No one popped into her mind, so I threw out some names—Oscar, Otto, Owen, Oliver. Jake hadn't mentioned any of them. Then I asked her if the name Thatcher sounded familiar. Jewel remembered that name as a town councilor's. I named other people on the council. A few of them sounded familiar too."

"So Thatcher wasn't special, just part of the town power structure that Jake wanted to break into." They stopped walking as Muffin sniffed around a tree. "Could she shed any light on the other references to O in his calendar?"

Granddad followed as Muffin tugged on her leash. "Yup. I hit gold there. His calendar entry for the second weekend of October was *Wilmington O*. Jewel said that was when Jake went to a boat show in Wilmington, North Carolina, and he got a ride with someone."

"Someone whose initial could have been O. Did she see the driver or the car?"

Granddad shook his head. "Jake wasn't picked up at the house. He drove somewhere to meet his ride. On the weekend before that, the calendar note for Saturday was *Annapolis O*. That's when the big boat show in Annapolis was held."

"Chatty told me Jewel spotted him at that show after trying to trace him for months. From then on, she stuck to him."

"When Jewel and I were looking at the calendar for that day, she said she saw Jake walking with a man at the Annapolis boat show. When she came up to them, the other guy went off."

"She was probably reaming Jake out for deserting her. No big surprise that the other man didn't want to get involved. Could she describe him?"

"She wasn't focused on him. She remembered he was a little shorter than Jake. Most men, including Thatcher, are a few inches shorter than Jake, who was over six foot." Granddad stopped as Muffin sniffed around the curb. "Jake had an entry in his calendar in early September that said *Norfolk*. I checked if there was a boat show there at that time. There was."

"But no O next to Norfolk in the calendar?"

"Nope. I'm thinking Jake and O got acquainted at that boat show and decided to meet up at the Annapolis one. Then they arranged to travel to the Wilmington show together."

"That makes sense, Granddad." She patted him on the shoulder. "Your visit to Jewel was really worthwhile. I'd like to know if the Frosts' son was at those boat shows."

"Don't ask Franetta or Thatcher. If Jake's murder has

anything to do with their son, they'll know we're on the trail."

Val sighed. "We'll never convince the chief to look into Owen Frost's whereabouts without more to go on than a theory and an initial. We need to find another link between Jake and the Frosts."

Chapter 20

Val spent the remainder of the afternoon skimming online references to the Frosts—Franetta, Thatcher, and Owen. Nowhere did Jake Smith's name appear in connection with any of them. Val tried all the name variations Jake had used, according to the chief, but found nothing. If any link between Jake and the Frosts existed, it wasn't out in the open.

Around four o'clock Officer Wade escorted Bethany into the house. Muffin raced toward her, tail wagging, and Val invited the young officer in for a snack.

"Thank you. I wish I could, but I have to get back to work." He turned to Bethany. "I'll come by for you tomorrow morning. Please stay out of sight, Bethany, until we get this criminal behind bars." He'd echoed the chief's sentiments, but with an urgency that sounded more personal.

After he left, Bethany looked down at the dog gazing up at her. "Muffin wants me to take her for a walk."

"She's guilt-tripping you. Granddad brought her back from a walk ten minutes ago, right before he left for the supermarket. And that was her second walk of the afternoon." Val wondered how long her friend could put up with what she'd termed *house arrest* and the need for an escort. "Are you okay with Officer Wade as a bodyguard again tomorrow?"

"More than okay." Bethany smiled. "His name is Ryan. He's really nice, and he isn't as young as he looks. We're exactly the same age."

Both of them looked young to Val, and she was only six years older than they were. Could a romance be in the offing for them? "The chief thinks highly of Officer Wade—I mean Ryan. Did he say anything about the investigation?"

"Not much. On the way back from school, he asked me to show him where I saw the ghost on Saturday night. When we got there, he told me the police had searched that area this morning. I'd described it well enough last night that they knew where to go. They were looking for evidence—a footprint, a piece of clothing snagged on the bush, or anything else the ghost left behind."

Val wondered if they'd collected a pebble the ghost might have removed from a shoe. She wasn't sure DNA would stick to stone, but the foot of someone who'd walked on a hard object might have a bruise that matched the object's shape. Unless the police nabbed a suspect soon, though, the sore would heal. "I'm going to bake tonight's dessert. Do you want to keep me company and have a snack?"

Bethany glanced toward the kitchen, apparently tempted. Then she squared her shoulders. "To stay on my diet, I have to keep away from the kitchen. I'll go upstairs so I can't smell what you're baking. I need to call my mom."

"Are you going to tell her about the chocolates?"

"Definitely not. She'd freak out. We'll talk about Christmas plans." Bethany left with Muffin in her wake.

Val made a cranberry-apple crisp, popped it into the oven, and went back to the study.

She had an e-mail from her cousin, Monique, who'd attached a zipped file of the pictures she'd taken at the festival on Saturday. Val skimmed them, looking for ones in which the body language of Santa or the person with him suggested conflict. A photo time-stamped in the morning showed exactly that, and the person with him was Granddad as Scrooge.

In another photo from that morning, Jake in his red Santa suit and Franetta in white as the Ghost of Christmas Past appeared amiable. But in one taken later in the day, he was glassy-eyed and she annoyed, probably because he'd been at his flask since morning.

Val got up and checked on the dessert in the oven. She turned it so it would bake evenly and then went back to looking at the festival photos.

Half of Monique's photos were of posed groups, the rest were candid shots. Val scrutinized dozens of pictures of Santa and Mrs. Claus. Jake and Jewel smiled when they posed, but their candid pictures didn't suggest a devoted couple. In an unguarded moment a tight-lipped Jewel eyed Jake with narrowed eyes. Jake's smile was genuine, with crinkles around his eyes, as he presented

small gifts to children, but not when he looked at his
wife.

Val searched in vain for photos of him with Holly or
Shantell. In a picture Monique had taken late in the day,
Oliver and Cyndi posed with Santa and Mrs. Claus. All
four of them displayed say-cheese smiles.

The doorbell rang. Val went into the hall and looked
through the sidelight. Cyndi stood on the porch with her
husband. The last time Val had seen the Kenwigs, Cyndi
had yelled at her and thrown her out of the Naiman
house. Now she smiled tentatively at Val through the
sidelight.

Unless Cyndi was a good actress, Val had nothing to
fear from the couple. She cracked the door open. "Hi."

Cyndi looked relieved. She must have anticipated
Val turning her back on them. "Hello, Val. I came to
apologize for my outburst the night before last. I was
extremely upset and I took it out on you. I shouldn't
have done that." A cold gust blew her red hair into her
face.

Words weren't enough for Val. She'd forgive Cyndi
only if she made amends for damaging Val's reputation as
a caterer. "Come in, please," she said through tight lips.

"Thank you." Cyndi stepped inside.

"I'd like to get on the road home soon," Kevin said to
his wife in an undertone as he followed her into the
house.

Cyndi said, "We won't keep you long, Val. We made a
quick trip here to talk to Dad's lawyer about his estate.
Elaine's already on her way back to her house, but I really
wanted to talk to you before we left."

Without offering to take their coats, Val led them into the sitting room, sat down in the armchair to the side of the sofa, and motioned for them to sit on the sofa. She took perverse pleasure in subjecting them to the most uncomfortable seats in the room. And before they left, she would speak her mind about Cyndi's campaign against her.

Cyndi settled on the sofa, took off her knitted gloves, and unzipped her parka, though she didn't remove it. She slid over to make room for Kevin. After taking off his puffy quilted jacket, Kevin laid it over the arm of the sofa and sat down next to his wife.

Cyndi twisted the gloves in her hand. "I'd like to explain why I acted the way I did. I opposed the autopsy because I was afraid it would show Dad had deliberately overdosed on meds to commit suicide. I wanted to accept the doctor's conclusion of cardiac arrest, but that would have been a mistake. If it weren't for your suspicions about the chocolate, we wouldn't have known Dad was poisoned." She bit her lip, holding back tears.

Kevin reached for her hand. "Bad as poisoning is, at least we won't wonder forever if he took his own life."

Cyndi nodded. "And there's comfort in knowing he wasn't personally targeted. The police told us his death could be related to another poisoning."

Val wasn't sure whether the police had told them about an attempted poisoning with the same kind of chocolates that killed Oliver. She decided to pretend ignorance and mention only Jake's better publicized murder. "The police must have meant the man poisoned Saturday evening at the festival tea. I wonder why they think your father's death is related to that. Did he know that man, Jake Smith, or maybe it was John or Jack Smith?"

"I never heard him mention a man named Smith. Did you, Kevin?"

"No."

"My cousin was the roaming photographer at the festival. She sent me the pictures she'd taken. There was one of your father and you, Cyndi, with Jake and his wife, Jewel." Cyndi looked baffled, and Val added, "Smith was Santa at the festival and his wife was Mrs. Claus."

"Ah. I remember posing for that picture, but I didn't know Santa was the poison victim."

Kevin said, "At home we get news from Baltimore, not from this area, but I'm surprised Elaine didn't tell us that."

Cyndi shrugged. "She and I talked mainly about Dad's death, not someone else's."

Val said, "If you'd like, I'll send you a copy of the photo, Cyndi. Your father looks really happy in it." Happier than he looked on his birthday the following day.

"We finally coaxed him to go to the festival in the afternoon. It would have been too far for him to walk, but Elaine drove us as close as she could to the historical district, though she couldn't park there. Dad enjoyed seeing the decorations and the people in costume."

Val turned to Kevin. "Did you get to spend any time at the festival?"

"Only in the morning. Then I realized I'd forgotten to take along the tests and papers I needed to grade by Monday. I went home after lunch on Saturday."

"Forgetfulness has its rewards," Cyndi said. "Kevin

got to sleep at home that night. He hates the beds at my father's house."

"Two nights in a row on that mattress would have done my back in."

Cyndi handed Val a business card. "My e-mail address is on here. I'd appreciate a copy of that photo. It's a good memory for me."

Val tucked Cyndi's card in her pocket and decided to be blunt. "On Tuesday evening, Cyndi, you threatened to wreck my reputation as a caterer. Since then people have canceled contracts with me. I'd appreciate your walking back the negative things you said about me to your father's neighbors or anyone else."

Cyndi blushed. "Okay. I'll recommend you as a caterer and explain I was mistaken. I'll see a few of those people tomorrow. My father's funeral will be small, family only. But tomorrow night Franetta is having a get-together for his neighbors and friends to pay their respects. Will you join us?"

"I didn't know your father very well, but I'll stop by. What time?"

"Seven."

The hall steps creaked as Bethany descended. She came into the sitting room with Muffin at her heels. "Sorry, I didn't know you had company, Val."

Kevin put his jacket over his arm. "We were just leaving."

He couldn't leave fast enough for Val. She was afraid Bethany might mention something the chief had withheld from the Naiman family. If they were suspects in Oliver's murder, he might not have revealed the type of poison and definitely wouldn't have told them Bethany had been poisoned in a similar way. He'd kept her name and location a secret.

Val said, "I think Muffin's food dish is running low. Could you refill it?"

"Sure." Bethany headed toward the back of the house. "Come on, Muffin, we don't want you to go hungry."

As soon as they left the room, Kevin stood up and hurried to the hall.

Cyndi leaned toward Val and whispered, "Kevin's afraid of dogs. He freaks out if one comes near him." She stood up, put out her hand to Val, and raised her voice. "I hope you'll forgive my bad behavior."

Val shook hands with her. "I understand how stressed you were. I'm glad we cleared it up. I'll see you tomorrow evening at Franetta's."

As they joined Kevin in the hall, he opened the front door and stepped outside. "Sorry to rush off, but the bridge traffic is a bear this time of day."

Val closed the door behind them and went back to the sitting room.

Bethany bustled in with the dog on her heels. "Muffin had plenty of food. Who were your visitors?"

"Oliver Naiman's daughter and her husband."

"If I'd known that, I'd have given them my condolences."

And Cyndi would have asked how Bethany knew her father. Before long the fact that she'd been poisoned the same way would have come up. "Cyndi's husband is afraid of dogs and rushed out after spotting Muffin."

"How could anyone be afraid of Muffin?"

Granddad came in carrying grocery sacks. Val brought in the remaining sacks from his car while Bethany helped him unpack the food. Then the three of them had happy hour in the kitchen.

Muffin stood at the door to the kitchen with a ball in her mouth, apparently wanting a happy hour too. Bethany played fetch with the dog in the dining and sitting room, and Val went back to the computer. This time she focused her search on the Naimans. Twenty minutes of skimming everything she could find online about the father, his two daughters, and his son-in-law convinced her that they, like the Frosts, had no obvious connection to Jake Smith. But if the link between the killer and Jake involved something underhanded, it wouldn't necessarily appear online.

She sighed. The police had more resources for digging up information than she did. Her time might be better spent figuring out why the killer had targeted Bethany. If the motive stemmed from her encounter with the masked figure on Saturday night, the place to start would be where they'd met—near the intersection of Pine Street and Dixon Lane. Val would go there at night and re-create the scene with someone who could assume the part of the ghost. Not Bethany, who needed to lie low. Not Granddad, who couldn't easily crouch or bend over as the ghost had. Who else could she rope into this on short notice?

Possibly Bram. He was coming over later to take Muffin on a night walk. Would he mind playing the ghost? Only one way to find out. Val called him.

"Hi, Bram. I need a partner in my crime investigation. Are you willing?"

He said nothing for a moment. "I'm willing to be your partner in . . . anything."

The huskiness in his voice tempted Val to interpret his

words as applying to more than just tonight's venture. But that was wishful thinking. She reminded herself he was moving away.

She told him her plan and said, "Dress in black, or at least dark colors. See you later."

Chapter 21

B ram arrived at eight o'clock for the combo dog walk and ghost encounter reenactment. Val thought he'd done a decent job of dressing for his role. His pants, athletic shoes, and gloves were black. His hooded parka was navy. Ideally, he'd have worn a black robe like the ghost's. Not expecting him to do that, she'd found a substitute for it in the front closet.

"Dress warmly, Val. The temperature's plummeting." Accustomed to California weather, his face had turned ruddy in the cold wind.

Bethany looked up from leashing her dog. "Uh-oh. I'd better put on Muffin's overcoat." She coaxed the dog upstairs.

Val took the olive drab cloak from the closet.

Bram's brows rose. "That thing will keep you warm in any weather."

On Saturday morning, when Val had worn it to the festival, she'd ditched it before Bram saw her in the unattractive garment. Though she now had less reason to care if she looked attractive to him, she still couldn't bring herself to put it on.

She held it up. "This isn't for me. I'm hoping you'll throw it over your shoulders when we get to our destination. Though it will only cover you down to your shins, this big shapeless thing is the closest we can get to the ghost's robe."

"Do you have a mask too?"

"No, we'll just pretend your face is a mask. I have a gift bag for you to put on when we re-create what Bethany saw. I didn't cut eyeholes because you'll be standing in one place and won't have the bag on your head for more than a few seconds. I'll also bring this bag because the ghost carried one." She held up a festival shopping bag.

Val donned her parka, a knit hat, and gloves. Bethany came down the stairs with Muffin in his doggy hoodie.

Bram smiled. "Muffin is incognito. In the dark she'll look like a short-haired, black dog."

Muffin's ears moved forward as if reminding him of her silky, reddish hair.

Bethany handed Bram the leash. "Don't keep her out too long. She might catch a cold even in her hoodie. I'll also give you some treats as an incentive for her to follow you instead of where she might want to go on her own." Bethany left for the kitchen and returned with two packets of dog biscuits.

Val put them in her pocket and left with Bram and the dog. Muffin didn't do as much sniffing around as she usually did on a walk, possibly sensing they were on a mission.

As they walked to Pine Street, Bram said, "Something occurred to me as I was trying to get into character for my role tonight. Don't assume that the ghost was a woman, just because Bethany heard a female voice. If I were covered from head to toe and wanted to mislead people about who I was, I'd play an audio clip of a woman speaking."

Val took a moment to consider his idea. "Canned audio would explain the odd exchange between Bethany and the ghost. She said, 'Are you okay?' and instead of answering that question, the ghost said 'Happy Holidays' and nothing else." Yet Val wasn't totally convinced. "Where would the ghost have hidden the device that played the audio?"

"You'd be amazed what you can conceal up your sleeve or inside your glove. There are audio devices tiny enough to fit in the palm of your hand."

"How did the ghost find the button to play the audio in the dark?"

"I guess the same way I learn a magic trick—practicing until the action becomes automatic."

Though Bram's theory on the canned audio had merit, it didn't radically change Val's ideas about the murder. "I'll go back to using *he* for the ghost. It comes more naturally to me, but I won't rule out that a woman wore the ghost costume."

"You shouldn't. My point is only that you can't rule out a man."

The possibility of a male ghost added a new wrinkle to Val's suspicions about the Frosts. She'd figured out how Franetta might have managed two costume changes and the round trip to the bookshop within ten minutes, but it was tight. Franetta wouldn't have needed to do that, though, if Thatcher had played the ghost.

Val and Bram took the same route Bethany had taken on Saturday night. They walked along Pine Street past the church with the graveyard behind it. Muffin took the lead as they approached the corner of Pine and Dixon. She turned onto Dixon, possibly because this was a route home she recognized. No one else was walking or driving along Dixon Lane on this frigid night.

Val stopped when they came to a large cherry laurel with dense foliage overhanging the sidewalk. "This must be the shrub the ghost hoped would keep anyone from seeing what he was doing."

Though the house behind the overgrown shrub had a porch light on, the greenery was thick enough to keep most of the light from reaching the street. The only other illumination came from a streetlight at the corner and another across the lane, half a block from where they were standing. The sidewalk near the bush was in a pocket of dimness.

Bram put on the cloak and took the gift bag from the festival shopping bag. He gave Val the leash. "I'll stay close to the bush. You take Muffin back to the corner with you and then walk toward me."

Muffin resisted backtracking. Val reached into her pocket for the dog treat packet and shook it. That was enough to make Muffin trot alongside her. She gave the dog a treat when they reached the corner and then called out to Bram that they were walking toward him.

Like Bethany on Saturday night, Val saw only a dark mound near the bush ahead of her. But she could tell the shape was shifting. She'd suggested he mimic the act of emptying a pebble from his shoe. The mound got lower and then she was close enough to glimpse Bram's bare hands tying his shoe.

Val repeated the question Bethany had asked the ghost. "Are you okay?"

"Happy Holidays," Bram said in his own voice. He uncurled himself and stood upright. "Did you see me take off the gift bag?" When she shook her head he continued. "I bent over, slipped off the bag with one hand, and pulled up my hood with the other hand. All in one motion."

"The magician's hands are quicker than the eye. But I spotted those hands when you were tying your shoe. Bethany didn't see that. Could the ghost have kept his gloves on while tying his shoe?"

"No way. I wore gloves to untie my shoe, take it off, and put it back on, but tying the shoelaces was impossible with gloves. If I couldn't do it, neither could the ghost. The elongated fingers on his skeleton gloves would have gotten caught in the knot as he tied his shoes. But maybe he didn't need to tie his shoes because he didn't remove a pebble from them, or he wore loafers."

"*The Ghost Wore Loafers* would make a good book title, but I glimpsed the back of the ghost's shoe as he left the CAT Corner. It looked like a white athletic shoe." Val felt a tug on the leash as Muffin headed back toward the intersection, perhaps in hopes of another treat. Her two human escorts followed. "Let's assume the ghost had bare hands and was afraid Bethany had seen a distinguishing feature on them. In one of Granddad's favorite Hitchcock films, *The 39 Steps*, the villain is missing part of a finger. Something like that, or a scar, a birthmark, or a tattoo on the hand, could be the reason the ghost poisoned Bethany."

"As Sherlock Holmes says, 'There is nothing like first-hand evidence.' In this case, there's nothing like hand evidence. Am I right in guessing that you'll study the hands of all your suspects?"

Val laughed. As a fan of Arthur Conan Doyle's detective, Bram could find a Sherlock quote to fit any occasion. "I won't be able to stop myself from looking at their hands. But even if I see someone with a missing finger, the chief wouldn't consider that evidence because Bethany didn't see it." Muffin stopped and sniffed around a tree under a streetlamp. "Most people with motives to kill Jake were in plain sight at the tea and couldn't have poisoned him. And the people who could have dressed as the ghost and delivered the poisoned cookie don't have an obvious motive. It seems like an impossible crime."

"Sherlock to the rescue. 'When you have eliminated the impossible, whatever remains, no matter how improbable, must be the truth.'"

"Chief Yardley has sometimes dismissed my reasonable theories as improbable. If I came up with a really improbable solution, he'd call it wacky or, even worse, ditsy." A word Val hated because it was sexist, only ever applied to women. She looked up at Bram. "Got any other words of wisdom from Sherlock?"

Bram pointed to Muffin. "There's 'the curious incident of the dog in the night-time.'"

Val had heard that one often enough to recite the next line. "'The dog did nothing in the night-time.' And Muffin did nothing during the night between Sunday and Monday, when the killer left poisoned chocolates for Oliver. The curious incident was why the killer didn't leave the chocolates for Bethany that same night."

Muffin circled the tree twice, so Val did the same to unwind the leash. She felt as if she was going in circles on the poisonings too. After deciding that none of the victims were random, she was now second-guessing that. Could Oliver have been a random victim, meant to obscure the connection between the ghost and Bethany?

When Val circled back to Bram, he said, "I want to explain why I left your house so quickly on Monday night."

So his claim of not feeling well that night hadn't been the whole truth. "I'd like to hear your explanation. I was afraid it was something I said."

"It *was*. You described all the bad things Jake had done. Then you said that his worst act was jilting his fiancée right before the wedding, exactly what you'd expect from a jerk like him." Bram took an audible deep breath and released it. "I couldn't decide what to do. Admit being a jerk too? Defend what he did? Hide the truth and mislead you? I had to think before saying anything, so I left to do that."

Val took a moment to digest his words. They could mean only one thing. "You jilted your fiancée too?"

He gazed at the ground, where the roots of the tree stuck out. "Six years ago I got engaged. It was like getting on a train that made no stops. As soon as I realized I'd made a mistake, I pulled the emergency brake, but that wasn't until—"

"Until she was walking down the aisle?"

He looked up. "I'm not that much of a jerk. It was two weeks before the wedding. It was the right thing to do, but I felt terrible about how I'd treated her. I threw myself into work and avoided getting involved with anyone. The only girlfriends I had were as driven as I was in the workplace. They were no-risk relationships."

Why was he telling her this now, in his last few weeks before picking up his old life? She shrugged. "So you have commitment issues because of a previous relationship. Lots of people do, including me. That doesn't make you a jerk."

His face lit up with a big smile. "I'm glad to hear it, because I think I'm getting over my reluctance to commit."

And now he would tell her about the woman he'd left behind when he came here in October, and how absence had made his heart grow fonder. "Good to know commitment phobia doesn't last forever." Val tugged gently on the dog's leash. "Time to head home, Muffin."

Main Street was less deserted than Dixon Lane. Couples came out of restaurants, singles went into bars, and families with children peered at the decorated shop windows. But it was a smaller crowd than Val remembered from last year's holiday season, either because of tonight's raw weather or the effect of three poisonings on the holiday spirit.

As they made the final turn onto Grace Street, Val shivered in the cold.

Bram held out the cloak he'd been carrying. "This will protect you from the wind."

"Thanks, but I'll make it the three blocks to Granddad's house without freezing." And without looking like a tent with feet.

"This afternoon I got a text from a real estate agent about a house that's going on the market after New Year's. She'll arrange for me to get a sneak preview of it. Then, if I like it, I can jump on it when it's listed for sale."

Val hadn't expected him to go away quite so soon. "So you'll fly to California before Christmas to see the house?"

"The house isn't in California, Val. It's here."

What would he do with a house here if he was moving

away? "Are you buying it as an investment, a rental property?" Or maybe to replace the tiny house his mother was
renting.

He peered at her as if she'd just spoken in Swahili.
"I'm buying the house to live in. When I came here to
help Mom open the bookshop, the two rooms over the
shop were fine as temporary lodging, but it's too cramped
to stay there long-term. I thought I told you I was moving."

But he hadn't said where, and that was her fault. "You
told me, and I jumped to the conclusion that you'd
changed your mind about staying here and were returning
to California." And she'd cut off discussion of his plans
to spare herself pain. Now that Val knew he wasn't leaving after all, she felt a warmth inside her that the north
wind couldn't penetrate. She reached for his hand. "I'm
glad you're staying. Tell me about the house."

"I don't know much about it, but I'd like you to look at
it with me and get your opinion."

"I'll give you my opinion. When have I ever not?"

Muffin picked up the pace, and Val felt as if she was
floating behind the dog. It wasn't going to be the miserable Christmas she'd feared. She would get to introduce
her parents to Bram after all. She envisioned them all at
the table and the food they'd share.

As they approached Granddad's house, the chief's car
pulled up to the curb, and Val came back to earth. A cloud
still hung over the holidays. Only one thing would lift
that cloud—solving the murders so Bethany could have a
happy Christmas, free of fear that a killer would target
her again.

The chief climbed out of the car. "I'm glad to see you

two out walking Bethany's dog. She's inside with your granddaddy?"

Val nodded. She'd planned to ask Bram to come in, but he said a quick good night and left. Just as well. The chief might not be as forthcoming with another person there as he would be with only her, Granddad, and Bethany present.

Val sensed he'd come to deliver bad news.

Chapter 22

Val felt the tension in the sitting room. Granddad sat on the edge of his favorite chair, feet on the floor, instead of lounging in it as he usually did. Val perched on the arm of his chair. Bethany sat stiffly on the sofa next to her squirming dog. Everyone's attention was on Chief Yardley.

He took the armchair near the fireplace, but he didn't lean back. "I have some updates. Chemical test results show the residue in Jake's flask, teacup, and water glass contained nothing unusual. Everyone at the table ate the same food he did without ill effects. Unless Jake consumed something else that no one noticed, the gingerdead man must have contained the poison."

Val exchanged a look with Granddad. Nice that science confirmed the assumption they'd made from the beginning. She understood why the chief was updating them. He was now convinced Bethany had talked to Jake's murderer. That was why she'd been poisoned. "Did the police hear from anyone else who spotted the ghost?"

The chief nodded. "Two people. One of them saw the masked individual not far from Bethany's house on Saturday evening, soon after she walked home from Dixon Lane."

Bethany's face puckered up with worry. "The ghost followed me home."

Granddad said, "If Bethany was such a threat, why didn't the ghost get rid of her right away? By strangling her if he had no other weapon."

The chief said, "Choking the life out of someone is harder than using poison."

Bethany clutched her throat. "Also, people were walking home from the festival on the streets around Dixon Lane. Someone could have come along at any moment."

"Where did the other person see the ghost, Chief?"

"In the festival parking lot around seven o'clock."

Fifteen to twenty minutes after running into Bethany on Dixon Lane, the ghost was still wandering around in a costume. Though that information didn't tell Val who had dressed as the ghost, it told her who hadn't. Franetta had been only a few minutes late for tea. She wouldn't have had the time to follow Bethany home, walk to the parking lot halfway across town, change costumes, and get back to the bookshop in time for tea.

Granddad leaned forward. "Did the witnesses talk with the ghost?"

"The one in the parking lot did. He said, 'Good evening' to the ghost, who replied, 'Happy Holidays.'"

"In a woman's voice," Val said.

When the chief didn't contradict her, she told him Bram's theory about an audio clip. The chief sat back and heard her out, but she couldn't tell from his face if he would accept or reject the theory.

When she finished, he said, "Canned audio matches this killer's style. This is a belt-and-suspenders person, overcompensating for anything that might go wrong. He limps to disguise his walk and plays canned audio to hide his voice. He uses a mask, a hood, and a gift bag to hide his face, and two sets of eyeholes in the bag to obscure his height. And, on the slight chance that Bethany saw an identifiable feature, the ghost poisons her."

Bethany rubbed her forehead as if she had a headache. "Are you ruling out that a woman did it?"

The chief shook his head. "I'm not ruling out anything. Someone with this killer's personality will try again after failing the first time. The ghost knows where you live, Bethany. Don't go near your house until we catch this person. If you need anything from your place, an officer can pick it up for you."

Muffin snuggled up to her owner. Bethany spoiled her pet, but she derived a lot of comfort from the dog. She stroked Muffin. "What's important to me is already here. I can manage, at least for a while."

Val said, "You came face-to-mask with a killer, Bethany. So did the other people who reported seeing the ghost, but they didn't get poisoned. Why you? You either saw something they didn't, or the ghost thinks you did. When you first described the ghost bending down, you said it looked like someone tying their shoes. Did you see the ghost's feet or hands?"

"Not the feet." Bethany squinted like a nearsighted person trying to make out a distant object. "I saw a hand for a second before the ghost pulled a glove over it. The person had light skin. It was so dim that I'm not sure if the hand was a woman's or a man's."

The chief said, "Did you notice any jewelry or a tattoo?"

"No. I had a side view, like you'd see from above if someone was going to shake your hand." Bethany held out her hand with only her thumb and index finger visible.

Val wasn't ready to abandon the idea that the ghost's hand had an identifying feature. Though Bethany hadn't observed anything unusual in the dark, the ghost had no way to know that. "You just stuck out your right hand, Bethany. Was it the ghost's right hand that you glimpsed?"

Bethany nodded.

"Call me if you remember anything else, Bethany." The chief turned to Granddad. "One other thing before I go, Don. You've been to Jewel's house a couple of times and the evidence you acquired there will be useful, but I want to warn you against seeing the woman again."

Granddad was taken aback. "I'm not *seeing* her. She hired me to do a job at her house."

The chief continued as if Granddad hadn't spoken. "She's been involved in frauds, including at least one sweetheart scam. She got gifts and loans from a widower who was convinced she loved him. She would have emptied out his bank account if the family hadn't stepped in."

"She may be trying that, but she's not my type," Granddad said.

A few months after moving in with him, Val had worried that he would fall for a sweetheart scam, but this time she was sure he could see through it. With Dorothy around Val figured he was immune to Jewel's "charms."

The chief stood up. "You all have a good night. Sit down, Don. I'll let myself out."

Granddad ignored him and levered himself out of his chair. "I get stiff if I sit too long. By the way, did Jake have any history of blackmailing folks?"

"We didn't find any record of it. Blackmailers and their victims don't usually report their dealings to the police. You have a reason to think Jake was blackmailing someone?"

With the two men now in the hall, Val couldn't catch every word they said, but she heard enough to know Granddad was telling the chief about the drowning incident Oliver had mentioned involving the Frosts' son. Granddad suggested Jake might have heard about the drowning while hobnobbing with town big shots. If he'd tried to blackmail the Frosts or their son, they had a motive for murdering him, as well as Oliver.

The chief thanked Granddad for the information and left.

As the heavy front door closed behind him, Muffin perked up. She settled down when Granddad returned to his chair.

Val glanced at the dog snuggling next to Bethany. "Does Muffin usually bark when people walk near your house?"

"Not if they stay on the sidewalk or the street. But as soon as they approach my door, she barks. That's her territory to guard."

"Did she bark at all Sunday night?" That would have been the earliest someone could have left the chocolates that Oliver found the next morning.

"No, and there was a lot of activity. My neighbor across the street was having a big football watching party.

Muffin had no problem with people coming and going or standing outside smoking."

Val suspected the poisoner had more of a problem with the neighbor's guests than the dog did. "Whoever left chocolates at Oliver's house that night probably planned to leave them at your place too, but was afraid the party-goers would spot him. That's why the poisoner postponed your delivery."

Bethany nodded. "Until one in the morning on Tuesday. Muffin barked then."

Granddad frowned. "Makes more sense for the killer to return later the same night. Why wait another twenty-four hours before doing the dirty deed?"

Val shrugged. "The poisoner didn't wait to stay up or had to be somewhere else."

Bethany shifted her position on the sofa, rousing Muffin from a snooze. "I'll say good night and head upstairs. I need a rest from talking about murder."

And probably from the sagging sofa. Val stood up. "I'll look again at Monique's festival photos in case I missed something." She started toward the study, stopped, and turned back toward Granddad, remembering that he too had a photo. "I've been so busy following leads that I forgot about the picture you took of the table right after Jake keeled over. I was there and saw the table, but so much was going on, I didn't concentrate on it."

Granddad took his phone from his shirt pocket and brought up the photo. She sat back down on the arm of his chair so they could both look at it. By the time he'd snapped that picture, everyone had left their chairs to cluster around Jake, but Val had no trouble recalling where they'd sat. Jake had been at the head of the small rectangular table and Jewel on the side to his right, with

Shantell next to her. Holly had been on Jake's left with Franetta next to her, and Granddad at the foot of the table.

"Irene and I set the table the same way for every tea," Val said. "Cup and saucer above the knife on the right side of the plate and the water glass to the left of the saucer. Look where Jewel's cup is."

Granddad enlarged the part showing the table where Jewel and Jake had sat. "It's to the left of her plate, next to Jake's cup." He reduced the size of the photo again.

"Unlike the other cups at the table, hers was positioned with the handle on the left side." A possible explanation for the cup's position occurred to Val. "Did you notice if Jewel is left-handed, Granddad?"

"Yes. She was jotting notes with her left hand when we looked at Jake's files. I watched her because I wondered how she could write with her long talons." He wiggled his fingers. "She must have moved her cup to the left after she sat down."

The photo showed another change that had occurred during the tea. Sitting on Jake's left, across from Jewel, Holly had moved everything near her beyond the range of Jake's coughs and sneezes. At a table that was snug for six people, Holly had crowded next to Franetta.

Val focused on the gift bags. Jake's bag was lying sideways on the table, next to his water glass. The remaining five bags were upright and distributed around the table, but with more of them at Granddad's end of the table than at Jake's. She pointed to the place where Granddad had sat. "You could reach two gift bags from your seat. Which did you think was yours?"

"I wasn't sure. The one on the left was closer, but the one on the right was near my glass and cup. It's the same problem you have with bread plates at a small table. Nobody knows which plate is theirs until the first person to take bread makes the decision."

And Jake was the first to choose a gift bag. "The photo shows everyone can easily reach either of two bags except Jewel. The nearest gift bag to her is closer to Shantell's plate." Val got up from the arm of Granddad's chair. "I have to call Irene. She poured the tea and might have noticed the position of Jewel's cup."

"Does that matter?"

"*When* Jewel moved it might matter." Val fetched her phone from the study, apologized to Irene for calling so late, and said she had a few questions for her. Val put the phone on Speaker so Granddad could hear. "As I remember it, you didn't pour the tea on Saturday night until after the costumed visitor left the gift bags."

"That's right."

"When you poured Jewel's tea, were her cup and saucer in the usual spot?"

"Why on earth would I remember that? Oh. Actually, I do. I was reaching out to pour when she moved her cup. She said she liked holding it in her left hand."

Now for the key question. "Did she move anything else?"

"She had to push a gift bag out of the way to make room for her cup."

So the gift bag had been to the left of Jewel's plate until then. "Did she put it where the cup and saucer had been?"

"No, she just nudged the bag away. Toward Jake, as best I can recall."

Yes! Val wished she could high-five her assistant manager over the phone. Irene had turned the investigation into Jake's death in a new direction. "Thank you, Irene, you have no idea how helpful that is."

"I sure don't. If you've got more questions, wait until tomorrow to ask them. I'm going to bed now."

"Good night, and thanks again." Val hung up and glanced at Granddad's photo of the table. No doubt about it. Everything they'd thought about Jake's death had been wrong. "I think Jewel was supposed to eat the poisoned cookie, not Jake."

Granddad tipped his head to one side and then the other, weighing her conclusion. "Explain."

"The ghost put a gift bag to the left of each plate, above the fork. There was no room for the bag on the right side of the plates because the glasses and teacups were there. When Holly shifted her setting away from Jake, she moved his gift bag too, probably assuming it was hers."

"So he took the gingerdead man from the only bag near him, which Jewel had pushed toward him." Granddad poked at his phone. "We gotta tell Earl. He may want Jewel watched. She could be in danger."

"It's been five days since Jake died. Two people have been poisoned since then, and Jewel wasn't one of them. If she was supposed to be the victim at the tea, why hasn't the murderer tried again?"

"Maybe he wanted to, but couldn't. Remember the man in a jogging suit Jewel saw near her house on Sunday morning? He looked familiar to her. He ran off when the police arrived. That could have been the poisoner, who's staying away from her now because the police have been there a few times since then."

Granddad might be right. The man across the street on Sunday morning was another piece of the puzzle that had to fit somewhere. "You might as well call the chief. We'd both feel terrible if anything bad happened to Jewel and we hadn't told the police she could have been the intended victim."

While Granddad left a voice mail for the chief, Val plopped into the armchair near the fireplace. Jewel had said the person who'd walked back and forth across the street from her house had worn a face-hiding hoodie. How does someone whose face you can't see look familiar? Val remembered Chatty's story about Jewel following Jake at the Annapolis boat show when he was with another man. Jewel had told Jake she recognized him by his walk. Maybe the man across the street had looked familiar to her for the same reason. She'd seen him before and noticed something distinctive about his walk. A swagger, a bounce, a trudge. Arms stiff, relaxed, or swinging.

Like everyone else at the tea, Jewel had watched the ghost who delivered a poisoned cookie walk into the CAT Corner, circle the table, and cross the room to go out the back door. If the ghost thought his victim might recognize him by his walk, limping with the aid of a pebble would keep that from happening. But the ghost was still at large and not limping. Jewel might recognize him by his walk if she saw him again. And if that man was also tied to Oliver, the police would have reason to investigate him thoroughly.

As Granddad put away his phone, she said, "The Frosts are having a get-together for Oliver's friends and neighbors tomorrow night at seven. The houses there are set back from the street, and visitors will have a long walk to the front door. If Jewel stands across the street and watches people going in, she might see someone who looks familiar."

"It will be like a police lineup, only the suspects are in motion." Granddad frowned. "But Jewel will be conspicuous hanging out or sitting in a car across the street."

"Not if she's with you and Muffin. There's nothing unusual about a man and a woman walking a dog." Though Granddad and Jewel would go up and down the same street several times, they'd be less noticeable than a woman alone. "You're probably the only person who can talk Jewel into this. She's sweet on you."

He groaned. "I know people on Bellevue Avenue. They'll see me, and word will get around that I was spending time with a woman."

Val understood. He was worried that Dorothy would hear about his woman friend. "No one will recognize you if you put on the outfit you used for your impersonation gig last January. Overcoat, driver's cap, and frameless, tinted glasses instead of gold-rimmed bifocals. And Jewel should wear something frumpy that will make her less recognizable too."

"You want her to wear the olive-drab cloak?"

Val laughed. "She'd never wear my invisibility cloak, but I'll bet she has a new coat and hat she bought for winter here. And, of course, Muffin will wear her black hoodie."

"Are you sure Jewel will see someone who looks familiar going to the gathering?"

"No. One person she won't see walking into the house is Thatcher Frost. He'll already be inside, greeting guests." Val would have to work out another way for her to watch Thatcher in motion.

"Is tomorrow two Fridays before Christmas?" When Val nodded, Granddad explained his question. "That's when the Chamber of Commerce holds their Holiday Happy Hour at the Bugeye Tavern. I went to it for years. Councilman Thatcher Frost will be there for sure, but he'll leave early to host his own gathering. If Jewel, Muffin, and I are in stakeout position by six thirty, we should see him going into his house."

"Great, but don't draw Jewel's attention to him or anyone else. The investigator holding a lineup isn't allowed to lead the witness."

"All I'll do is alert her when someone is approaching the Frost house. You stay away from us. Just go straight inside. If you and I need to communicate, we'll use a phone."

"Okay. We'll have to tell the chief what we're doing and why. He may think we're wasting our time, but he'll be annoyed if we don't alert him." Val crossed her legs, propped her elbow on her thigh, and rested her chin on her hand like *The Thinker* statue. "If Jewel was the intended victim, we have new avenues to explore. You and the police didn't find any connection between the two victims, Jake and Oliver. Could there be a connection between Jewel and Oliver?"

"Sure. She moved here two months ago. Nobody knows anything about her. This is just off the top of my head, but Jewel could be Oliver's illegitimate daughter. She's about the same age as his legit daughters. One of them coulda ordered a DNA profile and found out about this third daughter."

Val sat up straight. "That's really far-fetched, Granddad, but for the sake of argument, did Jewel know she was Oliver's daughter?"

He shrugged. "Not necessarily, but nothing stops her from getting her DNA done. Everybody's doing it. The family is worried she'll worm her way into their father's affections, he'll change his will, and she'll get a cut of the inheritance. Let's say the son-in-law decided to get rid of her. But once the murder plot against her failed, it was easier to bump off Oliver."

Val was impressed by his imagination, but not convinced by his logic. "It's too much of a coincidence that Jewel ended up in the same small town as the father who didn't know she existed." She stood up. "I'm holding out hope that tomorrow's stakeout will give us some new information."

Chapter 23

Val turned onto Belleview Avenue at seven on Friday evening. As her car approached the Frosts' Victorian house, she glanced across the street and spotted Jewel in a camel coat and a wide-brimmed, black hat that hid the top half of her face. Granddad had pulled his driving cap low and his collar up. He stood at Jewel's side, holding a leash as Muffin sniffed around a tree at the curb. With the streetlights far apart on this block, they could stroll along much of it in the shadows. They'd arrived earlier, so they must have walked back and forth several times by now.

The area around the Frosts' house was well-lit. Icicle lights hung from the front porch roof, and the path lights from the sidewalk to the door were closely spaced and bright. The house next door, Oliver Naiman's, was dark except for a pale light from a lamp in the living room. Val drove farther down the street, made a U-turn, and parked a few doors from the Frost house.

A silver compact sedan pulled into the driveway of Oliver Naiman's house. Kevin and Cyndi emerged from it as Elaine came out of the house. She hugged her sister. The three of them walked to the Frosts' house. Sitting in the car, Val watched other neighbors, including Holly, walk toward the memorial get-together and hoped Jewel was paying attention to the new arrivals.

Granddad hadn't been able to convince the widow that the killer tried to poison her. She was sure that the gift she'd moved toward Jake at the table Saturday night had been his, not hers. But she'd agreed to stand in the cold, watching people file into the Frosts' house, to help the police identify Jake's killer. Val suspected her real motive was to spend time with Granddad.

The chief had reserved judgment on whether Jewel had been the intended victim. He hadn't objected to Granddad and Jewel "dog walking" on Belleview Avenue, but warned them against going inside. He refused to assign an officer to patrol the area. Main Street would be crowded on a Friday night so close to the holidays. The Bayport Police would be busy directing traffic and possibly dealing with shoplifters.

Val was climbing out of the car to go to the memorial get-together when she saw Jewel dart across the street and up the path to the Frosts' house.

She pulled out her phone and called Granddad. "What just happened? Jewel wasn't supposed to go into the house."

"I couldn't stop her. She said a couple of people looked familiar and she needed a closer look."

· "Which people?"

"She wouldn't say. Twenty minutes ago Thatcher parked and went inside. She asked if he was Franetta's husband. She also asked about the people who walked over from next door. When I told her they were Oliver Naiman's daughters and his son-in-law, she wanted their names. She recognized Holly from the tea but had forgotten her name."

"No questions about anyone else?"

"Nope. It's possible no one looked familiar to her, and she went inside to warm up and eat the free food. She was complaining about the cold and asking me to take her to dinner."

"Are *you* warm enough, Granddad?"

"Yup. I got on a lot of layers. Muffin and I will hang out here for a while."

"I'm going in. I'll make sure she pours her own drinks and eats only what other people are eating."

When Val arrived at the Frosts' door, Franetta invited her into a roomy entrance hall with a curved staircase, its banister decorated with evergreen garlands. "Cyndi told me she'd asked you to come tonight. So glad you could join us. I know the food won't be as delicious as what you'd make, but platters from the deli and the bakery are the best I could manage on such short notice."

Val was relieved. Jewel would be safe as long as she chose her own food from the platters. "It's kind of you to do this for the Naimans. Oliver would appreciate it."

"He was a sweet old guy."

Thatcher joined them in the hall. "Welcome to our home. May I take your coat?"

"Yes, thank you." As Val gave it to him, she glanced at

his hands. Like many men, he wore a gold wedding band on his left hand. Nothing about his hands would identify him in bright light, much less in the dark.

"Drinks are in the kitchen. You can go straight through here." He pointed down the hallway toward the back of the house. "Or take the longer route through the living room and dining room."

Val glanced into the living room, where twenty or so guests had congregated. She recognized half of them as her café customers or prospective catering clients. Most of them wore conservative, casual clothes. Jewel was the exception in a red sweater with sequins along its plunging neckline, a black miniskirt, and the same thigh-high, black suede boots she'd worn as Mrs. Claus. Holding a plate of finger food, she stood near the fireplace, talking to Elaine Naiman.

Val made her way toward them, stopping to speak a few words to the guests she knew.

As she neared the fireplace, Jewel's voice carried toward her.

"It must have been a shock when your father died so suddenly," Jewel said. "I'm so sorry for your loss."

"Thank you." Elaine looked puzzled. "How did you know my father?"

"I never met him. I'm here to show my sympathy in a way no one else can. I understand what you're going through because I just lost a loved one too. My husband was poisoned like your father."

Elaine gaped at her. "Poisoned with chocolates?"

"No, it was a cookie that did in my husband. And I was right there when it happened, but I couldn't do anything to help him." Jewel pointed to Val. "She was there too."

Not the way Val wanted to be brought into the conversation. She stepped toward them.

Elaine looked warily from Jewel to Val, as if facing conspirators. "Hello, Val. You didn't mention you were on the spot at another poisoning."

Val heard an accusation, but of what? Knowing two poison victims and not informing the world? "Six people were there. The police asked us not to talk about it."

"I expected to see *you* here tonight because my sister invited you." Elaine turned from Val to Jewel. "Who invited *you*?"

Val cringed inwardly, anticipating that Jewel would name Granddad as the culprit.

Cyndi swooped down on them, and her sister's question went unanswered. "I'm glad you made it, Val." She turned to Jewel. "I'm Cyndi, Oliver's other daughter. Thank you for coming."

Jewel shifted her plate to her left hand and extended her right hand. "And I'm Jewel. Sorry about your father."

Her back was to the man who approached them with a glass of wine in each hand.

"Excuse me," Elaine said. "I see some old friends." She drifted away.

Cyndi took a wineglass from Kevin. "Jewel, this is my husband, Kevin."

Jewel peered up at him and smiled. "Hello. I feel like I know you from somewhere."

Kevin frowned. "I don't think we've met before. Jewel is an unusual name. I'd have remembered it."

"I don't recognize your name either, but I've definitely seen you somewhere."

Val would have stepped hard on Jewel's foot to shut her

up, but her foot was too far away. "That happens to me a lot, meeting a person who resembles someone I once knew."

Jewel stepped closer to Kevin as if she were near-sighted. "I'm sure I've seen you recently. Were you at the Annapolis boat show?"

Cyndi laughed. "That's like asking if the sun rises in the east. Kevin goes to every boat show he can."

"Just like my husband, Jake Smith. I think I saw you there with him."

Val cringed inwardly, but injecting herself into the conversation would serve no purpose. Jewel was nothing if not persistent as Jake had learned.

"Jake Smith?" Kevin shook his head. "I never met him, but I talk to a lot of people at boat shows without knowing their names."

Jewel squinted at him. "You were wearing a baseball cap with an orange brim."

"Kevin has a hat like that," his wife said.

He shrugged. "So do a lot of other people who live around here."

Including Granddad. Val pictured in her mind his favorite Baltimore Orioles cap with the team's nickname embroidered on it—*O's*. Did the O in Jake's calendar refer to the man he was meeting not by name—Jake had trouble remembering names—but by the big O on his hat?

Jewel continued her interrogation. "Did you go to the boat show in Wilmington, Kevin? Jake got a ride with someone."

Cyndi looked at her husband, perplexed. "Didn't you give someone a ride to the Wilmington show?"

"I intended to. The guy didn't show up." He held out his wineglass toward Val and Jewel. "Would either of you like a glass of white wine? I haven't drunk from it. If you prefer something else, I'll go get it for you."

Val glanced at the glass in his right hand. He held the stem with his thumb and two fingers just below the bowl. His ring finger and pinky were bent behind the stem. "I'll take the wine." She reached for the lower part of the stem.

In the instant he released the glass, she glimpsed a dome-shaped wart, half an inch in diameter, on the inside of his ring finger near the middle joint. He quickly hid the spot with his thumb, which he tucked under his index and middle fingers. Obviously he was self-conscious about the wart. Yesterday he'd covered his hand with his jacket when Bethany came into the sitting room. His rush to leave wasn't just fear of the dog, but fear of Bethany.

Val looked up at Kevin. His eyes were trained on her. He'd seen her staring at his hand.

"I'd like a diet cola if you have it, Kevin," Jewel said. "If I don't watch my figure, no one else will."

"Stay right here, I'll bring it to you."

As Kevin headed toward the dining room, Val noticed he was mildly duckfooted, his toes pointing outward instead of straight. His unusual gait wouldn't impinge on most people, but Jewel was attuned to how people walked. She was watching him now as he paused to talk to someone in the dining room and then went into the kitchen.

Kevin fit the mold of the killer, not just with his chemistry background, but also his kitchen expertise. Unlike his wife, he cared about food and did the cooking. He wouldn't have any trouble making gingerbread cookies or bonbons, and mixing in a little poison. He had a motive for Oliver's murder—a large inheritance his wife would share with her sister. But what on earth was his motive for killing Jewel or Jake?

An older woman Val didn't know came up to Cyndi and hugged her. "Sorry for your loss, my dear. We wish we could have come to your father's birthday dinner last weekend."

Jewel whispered to Val, "I think Kevin was the guy in the sweat suit hanging out near my house on Sunday morning."

Val wasn't surprised, though she couldn't imagine why he'd be there. She pulled Jewel aside. "Take the soda Kevin gives you, but don't drink it. Get out of the house quickly after that. You and I need to split up now and leave separately." Val didn't want anyone, least of all Kevin, suspecting an alliance between her and Jewel. "Okay?"

Jewel nodded and popped a cheese cube from her plate into her mouth.

Val set the wineglass Kevin had given her behind a trio of elves perched on the mantel. She grabbed her coat from the den. Avoiding Franetta, she slipped out of the house and joined Granddad across the street.

He motioned her into the deepest shadow. "Did Jewel recognize anyone?"

"Kevin." Val summarized the conversation Jewel initiated and concluded, "I'm not sure why Kevin would kill either of the Smiths, but—"

"I know why. Kevin and Jake spent twelve hours together on that Wilmington trip. They would have talked about their problems. Jake wanted to get rid of his blackmailing wife. Kevin wanted his father-in-law's money." Granddad watched the house across the street as he talked. "They traded murders, like in Hitchcock's *Strangers on a*

Train. That way they'd each have an alibi when the person they wanted dead was killed. Their scheme didn't turn out like the one in the movie. Jake was sick, tired, and drunk. He ate the cookie meant for Jewel."

Val stared at Granddad in the dim light. An improbable solution, but the only one that explained everything that had happened since the Dickens festival. "You nailed it, Granddad."

"Oh, no!" He pointed at the Naiman house. "Kevin just jumped into his car. I didn't see him leave the Frosts' house."

"He must have left by the door from the kitchen and crossed the backyards." Val watched him reverse out of the driveway. "What if he's decided he has to get rid of Bethany? Call Chief Yardley and tell him she needs protection." Remembering Kevin was afraid of dogs, Val grabbed the leash from Granddad. "I'll warn Bethany and follow Kevin's car."

"Text me where Kevin is or call the police, but don't go near him. I'll call Earl, tell him Kevin's behind the poisonings, and give him the car's description. I took down his license number."

Val sprinted to her car, tugging Muffin. They both jumped into the car as Kevin's brake lights went on at the end of Belleview Avenue. He turned off it. Val sped after him. She made the same turn he had and was relieved to see his taillights ahead.

She speed-dialed Bethany and switched the phone to Speaker. "The murderer is the man you saw at our house yesterday—Oliver's son-in-law, Kevin. He's on the loose, so don't open the door to anyone."

"Oh, Lord! Should I leave?"

"No. You're better off there. Kevin's afraid of dogs.

Did my grandfather ever show you his barking motion detector?"

"RoboFido. You want me to turn it on to scare Kevin away?"

"Yes. Fido's in the hall closet." Where could Bethany put the device so the barking would be heard no matter which door or window Kevin went to? "Plug it in facing the side vestibule but not visible from the window. You stand in the vestibule where you can't be seen. Then stamp your feet or wave your arms so Fido detects motion and keeps barking."

"I'll call Ryan."

"Yes, call your personal police escort, but set up Fido first. See you soon."

Bethany hung up. Val kept her distance from Kevin's car so he wouldn't notice her following him. He went past the street he should have taken to go to Granddad's house. Maybe he didn't realize it was the shortest way there, but it wasn't the only way. He would reach Main Street in another couple of blocks.

He slowed down almost to a stop and turned right onto Ad Hoc Lane, a road so small that it didn't appear on the town maps tourists got. The lane wasn't a dead end. Kevin could still drive from here to Granddad's house by a zigzag route. Or he could take a straight route on foot, cutting through people's yards.

Maybe he'd noticed Val's headlights and turned onto this obscure road to check if the car behind was following his. She cut off her headlights and turned onto the lane. Cars were parked along it, but only Kevin's vehicle moved. His brake lights went on, and he pulled over.

Val parked and called Granddad. She told him where Kevin was and said to send the police.

The streetlight illuminated Kevin as he got out of his car and bent down to look at his left rear tire. Was it going flat? He walked behind the car and opened the trunk. To get a spare tire or a weapon he could take to the place where he'd last seen Bethany—at Val and Granddad's home. But Bethany wouldn't let him in the house. Robo-Fido's barking should deter the dog-phobic Kevin from smashing a window to get in.

Val's blood ran cold as another kind of weapon occurred to her, one that wouldn't require him to go near any dog in the house. The chemistry teacher would know how to make a small incendiary device. He could toss it through a window and blow up the house with Bethany in it. The police should get here soon, but it might be too late if Kevin had a bomb.

Val had to delay him. The dog in her passenger seat put a paw on Val's leg. "C'mon, Muffin. We're going to keep Kevin away from Bethany. You're my shield." She clipped the leash onto Muffin.

Once out of the car, she closed the door softly and led Muffin toward Kevin, who was now rummaging in his trunk.

Val stopped in the road ten feet away from him. "Hello, Kevin." Muffin strained at the leash, ready to sniff him.

Kevin's face contorted in fear. He froze. "Keep that dog away."

"I will, as long as you stay where you are. Make a move, and I'll give the dog the attack command."

"Why? Are you crazy? I have a flat. I want to change my tire."

"The police can help you with that. They're on their

way." And they'd better hurry up. "They know about the scheme you cooked up with Jake."

"What scheme? What are you talking about?" He gestured wildly.

Muffin growled. Kevin stumbled back, almost falling over the curb.

"Stay still. The dog doesn't like sudden moves." Val made a show of pulling up on Muffin's leash. Confident that Muffin would hold him at bay, she moved closer to his car. "Your best bet, when the police show up, is to confess. So far you've gotten away with two murders, but you can't get away with another."

"Nothing you're saying makes any sense to me." He took his eyes from the dog for a moment and glanced at the trunk.

Uh-oh. He wanted something in that trunk.

She stepped forward until she could see into it. The cover was off the tire well. The spare tire was there. So was a handgun.

Chapter 24

Val's heart thumped so hard that she could hear it. Muffin was the only thing keeping Kevin away from the gun. If he realized the dog was harmless, he wouldn't hesitate to lunge for the weapon. Val had to beat him to it. She needed her right hand free to hold the gun, but to pick it up with her right hand, she'd have to twist around, losing a precious second and signaling to Kevin what she was doing.

She visualized a way to reach for the gun and then put her plan into action. She transferred the leash to her left hand, wrapped the loop at the end around her wrist, and gathered the rest in two large loops.

Keeping her eyes on Kevin, she sidled up to the fender with Muffin at her knee. Her hand had better be faster than Kevin's eye. She dropped the leash and stepped on it. Then she grabbed the gun with her left hand, switched it to her right, and pointed it at him.

She'd done it! But if he charged toward her now, she wouldn't know how to shoot the gun. Did it have a safety on it? Could he see that her hand was shaking?

"Are you nuts?" Kevin yelled. "Put that down!"

Muffin barked, objecting to his tone of voice. He eyed the dog without stepping back. Maybe he'd figured out that her aggression extended no further than barking.

Val heard the hum of a car driving on the street from the same direction she'd come. It was getting close to them, but she didn't dare take her eyes off Kevin.

"Help! She's holding a gun on me," he bellowed.

The engine quieted to a purr and the car door slammed. She sensed someone behind her.

"Give me that gun!" Granddad's hand touched hers. "I know how to use it and you don't."

Val yielded the gun and bent down to pick up the leash from under her foot. As Muffin greeted Granddad, Kevin ran off.

Val chased after him, not to catch him, but to see which way he ran so she could tell the police. Muffin, still tethered to her, came along.

"Stop! Come back, Val," Granddad called.

Kevin veered in front of his sedan and into the street, where Granddad's Buick was sitting, its engine still running. Kevin dashed around to the driver's side.

As he reached for the door handle, a black shape loomed next to him, tackled him, and held him down on the pavement. Muffin tugged on the leash, barking.

Granddad appeared, holding the gun. "Okay, nobody move or I'll shoot."

"Don't shoot me!" Bram said, still holding Kevin down.

Relief flooded through Val. Granddad had a gun, Bram had brawn, and Muffin had her bark. Kevin wasn't getting away after all.

A patrol car screeched to a stop in front of the Buick. Officer Ryan Wade leaped from the car. "Police! Don't move."

"Help!" Kevin whined. "I'm being assaulted."

The chief came out of the patrol car more slowly than Ryan. "What's going on here?"

Val pointed to the gun in Granddad's hand. "The man who just asked for help had this gun in his trunk. He was about to steal Granddad's car and Bram stopped him."

"You can get off him, Bram." The chief pointed at Kevin. "You on the ground, stay where you are! Wade, make sure he doesn't move."

Muffin pressed against Val's leg and whimpered. All the barking men were too much for her.

Granddad gave the gun to the chief, who held it gingerly with his hand wrapped in a handkerchief. "Now let's see what else is in that trunk of his."

Val, Bram, and Granddad clustered around the trunk as the chief trained a high-intensity flashlight on the tire well. The beam illuminated black gloves with white skeleton fingers and a container of caffeine powder.

"Looks like evidence," Val said. Evidence connecting Kevin to both poisonings.

Granddad said, "I'll go tell Bethany the good news. And I'd better get my car out of the middle of the street. Police will be crawling all over here."

As if on cue, another patrol car arrived. Kevin left in handcuffs, riding in the back of a patrol car.

Bram took Val by the shoulders. "Are you okay?"

"I'm fine. How did you get here at exactly the right moment?"

"I would have been here sooner, but Ad Hoc Lane isn't easy to find. Your grandfather called and said you might be in trouble. I rushed over." He pulled her closer. "I'll always be here for you."

"I can live with that." She nestled into him, and Muffin pressed against her leg. Val bent down and hugged the trembling dog. "Calm down, Muffin. It's all over and you did great. We'll go home to Bethany now."

Chief Yardley stopped by the house a few minutes later and joined Val, Granddad, Bethany, and Bram in the sitting room. The chief asked Val for a detailed account of what had happened at the Frosts' house and after she'd followed Kevin.

When she finished talking, Bethany said, "Ad Hoc Lane isn't on the way here. Was Kevin really driving here to shoot me?"

"I don't know," Val said, "but he might have shot me if Muffin hadn't kept him away. He was terrified of her. She protected me tonight. She was a heroine."

Bethany smiled at the heroine, who was snoring in front of the heating vent.

The chief said, "The route suggests he was heading out of town. I expect that's what he'll tell us, and it could be true. He had nothing to gain by killing Bethany now."

Granddad nodded. "Yup. Val and Jewel had already busted him."

Val hunched down, feeling deflated. Her spotting Kevin's wart and Jewel seeing him with Jake didn't constitute evidence. "Can you hold him on suspicion of murder based on what was in his trunk?"

"It's enough to get a search warrant." The chief must have noticed her disappointment. He continued, "The search will turn up evidence. The poisons he used probably left a trace. DNA can tie him to the gift bags or chocolates. And we can subpoena the toll plaza records from the Bay Bridge. We'll know when he crossed it."

"There goes Kevin's alibi," Val said with satisfaction. "He claimed he was going home to grade papers on Saturday afternoon. I think he went home to make gingerdead men and chocolates. Then he returned to Bayport in the evening to play the ghost, drove home, and came back Sunday morning. All those bridge crossings left a trail."

Bethany frowned. "Kevin killed Oliver for the inheritance, but why did he kill Jake?"

Granddad sat forward in his lounge chair. "I can answer that."

As he explained the murder swap, the chief kept a poker face. Bram on the sofa and Bethany in the chair by the fireplace looked dubious.

Val spoke up in defense of the theory. "Granddad has the only explanation that fits what happened. All the things that puzzled us make sense now, like why a man lurked outside Jake's house on Sunday morning. Kevin planned to pass the poisoned chocolates to Jake at the marina that morning. Then Jake was supposed to leave them on Oliver's doorstep at a time when Kevin had a solid alibi."

Granddad nodded. "But Jake never came because he was dead. Kevin didn't know that because the police hadn't released the information yet. He must have wondered if his co-conspirator had balked at doing his part. So he went to Jake's street. He wouldn't want to knock on the door where the woman he'd poisoned the night before lived. So he hung around, hoping to get Jake's attention. When the police came and Jewel opened the door, Kevin figured out the wrong person had eaten the poisoned gingerbread and he'd have to commit his own murder."

"Events made him do it sooner than he would have liked," Val said. "Sunday night Oliver announced he was going to marry Iska. For all Kevin knew, they might have already applied for a marriage license. So he had to poison Oliver right away." Val remembered Cyndi's sleepiness after Oliver's birthday dinner. "I'm sure Kevin drugged his wife's wine or coffee. After they left Oliver's house to drive home, he waited until she fell asleep in the car and drove back to leave the chocolates for Oliver. He had Bethany's chocolates too, but he couldn't wait around until the party on her street broke up. If his wife woke up, how would he explain being in Bayport long after they'd left her father's house? He delivered Bethany's chocolates the next night, when his wife was in Chicago."

Frowning, Bethany turned to Granddad. "Your murder-swap theory fits what happened, but how could two strangers with nothing in common decide to commit murders for each other?"

"They had boats in common. Jake was shopping for a getaway yacht in case his creditors or the law came after him."

Val nodded. "Even before I met Kevin at Oliver's birthday dinner, I heard that he loved being on the water. He probably planned to use his wife's inheritance for a boat. After a chance meeting at one boat show, a planned meeting at a second one, and a long drive to a third show, they found out what else they had in common—someone they wanted dead."

The chief turned to Granddad. "You could be right about who did it and why. Proving it is another matter. I know we'll get Kevin on the poisoned chocolates. Hard to argue that's not premeditated murder."

Bram scratched his head. "I don't understand why he still had the caffeine powder. It incriminates him."

The chief said, "The reason a killer keeps a weapon he used in a crime is so he can use it again."

Granddad broke the silence that followed those sobering words. "I'll bet the next victim would have been Kevin's sister-in-law. Most wills have a survivorship clause. You inherit only if you survive the will-maker by thirty days. If the sister died in the next few weeks, Kevin's wife would get everything."

"That won't happen now." The chief stood up. "You all had a hand in catching this killer, and you can sleep easier tonight."

Bethany's face lit up. "I can go home! But not 'til after dinner. I made a big pot of pea soup. There's plenty for all of us."

The chief passed on the soup. Val walked him to the hall. She no sooner closed the door behind him than Bram came into the hall and said he had to leave too.

"Mom's shorthanded at the shop tonight. I promised I'd get back as soon as I could." He gave Val a long kiss. "How about dinner tomorrow night, just the two of us?"

"I'd love that." Val saw him out and went back to the sitting room. "Let's adjourn to the kitchen. I'm starving."

While Bethany reheated the soup, Val made corn muffins and Granddad assembled a salad.

Bethany added water to the soup, which had thickened into a pea stew. "Did you know Kevin was the killer before you went to the Frosts' house, Val?"

"Not for sure. He went to the top of my suspect list last night, when the chief told us the places where the ghost was seen. A local person, like Thatcher Frost, would have removed the mask and robe in ten seconds and walked around town as himself, but someone who wasn't supposed to be in Bayport would have to stay in disguise. Kevin couldn't risk being seen by any of the Naimans or their neighbors because he was supposedly home." Val stirred the muffin batter. "Kevin also had the skill set to make sweets and handle poison."

"Why the two different poisons?" Bethany said.

"Two minds at work. Each man created a blueprint for the murder the other man would carry out." Val spooned the batter into the muffin cups. "Jake devised a dramatic murder scene with a party crasher in costume. Reflecting his personality, he threw in humorous touches like the gingerdead man and the Ghost of Christmas Presents. He even explained the pun in case we missed how clever it was."

"But he was deadly serious with his choice of cyanide." Granddad's knife thumped against the cutting board as he sliced a cucumber. "Jake needed a fast-acting poison so his wife would die at the tea table. He'd have witnesses swearing he couldn't have poisoned her. That's why he had to be there even though he had a terrible cold."

Bethany stirred the soup. "If I knew one cookie in a bunch was poisoned, I wouldn't eat any of them. Why did Jake even touch one?"

Val thought about what was going on at the table when

he opened the gift bag. "Jake had a problem. No one at the table had eaten a gingerdead man. If Jewel took hers home and ate it later that night or the next day, he'd lose his alibi for her poisoning. He'd be the only suspect. So he tried to convince her to eat it at the tea party. He grabbed the gift bag he assumed was his, wolfed down the cookie, and raved about how delicious it was."

"Until he keeled over." Granddad rolled his eyes. "His fancy murder plan tripped him up. Kevin had a better plan—use a poison that would look like a natural death and deliver it when no one was around to see."

"Yes, but someone other than Oliver might have eaten the candy left on the doorstep," Bethany said.

Val put the muffin pan in the oven. "It wouldn't have bothered him if his sister-in-law or Iska ate it."

Granddad looked up from the cutting board. "Speaking of Iska, I heard from her today. She asked me to give you a message, Bethany. She can't work for your *uncle*. She got a job as a live-in aide for an older woman."

"I'm glad to hear it. My conscience was bothering me about tricking her." Bethany adjusted the heat under the soup pot. "I feel really sorry for Kevin's wife, finding out she's married to her father's murderer. Do you think her sister suspected him?"

Val shrugged. "We'll never know her real reason for demanding an autopsy, but she was right to do it. The whole town is better off with the Christmas killer in custody."

"I can't thank you enough, Val, for risking your life to keep the killer away from me."

"You gotta thank me for one thing," Granddad said. "Kevin's flat tire. I thought he might run if Jewel accused him of murder at the Frosts' party. So I took the valve cap off one of his tires, put a small pebble in it, and screwed the cap back on. I knew the air would leak out little by little and the tire would be flat before long." He grinned. "We won't mention that to Earl or Ryan."

Bethany gave Granddad a high five.

A few days later Val got a call from the chief with an update. The police had evidence proving that Kevin had made the poisoned chocolates. They'd also substantiated Granddad's theory that Kevin and Jake had colluded. A search of their financial records showed that the two men had bought a yacht together. Jake had paid for most of it, expecting Kevin to reimburse him after Oliver died and Cyndi came into money.

At the Frosts' house, when Jewel revealed his connection to Jake, Kevin must have thought he'd soon be arrested for Jake's murder. As usual, he acted on the basis of the worst case scenario. He called the boatyard in Norfolk where the yacht was, said he was coming for it, and wouldn't need to moor it there any longer. When the police searched the yacht, they found nautical maps that would guide him from the boatyard to the Bahamas.

Val now understood what had motivated Kevin. He'd shared Jake's dream of fleeing the country, evading responsibility, and cruising around the islands.

Instead he'd spend the rest of his life in jail.

A satisfactory ending. When Val got off the phone with the chief, she made a batch of Christmas cookies.

Chapter 25

For the last six years, a spirit had visited Val on Christmas, when she was in the kitchen with no one else
around. She sensed Grandma's presence in that room
throughout the year, but it was strongest on the holiday
she loved. Grandma would be there again this year.

Dinner was over and the kitchen cleaned up before Val
had a chance to break away from the rest of the family.
Her brother and his two boys were on the sofa in the
study, watching Bram perform magic tricks. Her mother
and father chatted with Granddad and Dorothy in the sitting room.

Val turned off the lights over the kitchen island and sat
at the table by the window. She had a lot of news for
Grandma.

Granddad is doing well. He still misses you every day. His friend, Dorothy, is good for him. She's a bundle of energy and keeps him young. I knew they both loved old movies, especially Hitchcock's, but I found out only recently that she was a baseball fan too. That made my shopping for Granddad easy. For Christmas I gave him Orioles tickets, so the two of them could go to some games together.

Granddad's gift for me was a big surprise—a new sofa. It's a gift he'll get to enjoy too, but I can't complain. I did the same with Bram's gift. I'm treating us both to dinner at an elegant inn on the waterfront. Bram topped that by buying us both tickets to Paris. I should have suspected something like that because he'd asked me if my passport was current and whether I'd ever been there. That's where we'll be for my birthday. The weather may not be great on February 14, but good things can happen under the Eiffel Tower, especially on Valentine's Day.

Hearing footsteps, Val turned away from the window.

Bram stood in the doorway. "You're sitting here alone."

"I'm not alone." *Good night, Grandma. I miss you.* Val met Bram halfway across the kitchen and put her arms around him. "I'm not alone."

Acknowledgments

I owe thanks to many people who helped me as I researched and wrote *Gingerdead Man*. I would never write a mystery in which a character was poisoned without consulting two experts who generously answer questions that writers have about poisonings. Pharmacist and toxicologist Luci Hansson Zahray, the mystery community's Poison Lady, gave me information on the sources and effects of the poisons that play a role in this book. Physician and mystery writer D. P. Lyle, MD, provided details about the medical and forensic aspects of these poisons. Thank you to both of you. Any mistakes in the book on those subjects resulted from my misunderstanding.

For help on a different subject, I thank mystery author and professional Santa Claus, Bradley Harper, and his wife, Chere. Bradley gave me insights into the job of being a Santa in the modern world and into the growing and dyeing of beards. Chere told me about the important role of Mrs. Claus. She is a more traditional helpmate to Santa than the Mrs. Claus in this book. In case you were wondering, the IBRBS—International Brotherhood of Real Bearded Santas—is a real organization.

Words can't express how grateful I am to my critique partners and fellow mystery writers, Carolyn Mulford and Helen Schwartz. We started working together before any of us had published mystery stories or books. We've brainstormed plots together, offered chapter-by-chapter feedback to one another in our weekly meetings, and edited near-final versions of books and stories we were submitting. Every book in this series, from the first to the seventh, is better because of their comments and advice. Thank you, Carolyn and Helen.

My husband, Mike Corrigan, also read and commented on every book in the series. Thank you, Mike. I'd also like to thank Nora Corrigan and Cathy Ondis Solberg for reading the first draft of this book and providing feedback that made the book better. Carolyn Mulford brainstormed with me to fix the plot holes that the other readers found. She also did a thorough final edit under a tight deadline. Thank you for everything, Carolyn.

I'm grateful to my agent, John Talbot, for bringing the Five-Ingredient Mystery series to Kensington Books. I'd like to thank my editor, John Scognamiglio, and my publicist, Larissa Ackerman, as well as the production, marketing, and sales teams at Kensington Books who helped bring *Gingerdead Man* and the other books in the series to readers.

I couldn't have written and published seven books, or even one book, without Sisters in Crime—the national chapter, the online Guppies Chapter, and my local Chesapeake Chapter. Thank you for your vital support.

I'd like to recognize and thank some special readers. They generously contributed to literary charities by buying character-naming rights at auctions during the Malice Domestic and Bouchercon mystery conventions: Elaine Naiman, who is in this book; Ruth McWilliams and Sandy Sechrest, who had roles in *Crypt Suzette*; Linda Zaharee, who is in *S'more Murders*; and Judy Kindell, who asked for her father, Jerry Kindell, to be in *S'More Murders*.

Finally a huge thank you to all the readers who enjoy books about crime and detection. You keep the mystery genre alive.

The Codger
Cook's Recipes

GRASMERE GINGERBREAD

To make gingerbread (or gingerdead) men, you need more than five ingredients. You also have to roll out the dough and cut the shapes. Here's a gingerbread cookie you can make with fewer ingredients and without a rolling pin. This treat is so popular in England that people travel to the small town of Grasmere in the lake district just to buy it.

Preheat the oven to 350 degrees.

1 cup + 2 tablespoons flour
½ cup + 1 tablespoon light brown sugar
1½ teaspoons ground ginger
¼ teaspoon baking powder
10 tablespoons butter
1–2 tablespoons crystallized ginger, chopped (optional)

Line an oblong pan (approximately 7 x 11 x 2 inches) with parchment paper.

Mix the dry ingredients together.

Melt the butter and add it to the dry ingredients.

Add the chopped crystallized ginger to taste, one tablespoon if you're not sure if you like it and two if you know you do.

Spread the mixture over the pan in a thin layer, pressing it down lightly with your fingers or the bottom of a glass.

Bake 25–30 minutes until golden brown.

Cut the gingerbread into bars (approximately 1 x 2 inches) while it is still hot. Leave it in the pan until it cools. Remove the gingerbread by lifting the parchment paper.

Yield: 30–36 bars

Adapted from *English Food* by Jane Grigson.

ALMOND BRITTLE COOKIES

This is a hybrid dessert. A cross between candy and cookies, it's baked in a standard-size muffin pan. The recipe makes enough to fill two 12-cup muffin pans. You can use either a nonstick pan or a regular muffin pan with foil cup liners.

8 ounces (2 sticks) unsalted butter
1 cup sugar
$\frac{1}{3}$ cup honey
$\frac{1}{3}$ cup heavy cream
$4\frac{1}{2}$ cups sliced and (mostly) skinless almonds

Preheat the oven to 375 degrees.

Melt the butter over medium heat in a saucepan.

Add the sugar and honey. Stir until the mixture is smooth.

Stir in the heavy cream and continue stirring over low to medium heat until the mixture turns a light caramel color.

Add the almonds and stir until they are evenly coated.

Fill the muffin cups about $\frac{1}{3}$ of the way up and flatten the mixture by pressing down on it with a spoon.

Bake the cookies on the middle rack of the oven until the contents of the cups are bubbling and golden brown, about 8–10 minutes.

Remove the pan from the oven and cool the cookies in the muffin pan for 10 minutes. Use a knife around the edge to loosen each cookie from the cup. The bottom may be soft and the cookie a little floppy. Transfer the cookies to wax paper to cool and, once they're set, they will be flat.

If using foil cup liners, take the cups from the pan. When cool, remove the cookies from the foil.

Note: Using foil cups may result in caramel spikes sticking up from the top of the cookies. You can break them off once the cookies cool.

If using only one muffin pan and the foil liners, put in new liners for the second batch.

Yield: 24 cookies

Adapted from a recipe for Florentines by Bettyanne Hershfield (Winnipeg, Manitoba) via *Washington Post* recipe columnist Bonnie S. Benwick.

NO-BAKE CHOCOLATE CRANBERRY NUT MOUNDS

These bite-size candies take almost no time to make and have only three ingredients. Dried cranberries make them a festive holiday treat. You can vary the recipe by substituting raisins or other dried fruit for cranberries and by using a different type of nut instead of pecans.

12 ounces (2 cups) semisweet chocolate chips or chunks
    (milk chocolate also works)
1 cup coarsely chopped pecans
½ cup dried cranberries (or more to taste)

Line a baking sheet with parchment or wax paper and set it aside.

Put the chocolate chips in a microwave-safe bowl. Heat the chocolate at half power for 1 minute and stir. Heat the chocolate at half power for 30 seconds and stir. Continue to heat and stir, decreasing the heating time as the chocolate softens. Do this until the chocolate is smooth.

Combine the nut pieces and cranberries in a bowl. Stir them into the melted chocolate, coating them well.

Drop spoonfuls of the mixture onto the paper-lined baking sheet.

Refrigerate until the chocolate hardens, about 30 minutes.

Store the mounds in an airtight container at room temperature or in the freezer.

Yield: 18–24 pieces, depending on the size of the mounds

CRANBERRY-APPLE CRISP

Here's another cranberry treat suitable for the holidays and all year round.

Preheat the oven to 350 degrees.

2 cups fresh (or frozen and thawed) cranberries
5 cups apples, peeled and coarsely chopped
$1\frac{1}{2}$ cups sugar (separated)
$1\frac{1}{2}$ cups rolled oats
$\frac{1}{2}$ cup butter
$\frac{1}{2}$ teaspoon salt (optional)

Combine the fruit and half the sugar. Put the mixture into a buttered 9-inch pie pan or an 8-inch square baking pan.

With your fingers or a pastry blender, combine the oats, butter, remaining sugar, and salt (if using) until they make a crumbly mixture. Sprinkle it on the fruit mixture.

Bake for 1 hour.

Cool for 30 minutes.

Best served warm with vanilla ice cream, but good to eat at any temperature.

Serves 6–8

GRANDMA'S CHICKEN CASSEROLE

This is a variation on a recipe from decades ago that remains popular today. It makes enough for a crowd and keeps well as a leftover.

Preheat the oven to 275 degrees.

3–4 ounces low sodium chipped beef
8 chicken breasts, skinned and boneless
1 can cream of mushroom soup, undiluted
½ pint sour cream (more if you'd like more sauce)
8 ounces button or cremini mushrooms in ¼-inch-thick
  slices

Cover the bottom of a flat rectangular baking dish (approximately 8 x 12 x 2 inches) with chipped beef slices.

Lay out the chicken on top of the beef in one layer and wrap each piece with the chipped beef.

Mix the soup and the sour cream together, stir in the mushrooms, and spoon the mixture over the meat.

Bake for 2–3 hours, covered with foil for the first half and then uncovered.

Serves 8

SPICED CIDER

Spiced cider works well for any holiday or cool-weather party. This drink is also known as mulled apple cider. Like mulled wine, it's simmered with spices and citrus in an electric slow cooker or in a pot on the stove. The spices should include cinnamon and cloves at a minimum, but you can also add a star anise or grated fresh ginger if you like those flavors.

Put the smaller spices in a tea ball or wrapped and tied in cheesecloth. If you don't do that, you'll need to strain the cider before serving it. Simmer the spices and cider, keeping them below the boiling point.

$\frac{1}{2}$ gallon unfiltered apple cider
2 cinnamon sticks
10 whole cloves
$\frac{1}{2}$ ounce orange juice (or lemon juice, if you prefer a less sweet drink)
Sliced oranges and cinnamon sticks for garnish

Put the apple cider, spices, and juice in a large pot or Dutch oven.

Heat up to the point of boiling and then simmer for 1–3 hours. If you use a slow cooker, turn it to low and cook for 3 hours.

Turn off the heat and remove the spices from the pot, straining if necessary. Serve the cider warm, garnished with sliced oranges and a fresh cinnamon stick in each cup.

Connect with

Visit us online at
KensingtonBooks.com
to read more from your favorite authors, see books
by series, view reading group guides, and more.

for sneak peeks, chances to win books and prize packs,
and to share your thoughts with other readers.

facebook.com/kensingtonpublishing
twitter.com/kensingtonbooks

Tell us what you think!

To share your thoughts, submit a review,
or sign up for our eNewsletters, please visit:
KensingtonBooks.com/TellUs.

Grab These Cozy Mysteries
from
Kensington Books

Forget Me Knot Mary Marks	978-0-7582-9205-6	$7.99US/$8.99CAN
Death of a Chocoholic Lee Hollis	978-0-7582-9449-4	$7.99US/$8.99CAN
Green Living Can Be Deadly Staci McLaughlin	978-0-7582-7502-8	$7.99US/$8.99CAN
Death of an Irish Diva Mollie Cox Bryan	978-0-7582-6633-0	$7.99US/$8.99CAN
Board Stiff Annelise Ryan	978-0-7582-7276-8	$7.99US/$8.99CAN
A Biscuit, A Casket Liz Mugavero	978-0-7582-8480-8	$7.99US/$8.99CAN
Boiled Over Barbara Ross	978-0-7582-8687-1	$7.99US/$8.99CAN
Scene of the Climb Kate Dyer-Seeley	978-0-7582-9531-6	$7.99US/$8.99CAN
Deadly Decor Karen Rose Smith	978-0-7582-8486-0	$7.99US/$8.99CAN
To Kill a Matzo Ball Delia Rosen	978-0-7582-8201-9	$7.99US/$8.99CAN

Available Wherever Books Are Sold!

All available as e-books, too!

Visit our website at **www.kensingtonbooks.com**

Catering and Capers with
Isis Crawford!

A Catered Murder	978-1-57566-725-6	$5.99US/$7.99CAN
A Catered Wedding	978-0-7582-0686-2	$6.50US/$8.99CAN
A Catered Christmas	978-0-7582-0688-6	$6.99US/$9.99CAN
A Catered Valentine's Day	978-0-7582-0690-9	$6.99US/$9.99CAN
A Catered Halloween	978-0-7582-2193-3	$6.99US/$8.49CAN
A Catered Birthday Party	978-0-7582-2195-7	$6.99US/$8.99CAN
A Catered Thanksgiving	978-0-7582-4739-1	$7.99US/$8.99CAN
A Catered St. Patrick's Day	978-0-7582-4741-4	$7.99US/$8.99CAN
A Catered Christmas Cookie Exchange	978-0-7582-7490-8	$7.99US/$8.99CAN

Available Wherever Books Are Sold!

All available as e-books, too!

Visit our website at **www.kensingtonbooks.com**

Follow P.I. Savannah Reid
with
G.A. McKevett

Just Desserts	978-0-7582-0061-7	$5.99US/$7.99CAN
Bitter Sweets	978-1-57566-693-8	$5.99US/$7.99CAN
Killer Calories	978-1-57566-521-4	$5.99US/$7.99CAN
Cooked Goose	978-0-7582-0205-5	$6.50US/$8.99CAN
Sugar and Spite	978-1-57566-637-2	$5.99US/$7.99CAN
Sour Grapes	978-1-57566-726-3	$6.50US/$8.99CAN
Peaches and Screams	978-1-57566-727-0	$6.50US/$8.99CAN
Death by Chocolate	978-1-57566-728-7	$6.50US/$8.99CAN
Cereal Killer	978-0-7582-0459-2	$6.50US/$8.99CAN
Murder à la Mode	978-0-7582-0461-5	$6.99US/$9.99CAN
Corpse Suzette	978-0-7582-0463-9	$6.99US/$9.99CAN
Fat Free and Fatal	978-0-7582-1551-2	$6.99US/$8.49CAN
Poisoned Tarts	978-0-7582-1553-6	$6.99US/$8.49CAN
A Body to Die For	978-0-7582-1555-0	$6.99US/$8.99CAN
Wicked Craving	978-0-7582-3809-2	$6.99US/$8.99CAN
A Decadent Way to Die	978-0-7582-3811-5	$7.99US/$8.99CAN
Buried in Buttercream	978-0-7582-3813-9	$7.99US/$8.99CAN
Killer Honeymoon	978-0-7582-7652-0	$7.99US/$8.99CAN
Killer Physique	978-0-7582-7655-1	$7.99US/$8.99CAN

Available Wherever Books Are Sold!

All available as e-books, too!

Visit our website at **www.kensingtonbooks.com**